CW00504913

Baby's Got Blue Eyes

Baby's Got Blue Eyes

Ted Darling crime series

'A compelling début crime thriller'

L. M. Krier

Contents

About the Author

L M Krier is the pen name of former journalist (court reporter) and freelance copywriter, Lesley Tither, who also writes travel memoirs under the name Tottie Limejuice. Lesley also worked as a case tracker for the Crown Prosecution Service.

The Ted Darling series of crime novels comprises: *The First Time Ever, Baby's Got Blue Eyes, Two Little Boys, When I'm Old and Grey, Shut Up and Drive, Only the Lonely, Wild Thing, Walk on By, Preacher Man.*

All books in the series are available in Kindle and paperback format and are also available to read free with Kindle Unlimited.

Contact Details

If you would like to get in touch, please do so at:

tottielimejuice@gmail.com

facebook.com/LMKrier

facebook.com/groups/1450797141836111/

https://twitter.com/tottielimejuice

For a light-hearted look at Ted and the other characters, please consider joining the We Love Ted Darling group on Facebook.

Discover the DI Ted Darling series

If you've enjoyed meeting Ted Darling, you may like to discover the other books in the series:

Acknowledgements

I would just like to thank the people who have helped me bring DI Ted Darling to life: Jill Pennington – for reading the first few chapters and encouraging me to go on, Beta readers Emma Heath, Dave Ricketts and Mikki Ashe, Motorbike consultants – Em Faulkner and Dave Ricketts, aviation consultants – David Willerton and Alex Potter, additional internet research Peter J K Tither, Feline consultant – Sara Edlington

To Marty

Chapter One

Ted Darling snapped out an arm to stifle the strident ring of the mobile phone on the bedside table before it woke his sleeping partner. At the same time he smiled to himself at the absurdity of the gesture.

As he took the call, he looked over his shoulder to where Trevor lay spread-eagled between the tousled sheets. Trev always slept like a starfish, a dead one at that, taking up an incredible amount of space for such a slim, lithe figure.

Ted was reduced to a few meagre inches at the edge of the bed, with one arm and leg hanging out. What little room Trev was not taking up was occupied by an assortment of cats, seven, if they were all there as usual.

Trev was still sleeping the deep sleep of the innocent, silky-black curls framing a head-turning face. Outrageously long, thick black lashes to the lids concealed those devastating baby blue eyes which meant Trev was seldom refused anything.

'Hello?' growled Ted quietly. He had long since given up answering the phone using his surname – it took too long dealing with the inevitable wisecracks of his gruff voice opening the conversation with 'Darling'.

He listened, grunting a few times, then said: 'Shit. I'm on my way.'

The discovery of a body meant there was no time for a shower if Ted wanted to get there ahead of the circus, which was always his preference. He'd have to make do with a quick squirt of deodorant, a bit of mouthwash and finger combing his hair.

Ted was, as they say, small yet perfectly formed. So small that people seldom believed him when he told them he was a copper, despite the minimum height requirement having long since gone. He was in such good shape he would pass for ten years younger than his forty. Trev largely saw to that, along with the sports Ted packed into whatever free time he had. There was not an ounce of fat anywhere on his body, just hard, defined muscle.

His hair was the sort of thick dirty blonde which would probably never thin nor go grey. His eye colour would have artists and interior designers arguing for hours. Light hazel, tending to muddy green, depending on his prevailing mood.

He slipped on dark jeans, added a cotton polo, picked up his leather jacket and headed for the garage, car keys already in hand. The early morning was still cold and things were quiet in the cul-de-sac of modest semi-detached houses on an estate which had been reasonably respectable when he and Trev had set up home there nearly ten years ago.

Nowadays Ted tended to know more of his neighbours through his work than through any social life, although he largely kept to himself and left the Uniform branch to deal with the antics of the local scallies. The extra locks on the garage were not for his elderly but reliable Renault but to protect Trev's baby, a shiny Triumph Bonneville T100, with its red custom paint, largely paid for in instalments by Ted.

It was not far from the house to the location he had been given for the body, not even far enough for the Renault's heater to make any difference to the chilly interior. Ted swung off Marple Road and continued down a no through road towards playing fields at the bottom. He spotted an area car on blues, parked across the road at the end, and two PCs starting to unwind tape to protect and preserve the crime scene.

Ted pulled up, lowered his window, and greeted the two men with a, 'Morning, what we got?'

'Morning sir,' one of them replied. 'She's across the far

side of the fields, down the bank towards the river. A couple of your team are there already and the doc's just arrived.'

Ted gave them a thanks, then pulled out a packet of Fisherman's Friend lozenges from his jacket pocket. He waved them at the nearest of the PCs and asked: 'How many for this one?'

'You'll probably get away with one for this one, sir, she's fresh!' he called back cheerfully, pulling the tape back so the Detective Inspector could drive through.

Everyone had their own way of dealing with the gruesome side of the job. Ted's was his addiction to the strong menthol sweets he always kept in his pocket. It was a standing joke at the nick, how many the DI would need to munch his way through for the worst of the bodies.

Ted followed a tarmac road round to the far side of the playing fields, where the vehicles parked told him that most of the Scenes of Crime and allied services had just arrived and were going about their business. A passing officer directed him over to the trees where he could see others making their way down a narrow path.

It was almost fully daylight now but it would be darker in the woods, especially underfoot, so Ted had taken his Maglite from the glove compartment before he headed in the same direction. The short path led down to the riverbank, opening out into a wide grassy space. Ted saw that two of his team were already on site.

DCs Tina Bailey and Rob O'Connell were good solid officers, so he knew the basic groundwork would be done faultlessly. He heard the police surgeon before he saw him. Tim Elliott seemed to have a perpetual cold or a succession of allergies. If it was true that sneezing destroyed brain cells, it was a wonder he was still functioning at all, let alone as a doctor.

In his usual way, the doctor started speaking even before Ted had reached him, with no sign of a greeting, just plunging

straight in with whatever chaotic thoughts were circulating through his brain.

'Definitely dead, definitely not natural causes, throat's been cut cleanly. Been dead anything up to forty-eight hours, I would say. Not killed here, killed elsewhere and brought here. Both breasts have been removed with what looks like surgical precision.

'Bizarrely, on first examination, it looks as if all her body hair has been removed very recently, possibly after death, and the body may have been cleaned in some way. Her head is shaved, pubic hair is missing, none anywhere else on the body. Going to be an interesting one.'

He was already walking away before he'd finished the last sentence, so Ted threw a 'goodbye' at his retreating back and turned back to his DCs.

'Fill me in,' he said.

'The guy over there found her, sir,' Rob said. 'Luckily he had the presence of mind to back away before he chucked his breakfast up, so the crime scene is relatively uncontaminated.'

He was remaining formal with the boss within earshot of other officers.

Ted shot a glance towards the man. 'What was he doing down here at that time of the morning?' he asked.

'Walking his dog, sir,' Rob replied. 'The German Shepherd attached to him by a lead is a bit of a giveaway.'

Rob knew he could get away with the odd wisecrack with the DI, who was the best he had ever served under. There was a line he knew it was unwise to cross, but he hoped that he had stayed on the right side of it, despite the look the DI threw at him.

'Must have been dark when he found her though. Bit of an odd time for a dog walk?'

'Have you seen the size of that dog, boss?' Rob answered. 'I wouldn't be worried walking anywhere at any time of day or night with that brute next to me.'

'Fair enough. Legit, do you think?'

'Yes, boss, definitely on the level, I would say. He looks really shaken up. I'll give him time to come to a bit before I get a statement from him,' Rob replied.

'Any ID on her? What do we know about her?'

Ted was looking towards the naked body all the time they spoke, munching his Fisherman's Friend, but he made no attempt to approach too close. He left that to the experts.

Tina answered this time. 'No ID anywhere we can see so far, sir, and no sign of a weapon. She was left totally naked, no signs of any clothing or personal possessions in the immediate vicinity. Alice looks to be in her early twenties from what we can see and from what the doc confirmed.'

Tina always gave a name to any unidentified body until the real ID was discovered. She said it was more personal, a way of humanising the victim rather than just referring to them as 'the body' all the time. Ted was in favour of anything to increase respect amongst his officers, so was happy to go along with it.

'Right, thorough ground work here, witness statement from the dog walker, knock on some doors on your way back. Quite a way to lug a body from the nearest place to park a car. Someone may well have seen or heard something. I'll organise some reinforcements from Uniform for a site search.

'We need to find a weapon, clothing, personal effects, anything at all to help us,' Ted told them. 'Let's try and get an ID as soon as we can, so when you get back in get started on checking Missing Persons for a possible match. I'm going in to brief the Boss. We're a team member down and we need someone good on this one, by the look of things.'

He'd just lost possibly the best Detective Sergeant he had ever worked with. When the shakes had first started, Jack Gregson probably thought, like the rest of them, that he'd been hitting the bottle harder than he realised. He even went on the wagon for a few months, but it didn't make any difference and his symptoms just kept getting worse.

The diagnosis of Parkinson's disease came right out of left field. It rarely affects people under fifty and Gregson had only just turned forty. It brought his career to an abrupt end and took away Ted's right-hand man and a good one, who would be hard to replace.

Time to turn up the pressure on Ted's boss, Detective Chief Inspector Baker, to get him the promised replacement. This case looked as if he was going to need his team up to full strength and with the best officers available to him.

Chapter Two

'Morning, Darling,' the DCI said as Ted walked into his office, after a peremptory knock.

'Morning, Super,' Ted replied, taking a seat in response to the boss's nod towards the chair.

The DCI leant his wardrobe-sized bulk back in his chair until it creaked in protest.

'Ah, the old ones are always the best, eh, Ted?' he smiled.

It was a long-standing joke between the two men, in clumsy camouflage of the deep mutual respect they felt. The DCI was not yet a Superintendent but his ambition to become one was no secret and it made the joke work better.

'Do you want some coffee?' he asked, moving towards the coffee machine in a corner of his small office, which always looked overcrowded and cramped with him in it.

'It's an offence under the Trade Descriptions Act to call the muck you make coffee. But I like to live dangerously, so I'll risk it,' Ted joked.

Once they were both sitting down to the evil, black brew the DCI called coffee, he switched into serious mode.

'I don't like bodies on our patch, Ted, so I hope you're going to wrap this one up with your usual swift efficiency. Fill me in on what you've got so far.'

'Nothing much to go on yet, Jim. No weapon, no clothing, no personal effects,' Ted replied.

Within the walls of the DCI's office, the two men were relaxed and informal in each other's company. If any of the team members were in earshot, it was always 'sir', or 'boss' at the least, and 'DI Darling'.

DCI Jim Baker liked Ted enormously, even if he didn't profess to understand how he lived his life. He knew he was without doubt the finest copper in the force, with an unrivalled mop-up rate, whose team thought the world of him and whose record was impeccable in all matters. No rough stuff in Ted's interviews, no late paperwork, just a tightly-run ship and an impressive list of cases solved and successful convictions.

Even though Ted's relationship remained a mystery to him, he did secretly envy its stability. He knew Ted and Trevor had been together for more than ten years and were still blissfully happy. All he had to show for a marriage twice as long was a bleached and Botoxed wife who gave him stomach ulcers, a permanent overdraft and credit cards in meltdown.

His wife's affairs were a badly kept secret. He knew she was shagging several younger coppers, as well as at least one local magistrate, to his certain knowledge. He knew too that some of his men were laughing at him behind his back because of it. It was one of the reasons he was pushing himself so hard up the promotion ladder. A higher rank would give him more ammunition for revenge.

'Not a lot to go on yet, until we get the post-mortem report. Young woman, early twenties, no ID, left naked, throat cut, breasts removed. Some strange stuff going on, like all her body hair removed, possibly post-mortem, which is going to make it harder to identify her as we don't know her hair colour for one thing.'

As Ted filled the DCI in, he saw a shadow pass over the other man's face. Jim's own rebellious daughter Rosalie had left home in her teens after endless violent screaming confrontations with her mother, and had not been in touch since.

'So, to sum up,' the DCI said, 'we have no ID, no murder weapon, no motive and presumably no suspects. Shouldn't take you more than a day or two then, Ted. Oh, some good news for you, I've got you a new DS. He arrives tomorrow. From his record, he should be able to hit the ground running and be an asset.'

'Do I know him?'

'Possibly not,' the DCI replied. 'He's coming from Stretford, name's Mike Hallam. Good references, they speak well of him there.'

'So why's he wanting a transfer?' Ted's antennae were immediately twitching.

'It seems genuine enough. The mother-in-law had a serious road accident not long ago which has left her disabled. The wife wants to live much closer to her so she can keep an eye on her as she's a widow, on her own.' There was a slight hesitation before the DCI added, 'There might just be one small problem though, Ted.'

Ted laughed good-naturedly and said, 'Don't tell me. Another case of an over-developed gaydar? He's heard about me and is worried I might have him doing embroidery instead of house-to-house?'

The DCI looked uncomfortable. Although he liked Ted enormously, trusted him completely and accepted how he was to the best of his ability, he knew there were still others who didn't. He did his utmost to stamp out any form of discrimination amongst his officers, but this was always one area that left him feeling a little out of his depth.

Ted chuckled, sensing his discomfort. 'Don't worry, I'll lay out the ground rules for him, set him straight - pun intended. He's probably not my type anyway. You know I like pretty toy-boys, and I'm happy with the one I've got.'

By now the DCI was squirming. Ted's sense of humour about his relationship was a bit of a step too far outside his comfort zone. He'd met Trevor on many social occasions and got on with him really well, finding him incredibly intelligent. But he was still old-fashioned enough to struggle with thoughts of him and Ted .... he brought himself up short from such mental images.

Ted stood up to release him from his discomfort.

'Right, boss,' he said, back to briskly professional. 'Tina and Rob are in the field and once they get back in I'll get the team together for a briefing and see what direction we're going in. Meanwhile I'll start the team on a trawl of Missing Persons, see if we can get at least a few vague leads.'

He hated even mentioning the words and watching the emotions they caused to ripple over the boss's face. Every time Ted got a shout of a young woman's body being found on his patch, he dreaded arriving on the scene and discovering it was Rosalie. Selfishly, he feared even more the thought that if one day it was her, it would be up to him to break the news to the Big Boss.

It was worse at this time of year for the DCI and for the families of other missing persons. With Christmas looming, there was always that forlorn hope that this might be the year for the card, the phone call or even the visit which would finally put an end to their suffering. That day had not come yet for the DCI and the longer time went on, the less likely it looked.

The two men nodded to each other, unspoken volumes behind the gesture, and Ted went back to his own domain to assemble his team and get the enquiry under way.

Rob and Tina had just got back. Crime scene investigators were on the case now and door knocking had revealed no one at home who had seen anything. They would need to schedule more house-to-house at different times of day, just in case of any witnesses. The rest of the team members were also in and waiting on his briefing.

Maurice Brown, already several pounds overweight, had arrived with a large bag of sugared doughnuts. He did at least hand them round, but Ted noticed that he was still left with three in the bag for himself.

Dennis Tibbs, fortunately a black officer with a sporting

sense of humour since everyone from the DCI down called him Virgil, which he didn't seem to mind in the least and would not have hesitated to say so if he did. It was a reference to a Sidney Poitier film with a black police officer called Virgil Tibbs in it.

Abisali Ahmed, universally known as Sal, intelligent, hard-working, multi-faceted was also at his desk. Finally the baby of the team, Trainee Detective Constable Steve Ellis, shy, extremely geeky and still finding his feet, but by far and away the best of any of them armed with a computer.

'Right team, settle down,' Ted gave his customary call to order as they fell expectantly silent. Virgil had already started a whiteboard with a photo of Alice's body and brief details of what information they had so far.

'First and most important thing is let's get Alice identified for who she really is. She's someone's daughter, sister, girlfriend, maybe even mother, and they need to know the news as soon as possible. Steve, Missing Persons, that's your task. Don't leave that computer until you have some leads for us.'

The young TDC went bright red at being singled out and spoken to first. Ted was never sure whether it was his rank or his sexuality which made the young officer so uncomfortable, or whether he was just naturally shy and unlucky enough to blush easily.

'The rest of you, we need some house-to-house until we get a sniff of something. Sal, sort out a rota to get it covered until we do. Ask for some help from Uniform.

'Without an ID, a motive is going to be next to nigh on impossible to figure out but does anyone have any early ideas? Especially with what was done to Alice. Any theories on the reasoning for that?'

Ted's team knew that each of them was entitled to voice an opinion, as long as they kept their remarks within the strict code of respect set by the DI. Maurice could always be relied on to break the code first which he did immediately, spitting sugary crumbs as he did so.

'A woman-hater, boss. Why else cut off the hair and the tits?'

There was a long silence, an extended pause, while Ted's eyes changed from warm rich hazel to a warning shade of green. Eventually even the totally insensitive Maurice realised he had crossed way over the line. He mumbled a hasty 'Sorry, sir,' and much to everyone's surprise, turned and added, 'Sorry, Tina. I should have said breasts. Why cut the breasts off?'

Ted was staggered but hid it well.

'The choice of words was inappropriate Maurice, but I think you may have something there. Let's not get carried away and think Yorkshire Ripper just yet, but it's a line to keep in mind. Any thoughts on the hair?'

Tina spoke up. 'It's possible Maurice might be on the right lines, boss. Shaving the hair off could delay us but it might also be a way to de-feminize Alice, especially if her hair was very much a feature.'

Ted had heard it all now. The two most diametrically opposed members of his team, the fiercely feminist Tina and the original male chauvinist Maurice, in agreement over something.

'Right, you know what you need to do, let's do it. We can't give this young woman back to her family alive but let's at least put them out of their misery of waiting for news in time for Christmas. And let's get this bastard off the streets before he goes for a repeat performance.'

Chapter Three

Trev's baby was already safely back in the garage when Ted got home later that evening, after what felt like an extremely long day. Trev himself, still damp and fragrant from a recent shower, was sprawled on the sofa, impossibly long legs up on the reclining foot-rest, sporting an over-sized Queen T-shirt and sweat pants.

Almost every inch of his body was covered in cats, leaving him just enough room to balance a mug of the noxious-looking thick blackish beverage he called tea, with just a cloud of milk, strong enough to trot a mouse across.

'I cannot move, I am with cat,' Trev smiled up at a weary-looking Ted, picking up a seal-point cat with blazing blue eyes to match his own to make room for Ted to sit. 'Move up, Freddie, let Daddy sit down. You look knackered. Long day?'

Ted tossed his leather jacket onto the armchair and sank gratefully into the space left by the disgruntled-looking cat.

'Very long. I got a shout about five o'clock, a body found down behind Goyt Bank.'

Trev had the television turned on to a news channel but had reached out a languid hand to the remote to mute the sound when Ted came in.

'There's a chicken casserole in the oven. I saw it on the news and assumed you wouldn't want to go out tonight. Sorry I didn't wake up when you went out.'

Ted leaned back with a sigh as cats started to climb onto him, too.

'You are a mind-reader. And an angel. Maybe a fallen one.

What did they say? We're trying to keep a lid on the details for now; we've not got a positive ID yet.'

'Not a lot really, details were pretty sketchy. Was it gruesome? How many Fisherman's Friends?'

Ted's eyelids were starting to droop from the soporific effect of quadraphonic purring cats. He held one finger aloft.

'Come on, Mr Sleepy,' Trev randomly picked up cats so Ted could move. 'No use falling asleep there, go and get a shower while I sort food out. It will be ready by the time you come back down.'

Ted smiled gratefully to himself as he headed upstairs to the bathroom. He wondered what sort of a welcome home the DCI had had at the end of a long and difficult day. It would almost certainly have been to a cold and empty house, with nothing in the oven for him and his wife yet again out shagging someone or another.

His relationship with Trev was one of the longest and certainly the most solid he knew of amongst friends and colleagues in the force. The DCI's was a train wreck, Maurice Brown was recently divorced, Rob O'Connell and Sal were resolutely single, though never short of girlfriends. Tina seemed to have a steady boyfriend but there was no mention of marriage on the horizon. Virgil was recently married and already his wife was giving him grief about his erratic hours.

He and Trev were good. He often thought of the quote attributed to Paul Newman about not going out for a hamburger when there was steak on the menu at home. He never even looked elsewhere, he quite simply loved the bones of Trev and trusted him completely.

Trev was phenomenally clever, scarily so. He could have had literally any career he wanted, and top universities had been practically fighting over him when he was younger. But then he met Ted and his mind was made up. He loved Ted, cats, big bikes and the rock band Queen, in that order. He'd trained as a motorcycle technician and landed his dream job, looking after bikes in a big dealership in South Manchester.

True to his word, Trev had a meal on the table when Ted came back down, showered, refreshed and dressed in comfortable casuals. The food smelt sensational. Trev was a brilliant cook. He was brilliant at almost anything he decided to turn his hand to. He had poured a crisp, chilled white wine for himself, French, a good vintage, and there was sparkling apple juice for non-drinker Ted.

As Ted sat down and picked up his knife and fork, Trev looked at him and asked, 'It wasn't Rosalie, then? I know that's what always worries you.'

'No, I'm pretty sure it wasn't. Bear in mind I haven't see her for six or seven years but no, I don't think it was her,' Ted replied.

Trev reached over and laid a hand on Ted's.

'She may be all right, you know. You may never be put in the position of having to tell Jim.'

Ted shook his head. 'You know what the odds of a runaway returning are, especially after a long time.'

Trev squeezed his hand a little harder and said, 'Well, I just hope it's not you who gets the shout on that one,' before picking up his own knife.

'All those missing people out there, especially the ones nobody reports. It's too depressing. Let's change the subject. This meal is delicious, by the way, I think you've surpassed yourself this time,' Ted said.

Trev smiled at him and gave him a cheeky wink. 'I know you only moved me in here for my cooking skills.'

It was a long-standing joke between them as both knew nothing could be further from the truth. Ted had even mentioned the M-word but Trev wouldn't hear of it. His opinion was that Ted's relationship caused him enough of a problem in the work place without taking it to that level.

'Other than the body, any good news today?' he asked.

'Jim's found me another DS, who arrives tomorrow. Jim

says he may just have a few preconceived ideas about me.'

Trev groaned. 'Oh no, does that mean you're going to have to go all macho and start beating your chest and swinging from the light-fittings? One of these days I'm going to get one of your team to video it for me and send it to me as I've never seen it yet. Sal would do it for me, I've got him eating out of the palm of my hand, you know.'

It was Ted's turn to wink. 'Don't make me angry, Mr McGee, you wouldn't like me when I'm angry,' he said in his best Hulk voice.

'If you're going to start bursting out of your trousers, can you at least wait until we've finished eating? I've spent hours slaving over a hot stove to make you this, you know,' he said, deliberately batting those incredibly long black eyelashes over those intensely blue eyes.

There was a long gap between the main course and dessert that evening.

Chapter Four

It was unfortunate that the new Detective Sergeant, Mike Hallam's unprofessional opening words to his new team mates, a measure of how on edge he was, were, 'Is it true that the boss is a shirt-lifter?'

It was doubly unfortunate that he voiced them at the precise moment the DI left the DCI's office and came silently into the room behind him. Hallam knew immediately from the looks on the faces of the others that he had just dropped probably the biggest bollock of his entire career.

He spun round on one heel and snapped almost to attention as the much shorter Ted stood calmly looking up at him.

'Morning, sir,' Hallam snapped out. 'I'm your new DS, Mike Hallam.'

Still staying calm and controlled, Ted smiled icily and shook the other man's hand. 'Good to have you on board, DS Hallam. We're a team member down so you're doubly welcome. Just follow me into the cupboard they laughingly call my office then we can get some of the formalities out of the way.'

Ted led the way to his office, moving quietly and smoothly in his rubber-soled Doc Marten boots. His existing team were used to his silent but deadly stealth mode and they knew what it presaged. Hallam was about to find out.

As they got into the office, Ted said, 'I'll just shut the door so we won't be disturbed.'

Then he pivoted so quickly on the balls of his feet and let fly a karate kick so high and so powerful that Hallam cringed as it shot past him, close enough for him to feel the wind of its passing. The door crashed shut, shaking the whole partition wall, barely drowning out the guffaws of laughter of the rest of the team outside, who had witnessed the boss's 'kick-trick' on more than one occasion.

At nearly six feet tall, Hallam towered over his new boss but Ted made no move to indicate the spare chair, which was well out of reach. He wanted Hallam to feel uncomfortable while he made his point. Instead of trying to disguise their height difference, he accentuated it even more by perching on the edge of his desk so the DS had to look down at him whilst he spoke.

As ever, Ted's voice was calm, measured but commanding. Hallam was ashamed to find himself actually physically trembling, standing there in front of the man who was his new boss, not knowing whether he was about to get his marching orders before he had even got his feet under the table. He was imagining his wife's reaction if he had to go home on his first day to tell her he'd been booted out of his new post.

'Mike – it is Mike, isn't it?' the DI began in a deceptively friendly voice. 'I thought it would be helpful if I told you a bit about me and how I run this team before you get stuck in. You're going to have to hit the ground running, with a fresh and nasty murder case on our patch.

'My dad was a miner, Mike. He was paralysed in a mining accident in his thirties, confined to a wheelchair for the rest of his life. My mother left him shortly afterwards, because it turned out she liked shagging rather more than she liked her crippled husband and her young son.

'My dad got quite a bit of compensation for his injuries, because the mine owners were negligent and they couldn't wriggle out of their responsibilities. It was so he could afford proper specialist care for himself for the rest of his life. But I'll tell you what he spent most of it on, shall I, Mike?'

Hallam didn't dare respond as he feared that by this time

his voice would also be shaking, so he merely nodded.

'He spent it all on martial arts lessons for me, Mike. That's because when your name is Darling, you're a skinny little runt and you've known since the age of ten that you were - what was it you called it, Mike, a shirt-lifter? I prefer gay myself, but let's not split hairs - you need all the help you can get in protecting yourself. Billy fecking Elliott, eh?

'Especially when you also know from a very young age that you want to be a copper. Because let's face it, Mike, the force isn't exactly known for being all-embracing and welcoming of those, like me, who are a bit different from the norm. There are some officers, aren't there, Mike, even to this day, who take exception to people who are different, without taking the time to get to know them, and who try to make life difficult for them.

'So my dad paid for me to study judo, and karate and ju-jitsu and lots of others you may not have heard of. I was pretty good at all of them. I've got black belts in four of them. And I still keep it up because sometimes, Mike, I still have to protect myself, and protect my team, from the prejudice of others who are perhaps not very enlightened.

'My team includes a black officer, and a Muslim officer and a woman officer. And me. And guess what, Mike? We all get along really well. We respect one another, we work together, and that's why we are the best team, with the best results, in the whole division.'

By this time, Hallam was mortified to discover that not only was he visibly trembling, he was dying for a piss, utterly convinced he would soon be out on his ear and having to explain to his wife how he had totally screwed up his transfer on his first day. He just hoped he could hang on long enough to slink out with his tail between his legs and find the bogs before he pissed his pants.

'I know so many ways to kill with my bare hands that it would take too long to tell you about them all, Mike. So let me tell you a bit about my time in Uniform. Because I was an SFO, Mike. You know what an SFO is of course, don't you?'

'Specialist Firearms Officer, sir,' Hallam only just had enough control of his vocal chords to get the phrase out.

'Exactly Mike! The crazies! The ones even the SAS say are too mad to be let loose. But – now here's the very good news for you, Mike - I'm a peace-loving person. I keep cats, I grow lilies. I respect people, so I generally find they respect me.

'I'm not telling you any of this to brag, Mike. I'm telling you because it's sometimes easy to see a stereotype and not look beyond it. So if I heard you, for example, make a racist comment about our Virgil – it's not his real name, it's a joke, by the way, one he finds amusing, so it's different – or a sexist comment about Tina, or any bulimic gags about Maurice – just for example, Mike – I wouldn't be very pleased. In fact, Mike, I might just have to bounce your arse all the way back to Stretford, pretty sharpish.

'It's important to me that all my team members feel respected and respect one another. I respect you, and I know you respect all of us and are going to fit in wonderfully with the team. Welcome aboard, Mike, it's good to have you.' He stood up and once more shook Hallam's hand which was by now as damp and quivering as a fish out of water.

As Hallam scuttled back to the outer office, his new team mates were all at their desks chuckling, having undoubtedly heard every word the boss had said, despite his measured tones, through the paper-thin walls.

Maurice spoke up. 'You got the full kick-trick treatment then? Most of us have had that early on, except Tina 'cos she's Mother Teresa, and Steve cos he's too scared to say anything about anyone.'

Tina chipped in. 'If he's letting you stay, Sarge, he must rate you. You've got the best boss in the force in there, I hope you appreciate that.'

Maurice added, 'Oh, by the way, the bogs are just along the

corridor on the left!'

Hallam scuttled in the direction of his pointing finger and just made it in time to relieve himself and, to his eternal shame, to throw up his breakfast as the adrenaline really kicked in.

Chapter Five

DS Mike Hallam was already at his desk when Ted got in and Ted was usually in first, ahead of his team. He was impressed. His little talk yesterday seemed to have had an effect already.

The DS was still feeling uncomfortable around his new boss, totally unsure of his boundaries, so he made to rise from his seat when his senior officer came in.

Ted waved him down with a hand and said, 'No need for any of that old bollocks. What are you working on?'

'Well, sir, I'm trawling through these lists of Missing Persons, to see if I can get any solid leads that would be worth following up with a visit. Like you said, the sooner we get an ID, the sooner we can move forward,' he said.

Ted was pleased to hear him talking about 'we' – the team talk had worked.

'Must say I'm impressed with the work the TDC's done, very thorough job.'

'He's a good lad, is Steve. Make sure you tell him,' Ted said. 'He'll die of embarrassment when you do but everyone works better with good feedback, it's a powerful motivator.'

There was an awkward silence, then the DS spoke. 'Sir, yesterday,' he cleared his throat. 'I was bang out of order. I thought you were going to kick me out on my arse.'

Ted threw his head back and laughed, perching on the edge of the DS's desk. 'Shit, Mike, if I sacked everyone who ever made a homophobic remark about me, I'd have a real recruitment problem. I've seen your record. You're a good copper, I know that. You'll be an even better one now you know not to be judgemental. By the way, how's your mother-in-law?'

'It's difficult, sir. We've moved into her house for now. There's a house for sale in the same road and we've put in an offer on that,' the DS told him. 'It's just she used to be so independent, so active, always off out somewhere or other. Now she's stuck in a wheelchair the whole time and it's …'

He broke off suddenly and looked even more awkward, remembering what the DI had told him the previous day about his father.

'I know,' Ted told him. 'My dad was the same, especially when my mum walked out. Can I give you some advice, based on my experience?'

'That would be really helpful, sir,' the DS said. 'We're struggling a bit, to be honest.'

'Make her feel useful. Let her know that she's still needed,' Ted told him. 'Make sure you encourage her to do as much as she possibly can. Do you have kids?'

'Yes, sir, a girl and a boy, seven and nine.'

'Could she babysit?' Ted asked.

The DS looked a little uncertain.

'Why not?' Ted asked him. 'For half an hour, while your missus nips to the shops? Make sure the kids know how to help, what to do. You have taught them how to contact help when they need it, I take it?

Hallam looked sheepish.

Ted shook his head. 'Coppers, eh? Never ceases to amaze me how many of them don't even teach their kids how to dial the emergency services. She needs to feel needed or she will lose all self-respect. My dad did. What he didn't spend on karate lessons for me, he spent on drink and it killed him.'

His face clouded for a moment, then he stood up. 'Another bit of advice, Mike. When you get to the stage of knocking on to get a positive ID, try and make yourself look a bit less like a copper. You look like one from a mile away anyway, so try dressing down a bit. We're very casual here, look at me,' he indicated his customary attire of dark jeans, a polo neck and leather jacket, with his trademark soft-soled boots.

'The Big Boss is always telling me the opposite. Set a good example, wear a suit and tie. Can you imagine it? I look like bloody wee Jimmy Krankie dressed like that! Like this I can go in undercover anywhere and nobody thinks I'm a cop. And take Tina with you, she's very good at it. I take it you aren't sexist as well?' he said with a wink, then headed for his office.

He was hoping for the full post-mortem report on their victim today, which may enable them to move forward. He'd been at the PM yesterday, not his favourite activity, and had munched his way through most of a bag of Fisherman's Friends in the process. The pathologist had given him a brief resumé of his initial findings but Ted wanted the nitty-gritty details to give him more of an insight.

The report was waiting for him, as he'd hoped. The body was that of a young woman in her early twenties, in good physical shape, no signs of track marks. Probably not, therefore, a drug user, living on the streets or certainly not for any length of time, and not an addict.

Cause of death was a single clean cut to the throat from the rear, extremely efficient and precise, severing both jugular veins and the trachea, which meant death would have been relatively rapid. The weapon was interesting. A cut that clean and accurate suggested a precision blade; the pathologist thought possibly a surgical scalpel.

Ted knew that such a quick, clean cut was more difficult than most people imagined, which opened up some interesting possibilities. It was also a left-handed wound which might narrow the field of suspects down somewhat.

The double mastectomy was post-mortem, luckily, so they were not dealing with a sadistic torture element. The reason for it was still unclear. The body also seemed to have been cleaned after death and there was a likelihood that the hair removal was carried out post-mortem. This was not just a case of someone preparing for a night out by shaving their legs and having a Brazilian wax.

Ted was interested in the toxicology results which were still to come, to see if there were any indications of recreational drug use. There was the possibility that some substance may have been administered to prevent a struggle, something like the so-called date rape drug Rohypnol, although Ted knew traces of such substances quickly disappeared from the blood stream.

According to the pathologist's early observations, there were signs of recent sexual activity, as he put it 'rather rough but still probably consensual', with no signs of any physical restraints having been used. A condom had been used, so they were not going to be lucky with DNA on that score.

The victim had died about forty-eight hours before discovery. The pathologist noted that the body had clearly been preserved at low temperature to retard decomposition, though had not been frozen, so not kept in someone's domestic freezer.

DS Hallam knocked on his door and came in without waiting to be asked. Ted liked that, it showed the man was quickly settling down, after his rocky start yesterday. Hallam laid out four sheets of paper on the DI's desk and said, 'Got some possible matches in our area, sir. Thought I'd start local then work out.'

Ted glanced at the sheets of paper. So many people disappearing all the time. The thought always depressed him, especially as his mother had left without trace and he had never bothered to track her down. He didn't even know if she was still alive. Didn't much care, either.

He put his finger on the one on the right. 'It's not her, you can forget that one,' he said. It was Rosalie.

'Sir?' the DS sounded puzzled.

'Sorry, Mike, I should have made sure you were in the loop,' Ted told him. 'That's the DCI's daughter. I know her,

I've seen our body. It's not her.'

'Shit,' the DS looked visibly shaken at the news.

'My fault, I should have briefed you. She's been missing nearly seven years. You and Tina get round to the most likely first, start with the obvious. I'll send you a copy of the PM report, check it through for any more indications before you go, save a wasted journey, and save upsetting folks if you don't have to. Where are you putting your money?' Ted asked.

'This one,' the DS said decisively, pointing to the middle one of the remaining three. 'I'm starting off with the most likely assumption that with blue eyes, she was probably a blonde before someone shaved her hair off.'

'Dangerous assumption,' the DI told him. 'My partner Trevor has curly black hair and his eyes are as blue as ...' For a moment a faraway look came over Ted's face which made the DS feel decidedly uncomfortable, then the DI shook himself and continued, 'Blue. He has blue eyes. Blue and blonde don't always go together but it's as good an assumption as any to start on.'

Hallam turned to go and Ted said, 'Good work, Mike. While you're chasing down a positive ID on Alice, get young Steve onto finding anyone in our area with previous for using a specialised blade, anything like a scalpel. Someone who may possibly be a southpaw but don't get too hung up on that in case it's a blade expert who can use either hand, maybe someone combat trained.

'Then get Maurice onto checking where any likely suspects are at the moment and what they've been up to. He's a plodder, but a good solid plodder, very methodical. And Mike, don't forget ...'

The DS paused for a moment, looking a little confused. Then light dawned on his face. 'Got it, sir, give them positive feedback.'

Ted smiled. 'My work here is done,' he said, as he went back to his paperwork.

Chapter Six

Tina offered to drive her car while they went out trying to get a positive ID on Alice. Mike Hallam suspected this was yet another way of testing him, seeing if he was sexist enough to object to being driven by a woman. In fact Tina was an excellent driver and her car was a sporty Mini Cooper, a little on the compact side for his lanky frame but a fun ride nevertheless.

Inevitably, as well as talking shop, the DS was anxious to find out more about his unusual new boss, to avoid putting his size thirteens in it any more. They were heading to a smart suburb of South Manchester, from where their possible match had been reported missing by a flatmate. They were hoping to find the flatmate at home to be certain of an ID before they called on any family. Breaking the news of a death was something most officers dreaded. Getting it wrong was unthinkable.

Luckily Tina gave him the opener. 'So do you think you can work with us, Sarge? Not the most orthodox team in the division, eh?'

Mike laughed ruefully. 'I've certainly never had a welcome speech like that before. Have to confess I was bricking myself. I thought he was going to kick me straight out, literally. The missus would have killed me!'

'Any trouble in the team, he deals with it himself, in his own way,' Tina said. 'Saying that, he always has our backs, stands between us and any flak which might be heading our way. We all know he'd take a bullet for any of us too. He's not a pen-pushing sort of boss, always where the action is.'

'Ex-SFO, eh? I should have done my homework a bit better,' Mike laughed.

'We've never been able to find out if it's really true but urban legend has it he was offered a medal which he politely declined,' Tina continued. 'Well, not all that politely, the boss hates a fuss, but his boss refused it politely on his behalf.'

'I read up on it after yesterday's baptism of fire - something about him disarming someone with a knife?'

'Not so much a knife as two hooking big machetes, one in each hand,' Tina said. 'Guy ran amok in a crowded shopping centre. One fatality, lots of serious injuries and a hostage situation. Very difficult for the shooters to do anything. The negotiator was having no luck, the attacker didn't speak any English and they couldn't find out what he did speak. The boss just walked in and took the machetes off him, with some pretty nifty moves and no harm done.'

'You saw it?' the DS asked.

'Oh yes. Candy from a baby springs to mind,' she said. 'The DCI gave him a right bollocking for going in, we could hear it all round the nick, then he got offered a medal. We started calling him Mr Miyagi afterwards. You know, from The Karate Kid. But he didn't like that because he said it wasn't pure karate he used. He's a bit of a stickler for detail, is the boss. He can take a joke, as long as it's accurate.'

They'd turned off the main road into a pleasant, leafy, suburban street, lined with London plane trees, large Edwardian houses on both sides, most now converted into flats. Tina took the first available parking space and pointed a little further down the street.

'Flat 4B at number fifty-six is where our Alice lives, if it is her. It was her flatmate who reported her missing on Monday, after she didn't come home from work at the weekend. She works in a bar/bistro, not very far from here,' Tina told him.

'Do you want to do the talking while I observe?' the DS

asked her and added hastily, 'I'm not meaning you because you're a woman, nothing like that. I just thought, me being new to the team, maybe I should observe how you work first?'

He was sounding increasingly uncomfortable, aware of the elephant trap he was digging for himself, unintentionally stereotyping his female colleague.

'Relax, Sarge,' she laughed. 'I know the chances of you making a sexist remark after your initiation by the boss yesterday are somewhere between nil and bugger all. Happy to take the lead though, if you like, assuming anyone is in, of course.'

Flat 4B turned out to be the basement flat, down a separate flight of stone steps with iron railings at the side and small, high windows to allow in some daylight. There was a light on inside and the pounding whump-whump of music blaring out, making the sash window frames rattle.

They had to knock several times before there was the sound of someone coming to open the door. A young woman, late teens or early twenties, opened it. She had dreadlocks pulled back into a pony tail, a nose ring, a labret ring, and more earrings than it was possible to count at first glance.

Her face went pale at the sight of the two officers pulling out and showing their warrant cards.

'DC Bailey, DS Hallam. We're here about your report of a missing flatmate. May we come in?' Tina asked.

The girl looked scared to death. Both officers could easily smell the cause for her panic and Tina quickly reassured her. 'We're just here about Vicki Carr, nothing else. Can we come in?'

The girl stood aside and motioned them to a door on the left of the hallway which opened into a small but pleasant sitting room. Both officers studiously ignored the still-smouldering roach in the ashtray on the coffee table.

'May I have your name, please?' Tina asked as she and Mike sat down on the squashy sofa the girl indicated, while she turned off the music.

The girl had to clear her throat before she could reply successfully. 'Poppy,' she said. 'Poppy Adams. I'm Vicki's flat mate. I'm a student, reading law with criminology at Manchester.' She indicated an impressive stack of books on the floor. It may just have been a tactic to draw their attention away from the roach.

'Criminology, eh?' Mike said ironically, before he could stop himself, then surprised himself by immediately shutting up in the face of the withering look which Tina threw at him.

'Have you found Vicki? Is she in some sort of trouble?' Poppy asked.

'We're just carrying out enquiries at this stage,' Tina neatly avoided answering the question directly. 'Can you tell me when you last saw Vicki?'

'Saturday evening,' came the reply. 'She went out to do a shift at the bistro and didn't come back. I didn't think too much of it the first night.'

'Did she often stay out overnight?' Tina asked.

'Well, you know, sometimes, if she was with someone. Same as I do. Neither of us would worry about the other just for one night,' Poppy said.

'Was she seeing anyone in particular at the moment? Steady partner? Anything like that?' Tina asked, while Hallam made a mental note of Tina's careful use of the neutral 'partner' and logged it away for future use. He was learning.

'She did have a boyfriend up to a couple of weeks ago but she dumped him. He was getting a bit too possessive.' Mike and Tina exchanged a look and asked for details of the boyfriend which Mike duly noted.

'When did you start to worry?'

'Well, usually if one of us stayed out all night, we'd either come back around mid-morning or at the very least we'd text one another. I didn't hear anything from Vicki at all on Sunday and her mobile was going straight to voice-mail. That was very unusual as she had planned to go and have lunch with her parents and would usually have come back to change first.

'I phoned them to check that she hadn't just gone straight there, which she hadn't, so I popped round to the bistro and they hadn't heard anything either. So on Monday morning I went to the police station and reported her missing,' Poppy told them.

'Do you have any recent photos of Vicki, to help with our enquiries?' Tina asked.

Poppy pulled an expensive-looking phone out of the pocket of the baggy boyfriend cardigan she was wearing and started flicking through it. 'Loads of selfies. Who doesn't, these days?'

She found one and held it out to them. It was of her and a smiling young woman with long, unruly blonde hair. They were each holding a cocktail glass full of a vivid coloured liquid, rich in fruit, adorned with paper umbrellas and lit sparklers.

'That was taken at the bar. Vicki made it up. She wanted to call it "Better than a shag" but the owner wasn't keen. It was wicked,' Poppy told them.

Tina and Mike exchanged a look and tried not to make it too loaded. They had their positive ID. Their 'Alice' was definitely Vicki Carr, from Tina's observation of the body and the photos taken at the crime scene. Now they needed to go and do the dreaded knock on the door of the parents, whose address they already had.

Another leafy suburb, this time smart post-war semis, undoubtedly with a substantial price tag. Tina pulled up outside one with an obsessively immaculate front garden, bowling green neat lawn, late-flowering chrysanthemums standing in stiff rows like soldiers on parade.

Mike Hallam had heeded the Boss's advice and tried his best to dress more casually, less like a copper, but he was the first to admit he had little dress sense and his wife had given up on him long ago.

He obviously hadn't quite achieved what he'd hoped for though, as when a neatly dressed woman in her late forties opened the door and he asked, 'Mrs Carr?' she went ashen-faced and would have ended up on the floor had Tina not caught her deftly with a technique which spoke of practice.

Chapter Seven

The DS beat Ted in the next morning, too. Ted smiled to himself when he saw Mike working away at his desk. He stopped smiling when Hallam turned in greeting and Ted saw he was sporting an angry-looking cut high up on his left cheek bone, with the beginnings of a black eye forming above it.

The DS grinned and self-consciously touched the injury as he said, 'And the moral of that story is, when teaching your son how to swing a baseball bat, don't move in too close.'

Ted laughed. 'Are you into baseball then?'

Hallam shook his head. 'Not remotely, sir, not interested in any sports, to be honest, and I was rubbish at all of them at school,' he said. 'I just seem somehow to have spawned a son who loves sport and expects me to be able to teach him how to play anything and everything. I wish I could interest him in ping-pong instead, that might be less hazardous for me.'

'My partner Trevor and I run a self-defence club for kids. Might be good for your lad, and certainly less dangerous for you,' Ted told him. 'Anyway, I'd like you to brief the team this morning. I'd be interested to see how you deploy them. Up to you, but if I were you I'd put four on the Vicki Carr case, leave the others on existing cases. I take it you've brought yourself up to speed on what else we have on the books?'

'Yes sir, that's why I've been coming in early,' Hallam replied.

'See if you can get Steve out of the office a bit,' Ted suggested. 'Typical geeky type, he's happiest on his computer but a bit of fresh air would do the lad good. Don't put him on

L. M. KRIER

door-to-door on his own yet though, he'd never manage to say anything.'

'We need to start off with some questions at the bistro, staff and customers,' the DS said. 'I was impressed with Tina, I thought of sending the TDC with her on that, to get him started, if you think that's all right, sir?'

'Good idea, sound thinking,' Ted said. 'As soon as everyone is in let me know and I'll sit in. Good work, Mike, liking your enthusiasm and commitment. And it's fine to call me boss. I'm quite relaxed about it.'

Hallam was surprised at how pleased he felt at the boss's words. He'd never really given much consideration to this feedback idea before. Now he was starting to understand.

The DS noticed none of the team was late, they were all in ahead of time and ready for action. Maurice Brown was last through the door but still early, just. This time he came armed with a bag of still-warm croissants, which he handed round before tucking into the first of the remaining three.

The DI slipped quietly out of his office before Hallam needed to come and find him, and leaned against a desk, interested to see his new DS in action. He was amused when Hallam opened the team briefing with, 'Right, team, settle down.'

He was also impressed with the way the DS handled things. He used available manpower exactly as Ted would have done himself and showed that he had really done his homework in finding out the strengths and weaknesses of his new team. He'd also done his research on what the team were already working on and factored that in.

'We now have an ID, as you all know. Vicki Carr, twenty-three. Worked in a bistro, left work there Saturday night, never seen alive again. We need to know who she left work with, who she'd been talking to. It's a busy place, I hear, but had anyone there noticed anyone in particular interacting with her? Tina, you and Steve are on this. Get round there, talk to bar staff, customers, anyone else around.

'Next we need to find this ex-boyfriend. He sounds a possessive type. Maybe he didn't take the break-up all that well. Maurice, I need someone who knows the local area well to help me find him and ask him a few questions, see if we need to bring him in. You've got a car, have you? Easier for me to get my bearings if I'm not behind the wheel.'

Ted liked the master-stroke. Putting Maurice at the wheel meant he couldn't turn the outing into a pub crawl with a pint in every place they visited. The DS had quickly got his number. But Ted didn't envy him. Maurice's car was like a badly-kept dog kennel on wheels and stank of cigarette smoke.

Maurice had been trying to stop smoking for months, hoping to appease the nicotine craving with the sticky buns, but had just succeeded in having two addictions instead of one.

'Sal,' the DS asked, ' how's the fraud case going? You on top of it or do you need help?'

'Losing the will to live, Sarge,' Sal replied cheerfully. 'I wouldn't say no to a hand, but if there's none to spare, I can plod on with it.'

'Good,' the DS replied, 'because I want Virgil and Rob on this assault from last night. It's a nasty one, I want it mopped up fast.'

'Anything you want me to do, DS Hallam?' Ted asked quietly from the back. 'I'm one of the team, here to do what needs doing, don't forget.'

'You could make me some coffee while I get on with sorting these witness statements, boss,' Sal said with a laugh, with which the others joined in, including the DI.

'Just remember I'm here if anyone needs back-up for anything,' the DI said. 'And I do mean anything.'

Hallam was gobsmacked. He'd never before worked with a DI as relaxed with his team and they with him. His last one in Stretford had been a Class A bastard, impossible to read and certainly impossible to relax with. It was due in large part to severe haemorrhoids and a wife who nagged.

'I thought I'd leave you free for now, boss, in case Maurice and I find and pull in the ex-boyfriend and you might want to question him,' the DS quickly recovered his stride. 'But perhaps until we do, Sal would be glad of a hand? I think he takes two sugars.'

There was more laughter as the team went their separate ways. Hallam felt pleased with himself; he thought he'd got it just about right. The DI smiled and nodded at him. Another hurdle jumped.

DS Hallam was glad it was not a cold day. He needed the window wide open in Maurice Brown's battered old Ford to get rid of the smell of cigarette smoke. The car was a tip, fag ends and food wrappers everywhere, half an old meat pie in a paper bag on the front dashboard.

With his new resolution not to be judgemental, Hallam decided to put it down to the recent breakup of Brown's marriage. On the other hand, if he always lived like such a slob, that may have been one thing to help end the marriage in the first place.

He and Tina had got the ex-boyfriend's contact details from the flatmate before they had left the victim's flat so they started at the address they had for Robert Allen. It turned out to be another flat, this time on the top floor of a house not all that far from where Vicki had lived.

The house was tall and narrow, Victorian, much shabbier than where Vicki's flat was, in an area that was decidedly scruffy round the edges.

Hallam and the DC trudged up three flights of stairs to a dark and poky top landing with two doors opening off it. Hallam knocked on the one at which the ex-boyfriend apparently lived.

When there was no reply, he knocked again, more loudly. There was still no reply from within but the door on the opposite side of the landing opened and a tall, thin young man with tousled curly hair stood in the doorway, yawning expansively. He was wearing pyjamas and something which looked like a kimono over them.

Both men held up their warrant cards and the DS said, 'Sorry to disturb you, sir, we're looking for Robert Allen. Can you tell us where we might find him?'

'Oh gosh, I've no idea. The nearest pub, perhaps?' the young man replied. He was well-spoken, his voice well modulated, not a local accent.

'Do you have any idea what he does?' Hallam asked him.

'He drinks,' the young man said, as if it were self evident.

'For a living, I meant,' Hallam replied.

'So did I,' the young man riposted. 'Honestly, I have no idea how he earns a crust. He's always drunk or getting there. I've never seen him go out to work, he just seems to have a string of girlfriends from comfortably off families who seem happy to sub him. I can't imagine why. He's always behind with the rent, too. Find any pub or bar that's open anywhere round here and you'll find him or someone who's seen him recently.'

As the men trudged back down the stairs, Maurice said to the DS, 'Sounds a likely contender, Sarge. Vicki Carr's family were comfortable, by all accounts, and she was working. Asked her for more money, then got a shitty on when she refused, do you think?'

'Let's not put the cart before the horse, Maurice. Find him first then ask him.'

As the DS had hoped, Maurice Brown knew his patch like the back of his hand. He navigated them effortlessly round the local licensed premises and was greeted on first name terms in all of them. They finally tracked down Robert Allen to a wine bar where he was sitting on a bar stool, slumped over the counter, with half a glass of red wine in front of him.

The two men slid on to stools on either side of him, warrant cards in hand, and the DS asked, 'Are you Robert Allen?'

Allen, around mid-twenties, average build, with dark brown hair which flopped forward over his face, partly concealing spaniel-brown eyes, made a bleary effort to bring the man into focus and slurred, 'That, my friend, is a very good question, to which I am not entirely sure I have the answer.'

The barman came over. 'Good luck with that one, Maurice. Hard to get a straight answer out of him at the best of times, and he's been here since we opened. Usual for you, is it?'

Maurice threw him a loaded look, then looked at the DS as he said, 'Yes, that's right, Andy, the usual black coffee for me and whatever the DS is having. On my tab.'

Andy walked away chuckling to himself. He had never known Maurice order coffee in his life and he didn't have a tab. He wouldn't be allowed one. But he stretched a point and brought the two coffees the men had ordered plus another which he put optimistically in front of the extremely drunken Allen.

The DS asked, 'Mr Allen, we're here about Vicki Carr. I believe you know her?'

Allen was struggling to keep his eyes focused on the face speaking to him. 'I know her, in the biblical sense of the word, in every sense of the word. I knew her, I fucked her, she fucked me over.'

'When did you last see her, Mr Allen?' Maurice Brown asked him.

Allen swivelled his head owlishly in the direction of the new questioner.

'Shortly before she dumped me, by text. The bitch. The fucking bitch,' he said, his face contorting in anger.

'And where were you at the weekend, Mr Allen?' Brown asked, 'Say from Saturday night to Tuesday morning?'

Allen studied him long and hard. 'I don't even know when the weekend was, officer. That's because I have no idea what day it is today. Or tomorrow. I have no knowledge of the concept of time.'

The two officers exchanged glances. 'We're going to have to take him in and dry him out first before we can question him some more,' the DS said.

'Er, Sarge, we can't put him in my car, the springs have gone in the back seat,' Brown said apologetically.

Hallam shook his head and sighed at the news. 'Get on the blower, get the station to send a car. And let the Boss know we may have a possible suspect coming in.'

Chapter Eight

When the DS and Maurice got back with the ex-boyfriend, they checked him in with the duty sergeant then had him put in an interview room and plied with strong coffee while they went upstairs in search of the DI.

Tina and Steve were also just back in with their findings, which didn't amount to a great deal, and were briefing the DI on what they did have. The bistro was always packed at the weekends, no one had noticed anyone paying particular attention to Vicki, nor did they notice if she had left with anyone. Tina had been thorough and asked about the ex-boyfriend.

Yes, the manager and the staff confirmed, they knew him and had been highly relieved when Vicki had finished with him. He had a habit of turning up outrageously drunk and trying to talk to Vicki while she was working. He'd had to be thrown out on several occasions and on one memorable evening he had been drunk enough to throw up all over a table set out for a hen party. They hadn't seen him since the break-up and almost certainly would have remembered as he was barred and would have been unceremoniously evicted.

Hallam told them they had just brought the ex-boyfriend in for questioning.

'He's very drunk, boss,' he told the DI, 'but from what we hear, that's his normal state. He's downstairs. I've got them making him coffee, a lot of it. I thought that at least if we brought him in, he could start drying out. He couldn't offer us any alibi for the weekend and he did get very angry talking

40

about Vicki. He didn't indicate if he knew she was dead but then he didn't seem to be all that much in touch with reality.'

'Good work, all of you; it's a start and we need a start,' Ted said. 'I'll go and begin interviewing him, at least. See what else you can find out about him. Not you, Steve,' he said as the young TDC headed automatically towards his computer. 'You come and sit in with me on this one.'

The young man looked panic-stricken but followed the DI down to the interview room. Robert Allen was slumped at the table, making an effort to drink some of the coffee which had been provided for him. He was succeeding in spilling more than he drank each time he lifted the cup with a badly shaking hand.

There was a PC babysitting him who left when the DI and TDC came in. Allen smelt like a brewery and also smelt strongly of piss, which was not all that pleasant in the small room. Ted was not yet entirely sure if he was going to be fit to be interviewed. But he began the formalities and explained carefully that Allen was not under arrest, just helping with enquiries.

Allen's blurred eyes made unsteady contact with the DI's face as he said, 'How marvellous. Helping the police with their enquiries. That always sounds so ...' he broke off while he searched for a word. 'So noble.'

'Mr Allen, are you aware that Vicki Carr is dead?' Ted asked him.

'Is she?' Allen asked, then, with more emphasis, 'IS she now? Well, that just goes to show. When you wish upon a star, your dreams really do come true. Because, you see, Mr An Inspector Calls, I wished that bitch dead after she dumped me. I really did. I just looked up at the stars and I wished her dead.'

'Mr Allen, what is your profession?' Ted asked.

'Ha!' the young man exclaimed. 'My profession? Nothing! I am nothing. I am no one. I was going to be an ac-torrr,' he said, drawing the word out to the maximum. 'I signed on at the

Arts School. I was going to tread the boards. But then, you see,' he leaned conspiratorially closer to Ted and said wistfully, 'two small problems got in the way. First, and no one told me this, it seems you have to go to lectures and such things. And second, I didn't have any talent. None at all. Zilch.'

He spread his arms expansively wide and blinked rapidly.

'Mr Allen, where were you at the weekend?'

'Somewhere,' Allen said enigmatically. 'Somewhere over the rainbow. In the gutter, looking at the stars. I have not the first fucking foggiest of an idea, actually.'

'Mr Allen,' Ted said, 'I would like to question you further about the death of Vicki Carr and in particular on your movements at the weekend. However I don't believe you are currently in a fit state to answer such questions. I would therefore like to arrange for you to have a lie down and perhaps a sleep until you feel a little more able to answer my questions and then we can talk again. Are you in agreement with that?'

'Ah, to sleep, perchance to dream. What a shame, what a waste of talent. I know all the fucking words; I just have no idea how to act them,' Allen said, subsiding back over the table and looking as if he were about to go to sleep there and then.

Ted turned to the young TDC. 'Come on, I'll ask the PC to put him in a cell for now. We'll go back upstairs and come down when he's had chance to sleep at least some of it off, see if he doesn't make a bit more sense when he's sobered up somewhat. Do you have any initial thoughts?'

Steve trotted up the stairs in the DI's wake, uncomfortable as ever at being asked to voice an opinion, but he did say, 'I don't see how it can be him, sir.'

Ted stopped and turned back to look at the young TDC who was standing on the stair lower down.

'What's your reasoning?'

'Well, sir,' the young man was positively squirming. 'It's the sex thing.'

42

'The sex thing?' Ted asked, intrigued. 'Go on.'

'Well, sir,' he said again. 'Didn't the pathologist say there had been recent rough sex? And hasn't everyone we've spoken to said he's always that drunk, all the time? Well, sir, I just don't see how he could, you know, could even get it up when he's as drunk as that, sir.'

Ted suppressed a smile. He wondered if the young man were speaking from personal experience. 'You know what, Steve?' he said. 'I think you may well be onto something there. Come on,' and he continued up the stairs, two at a time.

Tina, Maurice and Mike Hallam were still there when they went in.

'Gather round,' Ted told them. 'Steve has a theory, and I think it's a credible one.'

Steve threw him a pleading look, going red in the face again. He was clearly not looking forward to discussing alcohol-induced erectile dysfunction in front of Tina but she remained professionally silent while he set out his theory and added, 'I mean, he smells as if he's wet himself, a few times, so if that's his usual state, I can't see how he would be having any sex with Vicki at all, never mind recent rough sex.'

'It's a good point, boss,' Tina said. 'If she'd dumped him and he was barred from the bistro, what was he going to do? Lie in wait for her outside then take her somewhere and persuade her to have sex with him, which then got a bit rough? It's not sounding very plausible.'

'We had to bring him in, sir, he has a pretty strong motive,' Hallam said defensively. 'He looked like he really hated her when he was talking about her dumping him.'

'Of course you did, Mike. You did right, he's the obvious suspect to start with,' Ted reassured him. 'Right, while he's hopefully drying out enough for me to have another go at him, let's sort out a quick search of his place, if he agrees to give us his keys.

'We've got no DNA on the body from the killer but let's

43

check his out anyway and let's look for any previous form of any sort, especially with violence or rough stuff involved. And as he doesn't seem to know where he was, you four get back out there and check out an alibi for him.

'If he's the famous pissing and puking local drunk, people will remember if he was in their bar at the weekend. And check especially for Monday night when the body was dumped. If he was in that state, it's looking less and less likely that he's our man.

'Find out about a vehicle, too. Does he have one? Could he even have driven one in that condition? I don't see how he could have trotted across town balancing a body on his shoulder so how could he have got it to where it was dumped? Still a lot of work to be done. But good work everyone. Especially you, Steve.'

The young man looked about ready to die of embarrassment, especially when the DI added, his eyes twinkling, 'Not being a drinker myself, I hadn't considered the correlation between alcohol intake and performance in the sack.'

Chapter Nine

Inquests were a part of his job which Ted didn't enjoy too much, largely because he had to make an effort with his appearance and ditch his usual casual look. He always insisted he looked like a schoolboy in a suit and tie, despite Trev telling him it made him look sexy. In fact women found him irresistibly attractive at the best of times, even more so when done up for a court appearance. Knowing his sexuality just made him more of a challenge.

He absolutely drew the line at formal suits, which he claimed made him look ridiculous, compromising instead with warm caramel chinos and matching jacket, which he could buy from a travel and outdoor clothing supplier so they didn't feel too formal. With Trev's guidance, he accessorized with a soft sage green shirt and a loosely done up tie in tones of fern and bracken, just about hiding the open top button. Soft suede desert boots completed the look.

Some senior police officers found Ted and his style far too informal. He didn't give a stuff. His boss was cool with it, which was good enough for him, as long as he made an effort for court appearances.

He generally preferred inquests with the area coroner in charge. She was a no-nonsense 'bish-bash-bosh-done' sort of coroner, which suited him. But for a violent death it had to be the senior coroner for the division, who was dry and pedantic and clearly disapproved of everything about Ted, not just his sartorial style. He could never fault him on his presentation or delivery of evidence, but it clearly pained him not to be able to do so.

In the case of Vicki Carr, the inquest was just a formality to take evidence of identification. It was then adjourned and would be resumed once the police enquiry was finished and its findings made available. At least it was over in time for Ted to have a swift drink in a nearby watering hole. Although he didn't drink alcohol, post-inquest lunches were always a good way to catch up with officers from other areas and get up to speed with divisional goings-on.

The pub of choice was called The Grapes. Some literary wag had shinned up its sign-post to spray 'of Wrath' underneath, which had so tickled the landlord that he'd never bothered to get it removed.

It was a dying breed of old traditional pub, half-timbered in the architectural style typical of the region. It had somehow escaped the fashion to convert everything into wine bar or gastropub and had kept its smoke-blackened beams. It also retained a whiff of cigarettes despite the length of time since the smoking ban. It begged the question as to when its soft furnishings had last been cleaned.

'Gunner, please, Dave, when you have a minute,' Ted said to the landlord as he went in.

'If I must,' the publican responded cheerfully. He liked Ted, liked his quirkiness. Ted was certainly the only one of his customers who drank ginger beer split with dry ginger ale, with freshly squeezed lime, 'without the Angosturas,' as Ted was often reminding him.

The place was already crowded and, glancing round, Ted could see that it was largely the court and police crowd. As Ted was waiting for his drink, a lanky young man sidled up to him and Ted groaned inwardly. He was a local reporter and Ted generally tried to avoid the press like the plague, preferring to leave that side of the job to the experts.

'DI Darling, what can you tell me about the murder case?' the reporter asked.

'Nothing more than you heard in court just now, Alastair. You need to speak to our press office for any queries, you know that.' Ted was even more averse to this particular journalist who had shockingly bad teeth and a disconcerting habit of playing pocket billiards all the time he was speaking, which was distracting.

'Can't you give me anything more? I'd love an exclusive on this one,' the man wheedled.

'If I get anything I can pass on to you, I know where to find you,' Ted said, thankful that Dave was handing him his Gunner. He paid, excused himself to the journalist, and went across to find a seat with a few people he recognised.

He wasn't thrilled to find himself at a table with one of the pathologists, not the one who had carried out the PM on Vicki Carr, but his immediate superior. He was reputedly the leading forensic pathologist in the country, but Ted found him insufferably pompous and patronising.

'Ted, old boy!' the man said, moving his coat from a stool to make room for Ted to sit next to him. He was, as ever, in the company of a stunning woman, not one Ted had seen him with before, but that was hardly surprising since none of them lasted more than a few weeks at most.

This one was extremely tall, even by Ted's standards, with finely-formed features, high slanting cheekbones, sky blue eyes and a long veil of gossamer-fine blonde hair. If she wasn't a model, she certainly should be.

'This is, er …' there was enough of a pause for the blonde to start to look uncomfortable, until the pathologist pulled the name out of his memory. 'Willow. How's that gorgeous young man of yours, Ted? With that arse and those blue eyes, I could almost fancy him myself. We must get together again soon. What about another game of badminton? You and him, me and whoever is the current plus one for making up a foursome?'

He had a way of making almost everything he said sound lewd and suggestive, even when giving his own name.

'Roger Gillingham. With a hard G,' he always said, which had given rise to his nickname of Hard G, of which he was well aware and clearly approved. He had a way of drawling his vowels which made even Loyd Grossman's English sound flawless.

He was proud of his appalling reputation as a womaniser. He was not married, never had been, but was never short of an attractive younger woman on his arm. And if rumours were true, he was not averse to two at a time for all his recreational activities. Ted did wonder sometimes if they were from a high-class escort agency. But then Hard G's car was an ostentatious show of wealth and privilege – a rebuilt E-type Jaguar in British Racing Green, with cream Italian leather seats – which might prove an attraction in itself if his money and social position didn't.

He had no need to work. He was obscenely independently wealthy, money from the family pharmaceutical company shares, and plenty of it. The company owned its own jet aircraft and landing strip. Hard G used it as others would use a taxi. It was handy for his frequent trips to the various holiday homes he and the company owned around Europe and further afield.

He was apparently entitled to call himself an honourable yet chose not to, which always surprised Ted because of his pretentiousness. He owned a huge house in Alderley Edge, which even a footballer couldn't afford, and which had its own staff cottage in the grounds where he kept a cook/housekeeper and her husband, whom he employed as a driver/handyman.

Ted didn't envy the housekeeper. Hard G boasted of insisting on freshly laundered and ironed linen sheets on his bed every day and of changing his shirts three times a day. His suits and jackets were all tailor made and he had a penchant for wearing silk bow ties. He was tall and stately, still with a thick head of hair, which he wore unfashionably long, with full wings at the sides.

Ted and Trev had been to his house a few times for social occasions, although Trev didn't like going. Hard G had insisted on dancing with him one time and, according to Trev, had spent the whole dance fondling his bum.

'Fascinating case you've got there at the moment, Ted old chap,' Hard G said. 'I gave it to young James as he needs stretching a bit more and that one looked ideal. I do hope he did you proud?'

'First rate job, Roger, thanks, no complaints there,' Ted replied.

'Very unusual though. What are your theories?'

Ted glanced round, trying to locate the pocket billiard-playing journalist. He found Hard G's indiscretion disconcerting. He liked to keep a tight lid on all his cases.

'Maybe not the best place to be discussing it, Roger,' he said with a warning edge to his voice.

'Oh, nonsense, so much noise in here no one can hear a thing anyway,' Gillingham waved away his objections. 'I do hope you've not got another Yorkshire Ripper just setting out his stall on your patch?'

Ted was seething. He could just see that headline in the local rag if they were overheard. 'Can we discuss this at another time, Roger? I'd like to get your take on it but not here, not now.'

'Of course, my dear boy, you know where to find me,' came the oily response. 'But you know, if life were an Agatha Christie novel, especially with such a murder weapon, it would be a case of "cherchez le docteur". Amazing how often it was the doctor who done it in her books. I hope this one is as easy for you to solve as the ones she presented to her Monsieur Poirot.'

Ted drained his Gunner and got up to leave. He was keen to get back to his team, bring them up to speed on the inquest, although it had been a formality, and to start driving the enquiry forward.

The most obvious suspect to date was already looking unlikely – early enquiries showed that Robert Allen had no car and no licence to drive one. It was time to start digging deeper. Ted had a one hundred per cent success rate in the many murder cases he'd handled. He wasn't about to let this bastard slip through the net and spoil that record.

Chapter Ten

Trev was just taking a pasta bake out of the oven when Ted walked in.

'That looks and smells amazing,' Ted said, trying to pick off some of the crunchy cheesy crust, whilst Trev pushed him away, setting the dish down on the work surface next to the oven.

'Ah-ah, don't touch,' he said. 'Aren't we going to the club tonight? I thought we could eat after that, just give it a quick warm up.'

Ted leaned against the sink. 'Yes, club would be great. I really need to burn off some energy, if you're up for it.'

The club in question was not a nightclub but the martial arts club where Ted and Trev had first met. As well as attending regularly to keep their own skills up to the mark, the two men ran a self-defence club for children in a bid to combat bullying in schools.

In addition to teaching them basic self-defence and simple judo and karate moves, they concentrated on building self-esteem and teaching self-control and respect. Ted reckoned it was an insurance policy against the future, helping to reduce the crime rate on his patch by making the youngsters who came along into better human beings.

Ted and Trev didn't always spar with one another. Trev had the advantages of height, extra reach and speed. Ted was graded higher in all disciplines but in addition, his technical skills and ruthless accuracy made him hard to beat. Their randori was always fast, furious and prolonged, with neither

51

man giving quarter. The club's senior coach often had to step in to break it up when the pair were dripping in sweat and barely able to continue standing. Trev knew it was likely to be one of those nights tonight with the pressure Ted was under.

Ted tended to take murders on his patch intensely personally. With no real leads yet, he would have a lot of pent-up frustration to unleash and the disciplined control of the dojo was a good place to do it.

'Brian sicked up a mouse on the kitchen table today,' Trev said, nodding to a smug-looking cat with long grey fur. 'Don't worry, I have cleaned.' Nothing like inconsequential chatter to lighten the mood, he knew.

'Brian, you're gross,' Ted told the cat sternly. 'I've told you before, say no to the cull.' Then to Trev, 'Right, I'll just get my kit together and we can go, if you're ready?'

'Already packed for you and in the hall,' Trev told him. 'Just double check everything is there.'

'By the way, Hard G was asking after you today. He says you have a lovely arse, but I know that already,' Ted called from the hall, where he was checking his bag. 'He can't have you, though, you look after me too well.'

'Ugh, Hard On more like, revolting old lech. I didn't just object to getting my bum fondled.'

'He wants us to play badminton with him again soon,' Ted said, coming back into the kitchen with his kit bag.

'Let's do it,' Trev said, putting their supper safely out of reach of any thieving or vomiting cats. 'Unless his latest woman is a British champion, we can wipe the floor with him again and wipe the smug smirk off his face at the same time.'

The dojo was a brisk half hour's walk away and both men preferred to walk than to drive. It gave them time to warm up and loosen muscles on the way there and to do an equally important wind down on the walk back.

There was a good turnout of youngsters, as always. Both Ted and Trev, having themselves been bullied as kids, were passionate about the club and threw their hearts and souls into it, which inspired the children who attended. The schools of those participating were thrilled, reporting a reduction in bullying as children became more self-assured and less likely to become targets for bullies.

The children liked and respected Ted, working well for him, but they all, without exception, absolutely worshipped Trev, who was brilliant at inspiring them. Sometimes Ted and Trev would spar a little for them, to show what they could aspire to if they continued training. This evening they both knew that Ted wouldn't be pretty to watch.

Working a murder case meant he was seething with emotions that needed an outlet. Although he had supreme self-control, he knew it would be tested to the limit and any sparring was likely to be fast, furious and needing to be X-rated. He was in the mood for Krav Maga, another of his disciplines, but it was too far to go to his nearest club.

Once the juniors had left, the seniors took to the mats and worked a little on technique until chief coach Bernard started pairing them off for some randori. He knew Ted well, well enough to read body language signals from the other side of the dojo. He could see from the tight muscles along his jawline and the darkening eye colour that there was only one partner it would be safe to put him with that evening.

Bernard indicated each of them in turn and the other members cleared away to free the mat. There was palpable tension in the air as the two bowed to Bernard, then to each other. They moved slowly to the centre of the mat then began a wary circling, each trying to get a grip on the other's judogi.

Trev knew he had at all costs to keep Ted from getting him down on the ground where he could use his superior tactical skills and surprising strength. Ted's preferred throw was always uchi gari, one leg shooting out to hook Trev's out from under him to bring him down, then Ted following him to the mat for a stranglehold that would end the session.

Trev's best strategy was always to throw Ted as far as possible away from him, using his height advantage with throws like ippon seoi nage and tomoe nage to clear Ted out of his way and avoid close combat at all costs.

Ted's mastery of Krav Maga had honed the speed of his attacking moves so that they became a blur. Time and again Trev had to leap and dance away from that foot which threatened to sweep his legs out from under him and have him down. He kept trying to whirl himself round to position for a shoulder throw but Ted was like an eel, never staying where he needed him to be to complete the manoeuvre.

Both men were soon breathing hard and sweating but the speed of attacks and counter-attacks showed no sign of slowing. Trev constantly used his longer reach to hold Ted at arm's length and prevent him coming in for a throw but he couldn't match him on sheer strength and as he started to tire it was getting harder to do so.

Suddenly his fatigue cost him a split second's concentration, the hooking foot swept one leg out from under him and the solid force of Ted's weight took him down to the mat. Ted followed him down, forearms instinctively going for a shime-waza, choking technique.

Bernard was across the mat in no time with a barked 'Matte' command to signal a break. Ted appeared oblivious, so Bernard closed in swiftly and thrust his upheld hand in front of Ted's face with a repeated 'Matte'.

Instantly Ted's hands dropped to his sides, he rocked back on his heels and stood up, leaning forward, hands on the fronts of his thighs, while he brought his breathing back under control.

Trev rolled clear and sprang to his feet with surprising agility after such a bout. Both men exchanged bows then bowed to Bernard. Then Ted patted Bernard on the arm and panted, 'Sorry. Sorry Bernard, got a bit carried away there.'

Ted and Trev changed quickly into outdoor wear,

preferring to shower at home after the walk back. As they walked, Ted was quiet and subdued, not proud of himself for his near loss of self-control. He'd pushed himself right to his limits, but he felt better for it.

Reading his mind as ever, Trev put an arm round his shoulders and pulled him close.

'Have you any idea how incredibly sexy you are when you get mad like that?' he asked. 'Come on, let's get home. I'm starving – and not just for tuna pasta bake.'

Chapter Eleven

Another pre-dawn. His mobile phone yet again vibrating on the bedside table. Luckily Ted had remembered to turn off the ring tone before going to bed. Much as Trev adored Queen, he wasn't keen on being woken up early to the sound of Freddie and Monsarrat belting out Barcelona.

Ted picked up the call and said a low, 'Hello?' Next minute he was sitting bolt upright in bed and his 'Shit' was louder than he intended, loud enough to make even Trev start to stir.

As Ted swung his legs out of bed, Trev opened one blue eye and asked sleepily, 'Trouble at t'mill?'

'Another body,' Ted said tersely. 'And you'll never guess where.'

As Trev was now fully awake and sitting up, Ted put the bedside light on and went on, 'On the rec, more or less behind this place.'

'Really?' Trev asked. 'That's seriously creepy. Take care out there.'

Ted leaned across to kiss him then threw some clothes on and went out. No need to get his car out for this one. The house was at the bottom of the cul-de-sac and right next to their small garden, a ginnel ran down to open out onto a large playing field area, the local recreation ground.

The sergeant who had phoned him, who knew whereabouts Ted lived, said the body had been found on the side of the playing fields nearest to Ted's house. It was still dark but there was enough light around from street lamps to show Ted where the action was starting up, less than fifty yards from where the ginnel emerged.

Blue lights were flashing on a couple of stationary patrol cars, arc lights were being rigged up and a tent was already going up to protect the body and maintain the scene of crime. No one had yet taped off the entrance to the ginnel. Probably only locals realised it was there. He could see that Sal and Virgil were just getting out of Sal's car.

Ted emerged out of the gloom, hard to see in his dark jeans and leather jacket, the colour of old tobacco. A PC stepped forward to block his way then, recognising him, stood aside and said, 'Sorry, sir, I didn't see you arrive.'

'I only live over there,' Ted told him, jerking his head back towards the way he had come. 'You may want to tape off the ginnel. I won't be the only one to come down it, I don't suppose. There'll be a few early dog walkers no doubt. Is that who found her this time?'

'Yes sir, couple of local lads with those pit bull type things,' the PC said. 'Dread to think what they were up to. They obviously think they're a couple of hard cases but they lost their breakfast over this one. Hope you've come well supplied, sir, it's not pretty.'

Ted reached into his pocket for the first Fisherman's Friend then joined Sal and Virgil as they made their way over to the tent. The sound of sneezing told them that Tim Elliott, the police surgeon, was already on site to certify death.

Ted and the others ducked through the flaps of the tent where the doctor was clearly finishing up his preliminary findings. They could see that again the body was that of a young woman, once again completely naked. This time the long blonde hair was still in place but Ted reached for several Fisherman's Friends at once and stuffed them into his mouth when he saw that the victim's eyes had been removed, leaving gaping dark orbits where they had been. There was also a yawning cavity in her abdomen and the throat was neatly slashed through.

The one good thing, the only good thing, about the whole affair was that Ted could see straight away that it was not Rosalie. The body was far too short to be the DCI's daughter.

'Morning Ted, we must stop meeting like this,' Dr Elliott said in a rare attempt at humour. 'Death certified, took place elsewhere, not here, she's been dead between twenty-four and forty-eight hours. Eyes removed – I hope to God that was done post-mortem – and a thoroughly professional full hysterectomy carried out, though in a somewhat primitive way. Other than that I can't tell you anything more for now.' And with another resounding sneeze, he was on his way.

'Shit,' Ted said again, somewhat indistinctly through a mouthful of menthol sweets. 'What kind of crazy, sick type are we dealing with here?' he said to Sal and Virgil. 'Bad enough another body on our patch, but this one is practically on my doorstep. I want this bastard found, and soon. You two, witness statements from the two lads who found her. I'll get the rest of the team in early, start house-to-house as soon as we can. This stops now.

'I'll also get all available officers onto searching the site. We need to find the murder weapon, her clothes, mobile phone, credit cards, anything at all.'

He turned to go, then added, 'Oh, and if those two scrotes with the dogs are in any way involved in dog fighting, get them charged and throw the book at them. That's more filth I want off this patch.'

'Yes, sir,' Sal and Virgil said almost in unison. They were as angry as the DI at another violent death and both of them shared his hatred of the dog fighters and their ways. So many pet animals were reported missing regularly, many of them finishing up as bait for the fighting dogs.

Ted came out of the tent and took out his mobile. Scene of crime investigators were on site now and starting work. He hoped this crime scene would yield more information than the last one, which had given them literally nothing to go on.

DS Hallam's number was saved on his phone, along with those of the rest of his team. He pulled up the number and hit call. It was still early so he hoped the DS had his phone switched on and handy. After a couple of rings, he was surprised when a woman's voice answered. He thought it might be diplomatically prudent not to ask if she was Mrs Hallam.

Instead he said, 'I'm sorry to disturb you so early. This is DI Darling, I need to speak to DS Mike Hallam, please.'

'I'll get him,' the woman said rather abruptly. There was the sound of the phone being put down noisily, footsteps, raised voices and a door slamming.

'Hello, sir. Sorry, the wife was nearer the phone than I was,' the DS came on the line, sounding slightly breathless and flustered. Ted dreaded to think what he'd interrupted.

'Another body, Mike,' Ted told him. 'Similar MO, found on the playing fields behind my house. Sal and Virgil are on it. I want the rest of the team in early. Can you ring round, please, then come in. I'll be on my way shortly.'

Ted jogged back to the house for his car keys. The lights were on when he got there. Trev must be up. He let himself in and found his partner in the kitchen. As soon as Ted came in, he thrust a steaming mug into his hands. 'Just brewed, drink it before you go.'

'No time,' Ted said. 'This one's even nastier than the first and it's personal now, dumping it in my backyard like that.'

'So add cold water and drink it quickly,' Trev told him. 'You're going to need it.'

In copper company, Ted would drink coffee but his preferred beverage was always green tea with honey. He meekly did as he was told and gulped the steaming liquid in big mouthfuls.

'I'll be late tonight. Sorry,' he said.

'Of course you will,' Trev replied. ' I'll cook something that will keep. Give me a bell when you're on your way and I'll warm it up ready.'

'You're a diamond,' Ted told him as he picked up the car keys. 'Do I tell you that often enough?'

'No, nothing like often enough,' Trev laughed. 'Now go. I'll see you this evening some time.'

So many coppers' marriages hit the rocks when one partner complained about police officers' hours. Trev was completely understanding and supportive.

The team members were just arriving as Ted got to the station. There was no sign yet of the DS. Ted assumed the ringing round had delayed him somewhat but was surprised he was not in by now. He didn't really want to start briefing the team before Hallam arrived nor did he want to repeat himself, so he told them all to get a coffee while they waited.

After about ten minutes, he heard the DS come racing up the stairs, then he burst into the room, slightly out of breath. His left hand was clumsily swathed in a gauze bandage and it was clear he was in some degree of pain.

'So sorry, sir,' he panted. 'I was just filling up a flask of boiling water to leave for the mother-in-law and the stopper wasn't on properly.'

Ted nodded briefly and launched straight into telling the team what he knew so far, outlining what he wanted from them. Once again they would be starting from the position of no ID, which would make their task even harder.

When he'd finished, he turned to the DS. 'Mike, have you got a minute, please?' he said, and headed for his office. The DS followed him in, looking decidedly nervous, but this time the DI indicated a chair and invited him to sit down.

'Are you all right, Mike?' the DI asked, with real concern in his voice. 'You look to be in some pain.'

'Oh, it's nothing, sir. I'm just clumsy, it's just a scald,' the DS tried to laugh it off.

'Show me,' Ted told him, and it was not a request.

Hallam looked awkward. 'Honestly, sir, it's not serious.'

Ted said nothing but his look told Hallam all he needed to

know.

Looking acutely embarrassed, he undid the gauze bandage. Underneath was an enormous fluid-filled blister, reaching from the space between thumb and forefinger down to his wrist. The edges looked red and angry, the skin already starting to stretch tight over it. It looked like a special effect from Alien. Ted fully expected some extra-terrestrial creature to burst forth from the watery centre at any moment.

'For god's sake, Mike,' he exclaimed. 'That needs immediate medical attention. I'd say it's second degree.'

'Really, sir, I can get it looked at later,' Hallam said.

'DS Hallam,' Ted said formally. 'You're clearly not understanding me. This is not a suggestion. If you don't do something about that it is going to be serious and it is going to cause you a lot of problems and leave me a top man down when I can least afford it. Go to A&E. Go to a drop-in centre. Find a district nurse, if we still have any. But get it done. Get it lanced and properly dressed, or whatever they do to them these days, then come back to work fit for purpose.'

'Yes, sir,' Hallam said and leapt to his feet.

'And Mike,' Ted called in a friendlier tone as the DS put a hand on the door handle. 'Next time make sure the stopper is in properly.'

Chapter Twelve

'Another one, Ted,' the DCI sighed. 'Bad business. Not what we need. Coffee?'

He lifted up the glass jug of the coffee maker and held it aloft.

'Thanks – I think,' Ted said, trying to lighten the mood. Both men were at a low ebb. Another killing on the patch, with the first still unsolved, didn't please either of them. Ted filled the DCI in on the details while he poured out his evil brew.

Inevitably, for Jim Baker, at the mention of any young female body found, his first thoughts would always go to his missing daughter. There would initially be that sickening jolt in his stomach at the thought that it might be her. Then when it wasn't, the mixed emotions that ran through him. Sheer relief that it was not, that she may yet be out there somewhere, unharmed. Followed by the guilty empathy for the parents of whoever the latest victim would turn out to be.

'Same killer, do you think?' the DCI asked. 'Same MO?'

'I hope to hell it is the same person,' Ted said fervently. 'I'd hate to think we had two such sick buggers operating on the patch at the same time.'

'Of course once you have an ID you'll look for any connections between the two?'

'We're already starting to map out any similarities. I also want to know if the fact that she was found so close to my place is just coincidence or if there's some significance to it,' Ted said.

'A personal grudge against you?' Baker asked. 'Some sort

of personal vendetta? Is that a bit far-fetched, certainly at this stage?'

'It may be a complete coincidence but it's not something we can overlook until we have far more to go on,' Ted replied.

'Don't forget Wearside Jack was not the real Yorkshire Ripper, Ted. All that taunting of the police was just a different sort of sick bastard,' the DCI said. 'Dumping bodies in your backyard to send you a personal message seems a bit unlikely to me at this point of the enquiry.'

'It's just something I don't want to dismiss out of hand, Jim,' Ted told him. 'Given we've got bugger all of anything to go on so far, I'm not ruling out any possible lines of enquiry.'

'Fair enough. What about the Carr girl's ex-boyfriend. Is he definitely out of the frame for her killing?'

'We've got positive IDs of him in bars and pubs on all of the relevant days,' Ted told him. 'He's well known in the area as a total pisshead. Unless he's a much better actor than he claims to be and unless he was pouring his drink away rather than drinking it, I can't see him being in any fit state to kill her, let alone carry her body across a playing field and down a fairly steep path to the river bank. He doesn't appear to have a car in which to transport bodies, for one thing, nor even a driving licence.'

'That's the bit that puzzles me the most,' Jim Baker said. 'How can someone carry a body the distance this killer did on two occasions without anyone noticing anything?'

Ted shrugged. 'I think people are inclined to look the other way rather a lot these days, not wanting to get involved. Sal and Virgil will be back in soon. They've been asking around, to see if anyone did see or hear anything. Trouble is, if it's a hang-out for dog fighters and the like, I doubt anyone is going to say anything, even if they saw the whole thing.'

'Nice neighbourhood you live in, Ted. Can we get the dog fighters off the streets at least, if we can't get the killer yet?'

'Already on it,' Ted told him. 'I had a word with Uniform

when I got back. They're going to pay those lads a visit, have a closer look at their dogs. With any luck they're a banned breed, that will do for starters. Shame for the dogs but maybe we can find a magistrate with the balls to send them down for six months. That would send a clear message.'

Ted stood up. 'Right, another briefing to sort and it's time to up our game. Don't worry, we'll get the bastard.'

'See that you do,' the DCI told him, although he had faith in Ted. He'd never yet let him down.

DS Hallam was back in already, his hand looking properly dressed. Ted guessed he'd been to the nearby drop-in centre and got lucky with no queue to speak of. Sal and Virgil were still out, hopefully finding someone who had seen something and was prepared to talk about it.

'Mike, I'll leave you to brief and deploy again. I want to talk to Professor Gillingham about prioritising the post-mortem on this one.'

Although he knew everyone in the office called the pathologist Hard G as he did, Ted would never dream of using the nickname in the work setting.

'I just wanted to say that we're going to be in for some long and difficult days on this one until we get a result, so it would be good if we all got together after work today at The Grapes for a bit of a social. On me, of course.'

His team members looked pleased and chorused a 'Thank you, boss.' Only DS Hallam looked ill at ease.

'Sir, I'm sorry but I'm going to have to give it a miss,' he said uncomfortably. 'The mother-in-law has an appointment this evening and I have to take her. The wife can't lift her in and out of the car by herself.'

'No worries, Mike, next time. Despite what the team may tell you, I do open my wallet more than once a year,' Ted smiled. 'Give my best to your missus and don't forget, if ever there's anything I can do ... And take care of that hand when you're lifting.'

He headed for his own small office and put the kettle on. He was in urgent need of green tea and honey to take away the taste and repair the potential damage of the DCI's filthy brew, and to steel himself to talk to the odious Professor, with his smarmy line in chat.

Ted's call to Hard G's mobile phone number was answered on the first ring.

'Ted, my dear boy, great minds, and all that!' Even at a distance the smooth tone made Ted wince. 'I was just about to call you. I've heard about your latest special delivery. You certainly like to keep my team on their toes.'

'Morning Roger,' Ted replied. 'I was going to ask you for a time-frame on getting us some results on this one. We're up against it, as you can imagine, with this second one before we've got very far on the first. So anything you can let me have, the earlier the better, I would be most grateful.'

'Oh, how priceless, Ted. If you throw yourself on my mercy, I shall claim a forfeit,' Hard G said, leaving Ted wanting to throw up. 'What are we today, Wednesday? I'll clear my decks and do the PM for you myself tomorrow morning, but in exchange, you and the delicious Trev must promise to come and play badminton on Saturday with me and the blonde job. I'll book a court at the club. Maybe a drink or a meal there afterwards, if you like?'

Hard G always referred to his current other half as 'the blonde job', as they invariably were blonde and it saved him from having to remember their names.

Not for the first time, Ted counted his blessings for having an understanding partner. Trev would not be thrilled if he agreed but he would do it, in the same way he did whatever was necessary to support Ted in his work role.

'You have a deal, Roger,' he said. 'What time do you want me tomorrow morning?'

'I'll make an early start on the gruesome bits, spare you that. Come in about eleven while I finish up then I can give you my findings to date. It's certainly another interesting one,' Hard G said. 'Oh, and Ted? Bring plenty of your little sweeties with you, you might need them.'

As instructed, Ted sent Trev a quick text as he was leaving The Grapes following the after-work socialising, so that when he came wearily into the house, Trev was in the kitchen, the table was laid and food was appearing on plates. The radio was on low, and there was an Elton John track playing.

'I need therapy every time I listen to this track,' Trev said by way of greeting.

Ted sank gratefully into his seat, with only just enough energy left to slip off his jacket and hang it on the back of his chair. Cats immediately started to weave themselves in and out of his legs in greeting, vying for attention. He reached out an absent-minded hand to stroke backs, and to gently pull erect tails. He raised his eyebrows at Trev in query.

'This track,' he explained. '*Blue Eyes*. Hard G was playing it when he insisted on getting me up on the dance floor for a bum fondle and to rub his surprisingly impressive hard-on against me. Not my favourite track ever since.'

'You're not going to be best pleased with me,' Ted said. 'I've agreed we'll play badminton with Hard G and his latest blonde job on Saturday, with a meal afterwards. It was a bribe, in exchange for which I get the post-mortem on the latest victim rushed through and he'll do it himself.'

Trev put a plate of food in front of him and dropped a kiss on his head in passing. 'Sounds like a fair deal to me. And it means that you are going to have to work very, very hard to get back into my good books.'

Chapter Thirteen

Ted wasn't sure which he was looking forward to least, sitting in on a post-mortem examination, or spending time in close proximity to Hard G. Ted didn't consider himself a prude, but any time passed in the Professor's company, with his endless smutty innuendos, rapidly turned him into one.

He found a space in the hospital car park, used his official card to avoid the exorbitant parking charges and went off in search of the Professor, already starting on the Fisherman's Friends at the mere thought.

'Ah, Ted, dear boy, come in, this is an utterly fascinating case,' Hard G greeted him as soon as he arrived. 'She's young, poor cow, I'd give her nineteen at best. She's also probably been living quite rough. Malnourished, I would say, signs of a fondness for coke and I don't mean the drinking sort. Not averse to sticking needles in herself either, though not heavy use of those.'

Ted was munching menthol as fast as he could, steeling himself to look at the ruined body of a young woman, another life gone to waste.

'As with the last one, a single clean cut to the throat with a very sharp, thin blade, something very like a surgical scalpel, and again a left-handed cut. As young James said of the last one, I think, signs of recent sexual activity, "definitely rough but probably still consensual", as there are no signs of physical restraint. Though I can't, of course, rule out substances like Rohypnol as a restraint.

'As Dr Elliott said in his initial findings, she had been dead up to forty-eight hours, so there would be no trace left in the blood stream. I'm running a full tox screen just to be sure, though. Oh, and when I say recent sexual activity, she was soundly buggered. And not to put too fine a point on it, either your chap was hung like a donkey or he'd bought himself one of those, who do you call them, a strap-on dong?'

Ted tried to repress a shudder of disgust. He found Hard G's turn of phrase difficult to stomach at the best of times. In the presence of a young woman who had been brutally murdered, he found it distasteful in the extreme.

'Of course, talking of strap-ons, that does just raise the possibility that your killer is a woman who uses one,' the Professor leered with evident enjoyment. 'Now, onto the eyes, or lack thereof. Removed post-mortem, thankfully, for that much we can be grateful.'

'Any idea why anyone would do that?' Ted asked.

'Optography, dear boy!' Hard G replied. 'It was once believed that the eye was capable of capturing and retaining the last image it saw prior to death. It was tried on at least one of the Jack the Ripper victims, I believe. Your killer was worried his image would be imprinted on her eyes and could identify him, so he took them out to protect his identity.'

Then he threw back his head and laughed aloud. 'Ted, you are so easy to wind up! Optography itself existed but unless your killer is simple, he is very unlikely to believe that it works, so I have no other explanation.'

Ted ground his teeth on yet more menthol sweets, in an attempt to bite back the remarks he felt like addressing to the Professor. He may have been the country's leading forensic pathologist but Ted considered him a Grade A arsehole and constantly had to contain himself to avoid saying so.

'Of course I was teasing you, because it amuses me, but had I not been, that theory would fall down on a couple of factors,' Hard G continued. 'The first is that there is always the possibility that the victim never actually saw the face of her killer. The scalpel stroke was from behind. There is just a chance that our killer slit her throat whilst he was busy rogering her from behind, pun intended, and that death was during the act of sex, which is allegedly an extreme turn-on for some.

'The second is that the scalpel work of making the incision to remove the reproductive organs was quite neat. It suggests someone one who knew how to handle a scalpel with some degree of skill. This implies that they had at least been admitted to medical school, which hopefully implies in turn that they were not simple. Although I do sometimes have my doubts when I see some of the bright young things in medicine these days.

'With the amount of information available nowadays on the internet, almost anyone could bring their knowledge of anatomy up to the required level. But the actual physical manipulation of a scalpel, without leaving tell-tale mistakes, requires a certain degree of practice.

'Apart from the wound to the throat, the other incisions are made right-handedly so it seems that your killer maybe ambidextrous. As there has now been vaginal and anal penetration of the bodies, perhaps he is also ambisextrous too,' he smirked at his own sense of humour.

'So what kind of person does the scalpel use indicate?' Ted asked him, ignoring the rest of his lewd comments. 'Back to your theory of a doctor?'

'A doctor would be boringly obvious,' Hard G replied. 'But yes, a doctor, a surgeon, perhaps even a vet who had studied human anatomy to some degree. Although almost anyone could arm themselves with a scalpel and start practising on rats and mice, perhaps. Or cats,' he said, with an evil smirk, knowing how attached Ted was to his family of cats. 'It's not hard to get scalpel skills up to a particular level, enough for something like this.'

Ted was not entirely sure if he felt more inclined to throw

up or to punch the Professor's lights out. He struggled hard to suppress both urges.

'As for who else, well, perhaps a medical student, further on into training? I certainly wouldn't dismiss a vet out of hand. There was an interesting case of horses being sexually mutilated in their fields in the south of England some years ago and the police theory was that it was a rogue vet with a serious issue or two.

'Again I have no helpful theory for you as to why your killer might wish to carry out a full radical hysterectomy on this poor young woman, except presumably for his own amusement. And it was a radical one. That means that absolutely all the female reproductive organs were removed, womb, fallopian tubes, ovaries, even a part of the vagina.

'It was done abdominally, of course, hence the cut in the lower abdomen, which was left open for all to see. Equally, I have no theory as to why said organs were missing, unless your killer decided to eat them with some fava beans and a nice Chianti,' he added, making revolting Hannibal Lecter slurping noises, so that Ted had to swallow hard, repeatedly, to ensure his breakfast stayed where it was.

'One of the initial thoughts we've been kicking round,' Ted told him, when he had regained control, 'is that this killer might be a woman hater. DC Bailey suggested that the removal of the hair, cutting off the breasts and now this, of course, could be a way of de-feminising the victims, taking away their femininity.'

'That's a very intriguing theory,' the Professor said. 'I must say that young DC Bailey is very interesting in herself, I've always thought. Not my usual type at all, of course. So very, how shall I put it, androgynous, but she would present an amusing challenge, I would think.

'As for the killer being a woman hater, I would say that the violence of the sex suggests to me a man who had been dominated by women. Bear in mind that I am a forensic pathologist, not a forensic psychologist, but I would think a domineering mother, a hen-pecking wife.

'A lot of us like rough sex, but this was a bit beyond that,' he continued. 'I don't know what your personal preferences are, Ted ...'

'Nor will you ever, Roger,' the DI interrupted dryly.

'This was certainly on the brutally dominant side. That fits with a woman hater theory, I would imagine. But again, it is not really my specialist area - of forensics,' he added with a lewd wink.

Just for a moment, Ted allowed himself to fantasise on just which of the bare-handed killing techniques in which he was trained he would use to silence the odious man in front of him.

'There's something else you need to consider, Ted,' the Professor continued. 'These would have been very messy killings. A lot of blood. It would take a lot of cleaning up. Then the bodies have been thoroughly cleaned of any DNA, no traces at all to give us a lead. They've been kept at a cold enough temperature to delay decomposition. Almost as if they've been stored in a mortuary after death.'

'Are you telling me we're looking for someone with access to a mortuary?' Ted asked him, somewhat alarmed. 'Someone is doing this stuff in, what, a hospital mortuary, for example, and nobody notices? How can that be? Surely there are security checks on places like a hospital morgue?'

'Ah, when you think of what Jimmy Savile was apparently getting up to in the bowels of hospitals and seemingly getting away with it ... ' the Professor left the statement hanging.

'One thing that's been puzzling me a lot,' Ted went on, 'is how the killer managed to carry each body some distance and dump it without anyone noticing. Down on the river bank, fair enough, but he would still have had to carry it across fields. But behind my house, he would have had to carry this victim some distance, in full view of houses. Anyone happening to look out could have easily seen him, even in the dark, because of the surrounding street lights.'

'Oh, now that I can help you with, my boy,' the Professor said. 'You would be amazed at the British propensity to avert the eye. Sometimes if we go dogging to fairly inaccessible sites with a lot of people attending, the blonde job and I might have to walk some way from where we park. And if the blonde job has had slightly too much to drink, I may well have to half carry her at the very least. Nobody bats an eye if they see us.'

Ted thought he had heard pretty much everything in his line of work. He was seldom at a loss for words. He was now. He took another Fisherman's Friend to help him retain his composure.

'Of course, there is one potential prime suspect profile you should certainly not overlook,' the Professor continued. 'A forensic pathologist! Everyone knows we're all very strange and suspect, playing about with dead bodies all day long. We have medical training to a high level, access to scalpels and surgical implements, unrestricted access to mortuaries and of course, all the skills necessary to disguise DNA on a body. I wouldn't trust any of us an inch!' He threw back his head and laughed loudly at his own joke.

'So, Ted,' he continued. 'I'll look forward to seeing you and the gorgeous Trev on Saturday. I'll let you know what time of day I can get us a court, although they are usually very accommodating to me.'

Ted could imagine that the club would be. Hard G had a lot of money and he spent it lavishly and quite generously.

'Looking forward to it, Roger,' Ted replied. 'Does Willow play?'

'Oh, she loves to play,' the Professor smirked, 'but I have no idea if she is any good at badminton.'

Chapter Fourteen

'Sir!' it was Sal who took the call and shouted across to Ted as he was discussing things with Mike Hallam. 'Uniform just rang, they've brought a bloke in from the hospital. He works there, a porter or something. Someone called the police because he was spending a lot of time in the mortuary and acting weird.'

'Weird?' Ted queried. 'Acting weird is not a legal term known to me. Define weird.'

Sal shrugged. 'Don't know, boss, Uniform are just saying the hospital were worried because of his behaviour and when one of their managers asked him to leave the morgue, he got a bit weird. Their words, not mine. They've got him down in interview room No 1 and they want to know if you'll go down and talk to him. He fits the profile, doesn't he?'

Ted and Mike exchanged loaded looks.

'Let's not get too hung up on profiles,' Ted said. 'I'll take this one. Mike, you're with me. Sal, let the DCI know we have a possible suspect in.'

As they headed for the stairs, Mike asked, 'So is it good cop, bad cop, boss? Which one am I?'

Ted gave him one of his long looks and said, 'There are no bad cops on my team, Mike, only good ones.'

Seeing Mike look crestfallen at getting it wrong, again, he decided to cut him some slack and added, 'As you're new to me and my funny ways, I'd like you just to sit in and observe closely on this one without saying anything. I'll let you in on a little secret though. I don't actually need a bad cop as most people are usually quite happy to talk to me. I mean, how dangerous can an old queen who's knee-high to a grasshopper be to them?' and he gave Mike his broadest wink.

When the two of them entered the interview room, an officer from the Uniform branch was standing by the door and the suspect was sitting at the table. Ted dismissed the PC, did the preliminaries and set the tape running.

'For the purpose of the tape, can you please state your name,' he said.

The man sitting opposite him said simply, 'People just call me Jimmy.'

Ted could see why. The man was thin, tall and slightly stooped, but the hair was stunning. Shoulder-length and sparse, with a bit of a comb-over from the side to conceal a touch of thinning on the crown, it was on the whiter shade of silver and looked like natural premature greying. Jimmy Savile's hair, to a T.

'Could you state your correct real name please, sir, for the purpose of the tape.'

The man seemed to hesitate, then said, 'It's Oliver. Oliver Burdon. With a D, not a T.'

'And what would you prefer me to call you, Mr Burdon?' Ted asked patiently.

An even longer pause. Ted strongly suspected that very few people ever asked the man his views or preferences on anything. Then, 'Could I please be called Oliver?'

'Yes of course, Oliver, thank you,' Ted replied. 'Now, you don't currently have a solicitor and you are entitled to have one present. Would you like to have a solicitor before you answer any questions?'

Washed out blue eyes looked at him with a puzzled expression. 'I don't understand. I haven't done anything wrong. I thought solicitors were for when you had done something wrong?'

'Not necessarily, Oliver, but if you are happy to continue

you can. Just tell me if at any point you would like me to stop asking you questions and allow you to contact a solicitor. Are you happy to answer my questions?'

'Yes. I like you,' he said, but the pale eyes were looking towards DS Hallam and telling another story.

Ted read the look and said, 'I'm sorry, Oliver, has anyone offered you a drink? That was rude of me not to ask. Would you like something to drink?'

Again, the look of surprise. 'Can I have a coffee, please? With two sugars? And milk?'

'Of course you can. Mike, could you oblige, please? For the purpose of the tape, DS Hallam is leaving the room to bring refreshments.'

Turning back to the suspect he continued, 'Are you happy to answer my questions, Oliver?'

'Yes,' he said again, 'I like you.'

'Can you remember what you were doing on Tuesday evening?'

'Tuesday? Yes, that's easy, watching Holby City. I like that. I like Serena.'

'Can you remember what happened last Tuesday?' Ted asked.

'Oh, yes. Serena was sad so Raf gave her some wine and she got drunk. Some She-razz, he said it was. I would like to try some of that, but I don't know where to get it.'

Ted said helpfully, 'I think you can get it in almost any supermarket, Oliver.'

The suspect shook his head vigorously. 'I don't go in supermarkets. I don't know where to find anything. I get confused. I go in the corner shop. I know where to find everything in there.'

'What sort of things do you buy?' Ted asked, more for his own curiosity than for the tape.

'Weetabix,' came the swift response. 'And brown bread, cheese, butter. Sometimes baked beans.'

'Anything else?'

Oliver smiled guiltily. 'Sometimes some chocolate. I like white chocolate.'

'Oliver, do you know why you've been brought here?'

The man frowned. 'They said I was doing something wrong in the mortuary. But I wasn't.'

'Can you tell me what you were doing in the mortuary, Oliver?'

'Yes, I was trying to send a message to my mother,' came the simple reply.

It was Ted's turn to look puzzled. 'I'm sorry, I don't understand. Can you explain, please?'

The man nodded and leaned forward, with an earnest expression on his face. 'My mother died when I was quite young. They wouldn't let me see her. They took her away and I never saw her again. I wanted to talk to the people in the mortuary, the dead people, on their way to heaven, to ask them if they could contact her for me, to tell her I never stopped thinking about her.'

Ted cleared his throat, hard, to try to get rid of the lump which had suddenly appeared. He just about trusted himself enough to speak when the DS came back into the room, minus the coffees. He bent in low behind the DI and said, 'The team gave his locker at work a quick once-over, boss, and they've found a scalpel.'

'Shit,' Ted said quietly, for the DS's ears only then, aloud, 'Mike, can you delegate those coffees then sit in on this please?' Then, to the suspect, 'Oliver, my men had a little look in your locker and they found a scalpel. Can you explain to me what you use that for?'

Again the guilty look, and this time a mumbled response. 'I only used it once. It was for the chicken.'

Of all the replies Ted expected, that was not one of them. 'The chicken?' he queried.

'I'm sorry if it was wrong. My mother used to make me a

nice chicken meal. I wanted to try to do it but it wasn't right. It was a piece with a bone in and there shouldn't have been a bone. I didn't know how to take it out. They throw those scalpels away and burn them at the hospital sometimes so I thought it wouldn't matter if I took one. But I couldn't manage it very well.' He looked forlorn. 'I'm sorry if it was wrong. I took it back to work; I was going to put it where I found it.'

This time Ted had to clear his throat several times. Then he said, 'It sounds as if you got a leg joint, Oliver. You'd be better with a breast fillet, there's no bone in that.'

Burdon looked visibly shocked. 'I couldn't ask for that,' he said, in hushed tones.

'You'll probably find it on the shelves, without having to ask,' he said, then saw the look on the other man's face and suddenly understood. He asked gently, 'Oliver, do you have trouble reading some words?'

Burdon nodded slowly. 'Sometimes. Big words. Words I don't know. I'm not very good at reading.'

Ted thought for a moment then said, 'Oliver, here's what I'm going to do. We've taken up enough of your time. When you've had your coffee, DS Hallam here is going to get you a takeaway chicken dinner. And some chocolate. Some white chocolate.' He got his wallet out and handed Hallam some money. 'Then he's going to get someone to drive you back to your flat so you can enjoy your meal in peace.'

The DS opened his mouth to speak then, seeing the colour changing in Ted's eyes, said hastily, 'Of course I will, sir, no problem at all.'

'Here's my card, Oliver, there's my telephone number. If you ever need any help, any at all, you call me. And in the meantime, I'm going to see if I can find someone to help you a bit. Thank you for your time, and goodbye,' with which he swept out of the office and took the stairs three at a time.

After the briefest of knocks, he burst into the DCI's office where, even without the kick-trick, the force of his slamming the door shook walls throughout the station.

'It's not him,' he said emphatically. 'It's not sodding well him, I'd stake Trev's bike on it.'

The DCI eyed him warily. 'Ted, is this going to be one of those conversations where you kick things round my office and break things? Because I have to say, you are a little bit scary when you do that.'

'This is Timothy Evans all over again. The man is innocent, just not very bright. Far too simple for some of the stuff this killer has done. He was trying to talk to his dead mother in the morgue, for god's sake. He needs help; he needs a social worker. If the press get wind that we've had him in, it will be a repeat of the Christopher Jefferies fiasco. We're going to look completely stupid. It's not him, I'm sure of it. So if it's not him, then who the hell is it?'

Chapter Fifteen

'I'm really looking forward to this,' Trev said, as Ted parked his modest Renault in front of the club amongst the Bentleys, BMWs and Roger's E-type.

'You are?' Ted asked in surprise.

Trev leaned closer, a hand on his partner's thigh, blue eyes twinkling wickedly.

'Oh, yes. All the time we're playing, I'm going to be thinking up ways you're going to have to repay me for this.'

The club was exclusive. Had they not been guests of Roger, Ted doubted they would ever have set foot on its expensive carpets, let alone played matches in their hallowed courts. As it was, they had been a few times with Roger to play badminton, squash or tennis in the summer, or to use the pool, jacuzzi, hammam and saunas.

Roger and the tall, elegant blonde were waiting for them in the bar. Willow was sipping a slimline tonic with a slice of lemon. Roger's drink looked more like a gin and tonic, served as it was in a crystal spirit glass.

'Ted! Trev! Perfectly lovely to see you both,' Roger called, as soon as the two men walked into the bar. 'Ted, I think you've already met …' again the deliberate pause while he mentally searched for a name, 'Willow, haven't you? Willow, this is Ted's perfectly gorgeous partner, Trevor. What are you drinking?'

'Nothing for me before we play, thanks, Roger,' Ted shook his head. Trev did the same and added, 'You can buy us a bottle of bubbly when we thrash you again, Roger.'

Hard G laughed amiably. It was true that he had never managed to beat the two men, despite a string of different partners, some of them very good players indeed. The fact that Ted and Trev knew each other so well and anticipated each other's every move gave them an edge that was hard to beat. They hadn't played against Willow before and none of them, it seemed, knew what she could bring to the match.

'How's it going, Ted? Any more progress since Thursday?' Roger asked. 'Did I hear on the grapevine that you had someone in for questioning?'

'Expensive country club, a bit of badminton, few drinks, maybe a nice meal. Does that sound like a typical day at the nick to you, Roger?' Ted asked dryly.

The Professor laughed. 'Point taken, old boy. No shop talk for now.'

'Do you play, Willow? Trev asked her.

Roger interrupted with a lewd laugh. His hand strayed to Willow's behind which he squeezed, hard.

'Careful how you ask, Trev,' he said. 'You might find yourself with an entirely different après match foursome to what you perhaps had in mind.'

Trev saw the pained look that passed over the blonde's face and wondered if Ted would arrest him if he followed his instincts and karate kicked the crap out of the lecherous Hard G. Exercising all his self-control, he ignored the Professor and gently drew Willow aside by the arm so the two of them could talk without interruption.

Hard G laughed again, mockingly. 'Don't they make the perfect couple?' he sneered.

'Roger,' Ted said affably. 'One day you really will go too far and Trev will lamp you one. Don't be deceived by those baby blue eyes.'

An emotion Ted found hard to read flashed briefly across the Professor's face, his eyes clouding. Then he laughed again and said, 'Quite right, of course, dear boy. You know how much I love to tease. I just hope neither of you takes me seriously for a moment.' He drained his glass. 'Shall we all go and change? The court is ours whenever we want it.'

As they strolled along an impressive wood-panelled corridor towards the sports complex at the rear of the club, Trev slipped an arm around Ted's waist. He leaned close to say in a low voice, 'The payback rate has just doubled. No, trebled. That is, if you want me to promise not to kill him.'

Once changed, they assembled at their appointed court. Willow looked absolutely stunning in a pink skort and polo top, clearly expensive, top-of-the-range wear, as much fashion statement as sports attire. Her outfit was totally in contravention of the club's strict whites only rule but she looked so sensational that even the anal sports secretary was unlikely to object. She certainly looked the part, and her warm-up routine of jogging and stretching was professionally executed.

Ted and Trev took most of their sports seriously, though none quite so much as their martial arts. They liked to make a little joke of their badminton warm up, including a few karate movements in their stretching. They called it their personal haka, designed to intimidate the opposition.

They paired off, Ted and Trev at one end of the court, Hard G and Willow at the other, and began play. It was obvious right from the start that Willow was an extremely good player, possibly tournament standard. It was equally obvious that Hard G was set on doing everything he possibly could to humiliate her.

Although she clearly outclassed him and was certainly going to stretch both Ted and Trev, Hard G constantly leapt about the court taking shot after shot she could easily have taken and making a worse job of it than she would have done. His repeated interference gave Ted and Trev an easy victory in the first game when it was obvious that, had Willow been allowed to play unhindered, they would have had a much harder job of it.

Willow kept calling out to her partner to let her take the shot, but he either totally ignored her or blundered across her, preventing her from taking it and usually fluffing it himself. When he almost shoulder-charged her out of the way for one stroke which she could easily have taken with her deadly backhand, which had already proved too much for both Ted and Trev, she whirled round in fury and launched her racquet at him, before storming out of the court.

Hard G had his own racquet in his right hand but somehow managed to bring his left up to execute a deft catch of the flying racquet, before it made contact with his face. He laughed coarsely. 'Oh, dear, women's troubles, eh? Someone is clearly feeling a little pre-menstrual.'

Trev carefully put his own racquet down at the side of the court and sprinted out in pursuit of Willow. Ted walked round the net and up to Hard G, head and shoulders taller than him and still smirking mockingly. Ted's tone was low and measured but would immediately have sent his whole team, the DCI included, scurrying for cover.

'Roger, you really are a complete and utter piece of shit. And one day, someone is going to give you a short sharp lesson in manners around women,' he said conversationally. 'On that day, Roger, whether I am on duty or not, I strongly suspect I will be looking the other way.'

He collected up his, Trev's and Willow's belongings and made to leave the court.

'Please don't be a bore, old boy,' Hard G called after him. 'I only do it so I don't have to dump them, so they leave me. So much less messy. I've already been test-driving the latest model for a few weeks now and she has much better handling and manoeuvring skills, not to mention more thrust, if you know what I mean.'

'Goodbye Roger,' Ted said through gritted teeth, without even turning back.

'But what about our meal? I've booked a table,' Hard G said to his departing back.

'I hope you'll enjoy it. Bon appetit,' Ted said and only just restrained himself from slamming the door on his way out.

He found Trev and Willow outside the door to the women's changing rooms. Trev had his arms around the blonde, who matched his height perfectly. She was moulded to him, every inch of their bodies in contact. As she sobbed on his shoulder, Trev's hand gently stroked her long, fine, blonde hair as he murmured soothingly, 'Please don't cry, angel. He's such a piece of shit, he doesn't deserve you. You're so beautiful and you play so superbly. He's not worthy to be on the same court. Please don't cry, my sweet.'

He made eye contact with Ted over the top of her head and gave a little moue of apology. Ted nodded his understanding as Trev said, 'Willow is coming back with us today, and staying the night. I'll make a meal; she needs to be with people who appreciate her,' which made the tall blonde sob even more.

On the short drive home, while Ted drove, Trev sat with Willow in the back seat and kept up his low, soothing murmur until Willow's sobs finally stopped and she was patting her eyes and blowing her nose, apologising profusely for her outburst and thanking them both for their kindness and understanding.

Once inside the warm and welcoming kitchen, surrounded by purring cats, Willow squealed with delight and said, 'Ooooh, cats! I adore cats! Roger hates all animals – unless he's dissecting them,' she added, with a shudder.

She scooped up a particularly friendly Russian Blue, with striking green eyes, whose purring immediately doubled in intensity and volume.

'That's Mercury,' Trev told her, then asked 'Why on earth do you stay with Hard G?'

She smiled at the nickname. 'No more,' she said. 'That was the last straw. I could have wiped the floor with the two of you single handedly. No offence,' she smiled. 'But I'm a whore to my career – literally,' she continued. 'Being seen in all the best places on Roger's arm worked wonders for my modelling bookings. I almost convinced myself it was worth the price I had to pay.' She squirmed in disgust. 'But it wasn't, nothing is.'

'Honey, it's going to take me a little while to put together something edible for us. Ted will show you the bathroom, go and have a nice long soak. You can borrow my bath robe, it's the fluffy one on the door. And Ted will sort the spare room for you for tonight,' Trev told her as he started opening fridge and cupboards.

When Ted came back down, Trev said, 'How can anyone treat another person that badly? What kind of a piece of shit is Hard G really?'

'Don't worry, I told him exactly what a piece of shit he is,' Ted replied. 'It's going to make our next professional meeting a rather interesting one.'

Chapter Sixteen

Ted's first incoming phone call of the day when he got into work really surprised him. It was Hard G and he seemed genuinely contrite.

'Ted, I just wanted to apologise for yesterday,' he began. 'Utterly unforgivable of me. I should have sorted out dumping Willow in private rather than subject you and Trevor to such a show of bad manners. Please accept my sincere apologies.'

Ted was so gobsmacked he hardly knew what to say so he contented himself with, 'Thank you, Roger. I'll pass your comments on to Trev. And to Willow.'

'Ah, yes. The poor girl is so much better off without me. How is she?' Hard G asked.

'Relieved, Roger,' Ted said, acerbically. 'She spent the night with us. Good food, cat cuddles, hugs from Trev, a long hot bath, and she's on her way with her self-esteem higher than it's clearly been in a long time.'

Hard G sounded surprisingly subdued as he said goodbye and hung up.

Ted's next call was the DCI, summoning him to his office. Ted took the precaution of taking his freshly brewed green tea with honey with him, to save him from the mud-like coffee.

'Come in, Ted, sit down. You won't like it,' the DCI warned. 'Press conference, later this afternoon, hoping to hit the six o'clock national news. We need help with ID-ing the second victim and getting any leads on the first. I want you in on it.'

Ted made a face. He disliked any sort of what he called

fuss and appearing in front of the television cameras was definitely in that category, in his book. But he could see the sense of it in this case. Two bodies, only one ID and no suspects in the frame at all. They needed the public's help, and soon.

'Vicki Carr's parents are coming in,' the DCI told him. 'They're going to make an appeal, try to prick someone's conscience to come forward with any information they may have, even suspicions.'

'It's going to open the floodgates to the crank callers, malicious hoaxes and vengeance calls,' Ted warned.

'Of course, inevitably, and it's going to make more work for you and your team sifting through them,' the DCI agreed. 'But someone, somewhere out there knows something. There's no way this killer can be doing what he is doing without someone knowing or suspecting something. We need to prise that information out of them.'

'You don't want me to say anything do you?' Ted asked with a pained expression, as if the Big Boss had suggested he cross naked along a tightrope over Mersey Square on a unicycle, balancing a long pole and carrying a parasol.

'Press office will prepare you a brief of what to say and what not to say. Just stick to the brief, don't deviate from it at all,' the DCI told him. 'And don't answer any questions, no matter how leading they are. Leave all those to me. We'll have a photo-quality artist's impression of the second victim, see if anyone recognises that. If we can at least ID her out of it then it will be worth it.

'Oh, and Ted,' he looked at his DI, comfortable in his habitual get up of dark jeans and polo neck, Doc Martens and dark leather jacket. 'Go home and change, please. Suit, shirt, tie, proper copper gear. We need the public's help so we can't afford to have you sitting there looking like a Mossad agent.'

The prospect of the ordeal to come meant Ted was rather brusque in briefing his team. Those who had been with him for any length of time knew exactly what the cause was, once he mentioned the press conference. DS Hallam was already starting to know enough about him to understand.

Even before they got an ID on the second victim, whom Tina was calling Annabel, they were trying to look for any link at all, no matter how tenuous, between the two victims. So far, apart from the causes of death, they seemed to have little in common.

Vicki Carr was from a reasonably well-off family, in work, living in a flat and with no indication of any significant drug use, other than possibly sharing a bit of blow with her flatmate.

Annabel, they were presuming, was a runaway, possibly living rough, certainly a drug user, probably funding her habit by prostitution. That opened up the possibility that her killer had simply picked her up on a street corner, offering cash for sexual favours.

Ted was still troubled by the location in which Annabel was dumped. It was the first time in his career that a killer he was investigating had gone on to strike a second time, with him being no nearer to finding them. He was worried that it was becoming personal, that the killer knew he was leading the enquiry and was sending him a clear, direct message.

Appearing live on national television later that day may possibly increase the risk of it becoming even more personal between him and the killer. It would not be the first time on record that it had become a battle of wills between two individuals, with victims paying the cost.

Ted decided to go home early on to change into the hated court clothes. He wanted to be sure he was back in plenty of time to greet Vicki Carr's parents in person. He could barely begin to imagine what they were going through. It made him even more determined to catch the bastard who was doing this to these girls.

He took the time when he got back to walk through the ginnel to see if any progress was being made on the site where the victim's body was dumped. Uniform were still fingertip searching the area, looking for a murder weapon or the missing personal effects, so far with no results at all.

His team's house-to-house enquiries had similarly had no success. The only progress to date was that there were now two fewer fighting dogs and their owners loose on his patch. It was not enough. Ted didn't want killers of any description on his manor; he had too much respect for all life.

When he saw the state of Vicki Carr's parents as they turned up for the press conference, Ted felt ashamed that his first thought had been an objection to wearing a suit and tie. Her mother was ashen-faced, barely staying upright. The father was tight-lipped, only just in control.

Ted went across to introduce himself to them. The father's accusatory opening words were, 'Why haven't you caught this monster yet? Why did you let him go on to kill again?'

Having shaken the other man's hand, Ted held it a little longer and looked at him, frankly and honestly, straight in the eyes. 'I promise you, Mr Carr, I am doing everything I can possibly do to bring justice for Vicki, and for you and your wife. I will get him, you have my personal assurance on that.'

Carr obviously saw and heard what he needed to. He nodded his head, shook Ted's hand once more, then turned, supporting his wife, and they went to their appointed seats.

The DCI opened the press conference, outlining in a calm and matter of fact way all the information they had to date and asking for the public's help in identifying the second victim. He also asked for reports of any sightings of either young woman or of anyone behaving suspiciously in the locations involved or anywhere else on the crucial dates.

Mr Carr made an impassioned plea, to which his wife added a few brief words before she broke down completely in wracking sobs and her husband had to lead her from the room.

Then the DCI handed over to Ted, who said exactly what he had been told to say and, through supreme self-control, managed not to react to any of the hard questioning of him personally which followed, when the conference was thrown open to the floor.

Ted had already sent Trev a text to tell him he would be home late. He intended to watch the broadcast go out with the DCI in his office and then be available if any calls came in. DS Hallam had had to go to take his mother-in-law to another appointment but Sal and Virgil, Rob and young Steve were also at their desks manning the phones, ready to note any information at all that came in.

Ted was surprised at the speed with which the first call came through. The DCI answered his phone, said, 'Yes, he's here,' then handed it to Ted. 'Someone asking to speak to you and no one else.'

'DI Darling,' Ted said, as he took the phone. There was a long pause, then a hesitant voice said, 'Hello. It's Oliver.'

A call from Oliver Burdon, the strange but seemingly harmless porter from the hospital, wasn't what Ted was hoping for. Although he had told the man to call him if he needed help, he hoped he was not going to be wasting his time when he could be following up important leads.

'Hello, Oliver, nice to hear from you,' he said patiently. 'How are things with you?'

'Very good, thank you,' came the reply. 'I thought I was going to get the sack after that trouble. But when I went back to the hospital, they said you had spoken to someone and I could still have my job. They sent someone from Human 'Sources to talk to me and they're going to help me.'

'That's excellent news, Oliver, I'm pleased to hear it,' Ted said. 'I'm just a little bit busy right now, so could we perhaps talk again, at another time?'

'I want to help you,' the man said. 'You helped me, so I want to help you. I saw you just now, on the telly.'

Ted threw a loaded look at the DCI and put the phone onto loudspeaker.

'Oliver, are you telling me you have information concerning the murder enquiry?' he asked, mentally crossing his fingers that the hospital porter was not just a people-pleaser, trying to repay a kindness.

'Yes I do,' came the prompt and delighted response. 'I know who that young girl is.'

Ted and the DCI exchanged another look, not daring to hope that they might have a lead so early on.

'So who is she, Oliver?' Ted asked, trying to keep his voice as patient and neutral as he could.

'Well, on Saturdays, I go and help out at a place that makes food for homeless people; it's near the hospital. I go because they let me have my dinner there,' Oliver began, while Ted did his best to control his mounting impatience. 'That girl goes there. She's one of the homeless. She … ' he broke off and there was an awkward pause.

'Go on, Oliver, I'm listening,' Ted said encouragingly.

'She said she would do something to me, something dirty, if I gave her some money,' Oliver said hesitantly. 'I didn't want to get into any trouble, so I said no. They call her Mads or Mags, something like that.'

Ted did an air punch then said into the phone, 'Oliver, you have been extremely helpful and I am very grateful to you.'

'You were very kind to me,' Burdon said, 'I like you.'

'Tomorrow, I'm going to send one of my men round with some chocolate for you,' Ted promised. 'It's white chocolate you like, isn't it? I'm going to send you a load of bars of white chocolate, with my thanks.'

He rang off and went to speak to his team members who were waiting on his update.

'Got a lead,' he said. 'Two of you get round to the drop-in soup kitchen place near the hospital. Ask about a Mads or a Mags. Sounds like she may be in the habit of offering a blow job in exchange for money, presumably to buy drugs. It seems she may be our victim number two.'

Chapter Seventeen

Sal and Virgil hadn't had much luck at the soup kitchen. Everyone they spoke to knew the girl, but only as Mags or Mads. They knew she was living rough, most knew or at least suspected how she got her money, but nobody knew much about her background. One of the volunteers said her accent was more Black Country or Potteries than Stockport, but other than that, nobody really knew anything.

There had been the usual round of time-wasting phone calls, people reporting neighbours who 'looked weird'. Inevitably, they'd already had one confession, one of their regular confessors, a man they called Honest John who had so far claimed responsibility for every high-profile crime for miles around. He got his nickname because he punctuated every sentence he uttered with 'honest, it was me.'

They knew him well by now and knew the reality. The man was a sad, attention-seeking fantasist who lived in a cramped one-bedroom flat in a high-rise which he was unable ever to leave because of his clinical obesity.

Ted stood the team down as it was late, everyone was tired and they had at least had the glimmer of a lead with which to start fresh the next day. He went back to his office to get his jacket and decided to give his DS a quick call to bring him up to speed.

He was again surprised when the DS's wife answered the phone.

'DI Darling, Mrs Hallam, sorry to trouble you. I hope things went well with your mother this evening. I just need a quick word with Mike, if I may,' he said.

Once again the response was decidedly curt. Whatever her good points, graduation from charm school was certainly not one of them, Ted thought to himself.

'Hello, sir, sorry, I was just helping the mother-in-law,' Hallam's voice was apologetic when he came on the line.

'Just wanted to bring you up to speed with the night's results, so you know where to start if you're in before me in the morning,' Ted told him. 'We've got a partial ID on the second victim, homeless lass known as Mads or Mags, possibly a Black Country connection but no positive ID yet.'

Ted was just getting ready to leave when there was a timid knock on his door, so hesitant that he barely heard it. Through the glass panel he could see the young TDC standing outside, looking awkward.

He sighed and put his jacket back down. 'Come in, Steve,' he said, in as encouraging a tone as he could manage, knowing how nervous the young man always appeared to be.

'Sir,' Steve started, looking for all the world like a schoolboy in the headmaster's study. 'I did some digging again on missing persons. Because this latest victim is small, only five foot two, it narrowed it down a bit. I've got a possible match, a runaway, missing from Stoke-on-Trent for four years.'

He held out a computer print-out which Ted took as he leaned against his desk. 'Brilliant work, Steve, spot on. I'll eat my cats if this is not our Annabel,' then seeing the shocked look on Steve's face he added hastily, 'Joke, Steve, figure of speech.

'I'll send someone down to her last-known address tomorrow, see if we can dot the i's and cross the t's but I would say it's a racing certainty. Well done, Steve.'

The TDC scuttled out of the office, looking pleased with himself. Ted put his jacket back on and hesitated with his phone in his hand. He really wanted to fill the DS in with this further development, as he wanted to send him down to Stoke the following day, but he didn't want to disturb him if he was sorting out his mother-in-law. Ted knew from experience how difficult things could be, helping someone who had only recently lost their mobility and independence. Hallam was always in early, he could brief him then.

Only the next morning the DS was not in early. In fact he was not even on time, which did not please Ted. There was no sign of him, and no word from him. When Ted tried his mobile, it went straight to answering mode.

The message Ted left was abrupt. He wanted to move the enquiry on and he had planned to send the DS and Tina to Stoke-on-Trent for a positive ID as they were a good team for the job. He wanted to give Hallam the benefit of the doubt and wait for his explanation but time was getting on.

It was nearly lunchtime before the DS put in an appearance. He came slowly up the stairs and it was clear that every movement he made was causing him a lot of pain. When Ted saw him walk in, he called him over to his office, pulled out a chair for him and put the kettle on.

Hallam looked not just in pain but also extremely uncomfortable and on edge. 'Sir, I'm so sorry, I've been in A&E all morning. The lad left his baseball on the stairs, I didn't see it and I went full length from top to bottom. I've got four cracked ribs and quite a lot of bruising.'

'Sorry to hear that Mike,' Ted said. 'Would have helped if you'd phoned in to let me know.'

'I know, sir, and I'm sorry,' Hallam said, 'but my mobile was underneath me when I fell and it's not working. I did try to get someone to phone in for me from the hospital, but it seems like no one did.'

'All right, but make sure someone does let us know next time, please, if you're unlucky enough for there to be a next time,' Ted said. 'I need you to go to Stoke-on-Trent, to see if we can get a definite ID on this girl. Take Tina with you. Have you got your car?'

'Er, I'm not allowed to drive, sir,' the DS said apologetically. 'They've put me on some hefty painkillers and they advise you not to drive while taking them.'

'Get Tina to drive her car then, but get started as soon as you can,' Ted told him.

The DS looked extremely awkward and said, 'Sorry, sir, but can I send someone else? It's just I'm not sure I'm up to sitting in a car, even for a shortish journey. Especially not a Mini.'

Ted gave him a long look. He had the feeling there was something going on that he didn't know about and he didn't like that. 'Is there some problem between you and Tina?' he asked directly.

'No, sir, no, nothing like that,' the DS laughed off his suggestion. 'I'll be fine driving a desk for a day or two but honestly, it is very painful getting in and out of a car, and going anywhere might be a problem today.'

Ted still held his gaze. He was not convinced but he had more things to worry about than a possible office dalliance or a disagreement between colleagues.

'Send Sal then,' he said finally, 'he's very good with people, very courteous.

'Once we get a positive ID, we need to start mapping out any links, any similarities at all between these two victims, never mind how unlikely they seem. I have a horrible feeling this is a random killer, the victims are not particularly targeted, and you know how difficult those cases are to solve. But let's not overlook anything obvious in the meantime. Get someone out round any of Vicki Carr's haunts with pictures of this Mags, just in case there's any link.'

'Oh, before I forget, sir,' the DS had some papers in his hand and put them on the desk in front of the DI. 'The report on the scalpel found in Oliver Burdon's locker. Tests show that the only flesh it had contact with recently was definitely chicken, not human.'

Ted scanned through the report, then looked back at his sergeant.

'So, Mike, let me get this clear,' Ted said. 'You went ahead and ordered forensic tests on this scalpel after I'd released Burdon and said he was no longer a suspect?'

Hallam held his gaze levelly. 'Yes sir, I did.'

'In other words, if I'd made a complete tit of myself and let the real killer walk free, you had my arse covered by ordering the tests?' Ted asked ironically.

'That's right, sir,' Hallam replied. 'Just covering all bases.'

'Good work, Mike, thank you,' Ted smiled. 'Good to know you've got my back.'

Chapter Eighteen

'Poor old Sarge, in the wars again,' Sal said, as he and Tina set off for Stoke-on-Trent. He was more than happy to let her drive. She was an excellent driver and he liked the sporty little car. 'Do you think he drinks?'

Tina shrugged. 'I wouldn't have thought so, but who can tell?' she replied. 'The number of officers who do and get away with it for years is staggering.'

Thanks to Steve's work, they now had a possible name for Annabel, victim number two - Margaret Fielding, known as Maggie - and an address on the outskirts of Stoke-on-Trent as her last known place of residence. According to the information they had, she'd run away from home at the age of fifteen after some trouble involving the current live-in boyfriend of her mother. An all too familiar story.

The address proved to be a squalid-looking house on an estate. There was graffiti on every available surface around, mostly gang symbols, and a burnt-out car in the road a few yards away. Tina was a bit worried about the Cooper, so she parked as close as she could, where she could keep an eye on her beloved motor.

It took repeated loud knocks on the door before a woman came to open it. Both officers had their warrant cards in their hands. By silent mutual agreement, Tina did the talking.

'Mrs Fielding?' she asked. 'DCs Bailey and Ahmed. Can we come in, please?'

The woman had a partly-smoked cigarette clamped between wrinkled lips. She looked three sheets to the wind, her watery blue eyes having difficulty focusing on them. She and her clothes were equally dirty and there was a strong aroma of stale sweat and urine about her. She scanned Tina's face briefly then her gaze landed on Sal and stayed there.

'What do you want?' she asked suspiciously.

Tina would have thought it pretty obvious what an unannounced visit from two police officers was likely to mean to the parent of a reported runaway. But it seemed that the woman was too far gone to be thinking logically.

'It would be easier to talk inside, Mrs Fielding,' she said. 'Can we come in, please?'

Without saying anything, the woman turned and led the way down a filthy hallway, cluttered with old newspapers and bags of rubbish, to an equally squalid kitchen at the back of the house, with dirty crockery piled high in the sink and all around. She broke wind loudly and repeatedly as she walked.

There was nowhere to sit and the woman didn't invite them to. Instead she said, 'Have you found her then, the little tart?'

If Tina was taken aback, she was too professional to show it. 'We are here about your missing daughter, Margaret, yes, Mrs Fielding.'

'Missing?' the woman spat. 'She ran off when I caught her in my bed with my Henry, giving him a blow job. I only reported her because she ran off with all my housekeeping money. Have you found her, then?'

'Mrs Fielding, I have to tell you that we have found the body of a young woman and we have reason to believe that it might be your daughter,' Tina said. 'Do you have any photographs of Margaret, any others, besides the one you supplied to the police at the time of her disappearance?'

'Burnt them all,' the woman spat. 'Couldn't stand to look at the little bitch's face again, after what she did.'

Tina and Sal exchanged glances. Of all the reactions they'd encountered from grieving relatives, this was a new one on both of them.

'Mrs Fielding, we are going to need you to come to Stockport to view the body and tell us if it is your missing daughter,' Tina said. 'Do you have anyone who can drive you there?'

Sal hid a smile behind his hand. He had already realised that there was no way Tina was even going to consider putting this sad, stinking woman in her beautifully kept car.

'I've got no one,' the woman said, and just for a moment, the mask slipped and the two officers could see beyond to the human tragedy behind it. 'Henry fucked off just afterwards. He probably went after the little bitch with his dick in his hand, begging for more.'

'What I'm going to do then, Mrs Fielding, is phone the local station and arrange for a police car to take you up there,' Tina told her. 'What I would suggest is sometime tomorrow, to suit you. That would give you time to …' Tina hesitated for a moment, trying to think of a way to put it delicately. '… to prepare yourself. What sort of time would be convenient for you?'

The bleary eyes gave her a mocking look and the woman said, 'I'll have to check my diary, see what other social engagements I have. But don't make it in the morning. I don't get up in the mornings. It's too depressing.'

'All right, Mrs Fielding, I'll arrange it for the afternoon. May I take a phone number, so I can confirm the time with you?' Tina asked.

'No point, phone's been cut off long since,' the woman said with a shrug. 'Just tell the bizzies to knock on when they like. I'm not going anywhere.'

Once outside, the two officers gratefully gulped air. Even the polluted atmosphere of the neighbourhood tasted sweet and fresh after the inside of the house.

'How the hell do people end up like that?' Tina asked Sal, as they got into the Mini. Tina had first done an anxious check all round to make sure it still had all its wheels and there was no graffiti or any blade marks.

'It's the demon drink,' Sal, a non-drinker, said in reply. 'I wish people would wake up to the damage it does. It's just as bad as most of the drug-related stuff we deal with, and so much easier to get hold of.'

'Boss isn't going to be pleased we're going back without a positive ID but I don't see what else we could do in the circumstances,' Tina said. 'He's taking this one hard and personally.'

'He's always worried the next one is going to be Rosalie, I suppose,' Sal said. 'Can't imagine how the Big Boss gets through the day. I suppose, in a sense, there must be some sort of relief when parents of runaways know the worst is true. At least they can get on and heal in some way.'

'I just hope Sarge pulls his finger out a bit,' Tina said. 'What we really don't need on top of everything is him falling down on the job,' and they both chuckled at the weak joke.

Ted wasn't ecstatic at their news when they got back. His team were used to seeing him relaxed, confident and in charge, but this case was already starting to get to him and he was desperate for some positive progress. But as ever, he made sure the team got positive feedback from him. He didn't want them getting as discouraged as he was.

'Right, good, you did the right thing. Hopefully it's only a delay of a day before we get the positive ID,' he said. 'So far she's still the most likely match of any that Steve has come up with.

'So, let's start out on the assumption it is her. From what we know about her, start asking around on known pick-up streets, see if any of the regulars know her. Find out if she has a pimp and who it is. Let's start checking CCTV from likely venues, too. If she was picked up in a car, we may get something.

'Mike, sort out teams on this and get them started. Then go home. You look dreadful,' Ted told his DS. 'Have some more strong painkillers, have a day off if you need one, but get yourself as fit as you can. I need every member of this team on top of their game. I'm having this bastard off the street and soon. Two young women dead is two too many.'

Chapter Nineteen

If Ted was annoyed at the delay in formal identification of the second victim, he was incandescent with rage when he saw what the local papers had done following the press conference.

The pocket billiard-playing local reporter had the by-line for the story in the local weekly which started on the front page and continued over a double-page spread inside. Ted had to grudgingly concede that the journalist had done his homework and a lot of historical research had gone into his piece.

Unfortunately a lot of it was hysterical nonsense, which Ted could really have done without, notably the label of the 'Stockport Slasher' for their as yet unidentified killer. If the journalist crossed Ted's path in the near future, he was in grave danger of finding himself with nothing left with which to play pocket billiards, because of the mood Ted was in.

He'd clearly done a lot of digging for facts for the inevitable references to the Whitechapel killings of Jack the Ripper and the twentieth century murders of the Yorkshire Ripper. He'd also dredged up a lot of stuff on Stockport murders of the sixties, including one where a woman's body had been dumped in the car park of a police station.

He hadn't gone as far as to use the term 'serial killer', which would have been inaccurate with just two deaths so far. Had he done so, Ted would have wanted to create a new offence of breathing in and out in a public place, just so he could have had him arrested for it.

The journalist had also unfortunately overheard Vicki Carr's father's opening words to Ted and quoted them in full, whilst conveniently omitting what Ted had promised him in reply.

It was exactly the sort of scaremongering piece he had wanted to avoid at all costs. Ted was struggling to see how it would help the enquiry in the way it was intended to. Especially as it looked more than likely that they actually had a positive ID on the second victim on their own initiative, or rather on young Steve's, with Oliver Burdon's assistance, without the public's help.

He had arranged that he and Tina would go to the mortuary when Mrs Fielding arrived from Stoke-on-Trent for the identification. From what Tina had told him, it didn't sound as if she was going to be a grief-stricken parent, but it was a courtesy he would extend to any relative in the same circumstances, so he wanted to do it.

DS Hallam had come in, still looking in a lot of pain, but could easily hold the fort whilst Ted was out of the office.

When Mrs Fielding arrived, the officer who had driven her was having to support her gently by the elbow as she was so unsteady on her feet. It did not seem to be because of grief. She had at least changed her skirt for one which was marginally less dirty, but she smelled as if she had not changed her underwear in a long time.

Ted formally introduced himself and offered his condolences, but even he stopped short of shaking her hand, which was filthy.

'It's no surprise,' the woman said harshly. 'She always was going to finish up dead in a ditch somewhere, with her knickers round her ankles, the little whore.'

The identification was peremptory. The body has been made as presentable as possible, the eyelids closed. The woman barely glanced at her dead daughter before saying, 'Yes that's our Mags, poor little cow,' she said, although there was just the hint of some nostalgic affection in her tone of voice. 'Can I go now?'

Ted and Tina looked at one another.

'Mrs Fielding,' Ted said patiently, '*I* want to catch whoever has done this to your daughter,' he stressed the personal pronoun, with a touch of rebuke. 'I would really appreciate a few moments of your time. Anything at all you could tell me about your daughter may be helpful to my enquiry. Perhaps we could go and get a coffee?'

'I'd rather have a proper drink,' the woman grumbled. 'Who pays for the funeral? I can't afford to.'

Ted looked at the constable who had brought the not-so grieving mother and said, 'This officer will make sure you have all the information and support you need, Mrs Fielding. Now, shall we all go and get a coffee?'

He nodded to the officer to accompany them as they headed for the hospital coffee shop. She once again had to steady Mrs Fielding by the elbow a few times on the short walk.

Ted steered them to a table for four. 'What would you like to drink, Mrs Fielding?'

'I'd like a large gin, but I don't suppose I can have one. I'll have one of them fancy frothy coffees instead, with lots of sugar,' she said.

Ted produced his wallet and got out a twenty pound note which he handed to Tina. 'Can you do the honours, please, Tina? Whatever you and the officer want. I don't suppose they have green tea here?' he asked wistfully.

'You never know, boss, I'll see what I can find for you.'

'Mrs Fielding, I appreciate that you haven't seen your daughter for a few years but anything at all you can tell me about her, about what sort of person she was, may be of great help to me,' Ted began.

'A little tart is what she was,' the woman spat. 'Always at it, from very young. That time with Henry wasn't the first, it was just the last straw. He wasn't the first of my boyfriends who said she was always leading them on, always giving them the come on.'

Ted sighed. 'But Mrs Fielding, who was the instigator of those incidents?'

Seeing the puzzled look in the bleary eyes, the officer who had driven her translated for her. 'Who started it? Was it her or them?'

'She'd go with anyone, from a young age,' the woman said. 'For sweeties when she was little, then for money when she got older. Always had been like that.'

Tina came back with the drinks. She put an ordinary cup of tea in front of the boss, with his change, and reported, 'No green tea, boss, sorry, I got you this instead.'

'Mrs Fielding, we think your daughter may have been working as a prostitute to fund a drug habit,' Ted told her bluntly. 'It's possible she got into a car with someone who proved to be her killer. We're working on that assumption now.'

'Well, I hope the poor cow was getting paid better than just sweeties, at least,' the woman said, noisily slurping her cappuccino. 'I'm sorry she's dead, don't get me wrong, she was my daughter, but I'm not surprised. I hope you get whoever it was, though, the filthy bastard.'

Ted downed his tea fast and nodded to Tina to do the same with her black coffee. He stood up abruptly, motioning to the Uniform constable not to do so as she half rose. 'Can you see Mrs Fielding safely home, please, Constable, and please ensure she has some help available, so she knows what she needs to do.'

He surprised the constable by shaking her hand then steeled himself to do the same to Mrs Fielding, as a courtesy, before he and Tina left. He stopped at the first medicated hand-wash dispenser he came to and pumped out a generous quantity of gel which he massaged thoroughly into his hands as he and Tina walked back to her car.

'I could do with the mind bleach, too, after that,' he told

her. 'That poor kid, what chance did she ever have?'

'Abused by a string of the mother's boyfriends from an early age, do you think, boss? With a mother too drunk to know or care what was really going on?' Tina asked.

Ted shrugged. 'You know I hate to be judgemental,' he said. 'We can't know why that woman is like she is, what things in her own life brought her to the state she's in.'

There were some parts of his private life Ted didn't mind sharing with his team, like his father's accident and subsequent descent into alcoholism. He felt it helped them to understand him a little better. It certainly meant that none of them ever drank heavily in his presence, nor came into work complaining of hangovers.

'My dad was teetotal, you know, before the accident,' he reminded her. 'Brought up very strict Methodist, never touched a drop in his life until he lost his independence, his dignity and his wife. Then he became an alcoholic atheist.'

'But at least we now know who our victim is and have confirmation of her lifestyle. There's no question that she would have got willingly into a car with a complete stranger, and gone anywhere, not just up the nearest alleyway for a quickie. So it does give us a definite direction to go in,' Tina replied.

'And now I know her background, I'm not going to rest, and nor are any of the rest of you,' Ted warned, 'until we have some justice for this poor kid. It looks like there is no one else in this world who cares or cared for her.'

Chapter Twenty

'Mike, got a job for you today, if you're up to driving a bit now. Not too heavily medicated?' Ted said at the next team briefing.

The DS instantly looked decidedly wary but said, 'Yes, boss, I think I can manage that now. What's the job?'

'You look like the perfect mild-mannered family man, squeaky clean, nothing dodgy,' Ted told him. 'Later on this afternoon, once it's getting dark, the girls will start appearing on the streets. Find out from the team where the hotspots are and I want you to go cruising.'

Hallam's face was a picture. 'I haven't got my car today, boss.'

'No problems, take one from the pool,' Ted told him. 'Pick up a few of the girls, ask them what they know about Maggie Fielding, anything at all that might be helpful to us. They'll probably talk to you because of how you look. Let the missus know you might be a bit late, most of them don't come out to play early, just the ones who are desperate.'

'Yes, sir,' the DS replied, but he still looked uncomfortable. Ted couldn't quite tell if it was physical discomfort or something else.

He turned to the rest of his team. 'Tina, can you get round to the soup kitchen and ask some more questions? Talk to anyone who comes in, see if you can get any clearer idea of where Maggie's patch was, where she dossed. Did she mention any of her recent pick-ups to anyone?'

Turning to Virgil, he said, 'Virgil, huge apologies in

advance for the appalling racial stereotyping, but I need you working a late one this evening so take a bit of a break this afternoon in exchange. I also need you in your best pimp's threads.'

'Word, blud,' Virgil drawled with a wink and despite the seriousness of the briefing, the rest of them had to laugh, even the DI.

'That's the idea, method acting,' the Ted smiled. 'I need to know if this girl had a pimp, and who it was, or was she just moonlighting. Always worth looking at the pimp in a case like this although, of course, this world is light years from what we have found out about Vicki Carr. Which brings me on to links.

'Any ideas, any theories, anything, and I do mean anything, we need to explore them. Anyone got anything they want to propose?'

'Sir,' Steve said hesitantly, so much so that Ted was surprised he hadn't put up his hand before speaking. 'This may be nothing, but we now know both victims had blue eyes.'

'Yes?' Ted said encouragingly, pleased the young man was finding his voice a bit more.

'Well, sir,' the TDC continued, 'this is probably just rubbish, but as the second victim's eyes were removed, I just wondered if the eyes were significant in some way? Whether he was drawing our attention to a link, some sort of message ...' he tailed off, clearly thinking his idea sounded too far-fetched now he had voiced it.

'It's a point worth bearing in mind, Steve,' Ted told him. 'At the moment I'm not sure where it would lead us but it is a link and we need to look at them all. Well done.'

'Boss,' the DS asked, 'will you be using a psychological profiler on this case?'

There was a low chuckle from the longer-standing members of the team and even Ted smiled. 'DS Hallam,' he said, 'the rest of the team will tell you that whenever the words "psychological" and "profile" appear in the same sentence anywhere near me, the red mist starts to descend.

'There's been a study done which suggests it has no real-world value and can even take cases in entirely the wrong direction, which is the last thing we need. It works wonderfully on television. Some over-weight hard drinker with a Scottish accent comes along and tells us our killer had a troubled childhood and liked to torture small animals. I think we can probably work out for ourselves that these are not the actions of a normal and socially well-adjusted person.

'Having said that, if I thought me singing England's next Eurovision Song Contest entry would help us catch this killer, I would do it, willingly. We will do whatever it takes. Just promise me you won't suggest that idea to the Big Boss before we have exhausted every other possible route. In fact I'll talk to him first, nip any such idea in the bud.'

He looked round at his team then continued, 'Right, Maurice and Sal, I want you to dig deep into Vicki Carr's background and find any connection, no matter how tenuous, between her and Maggie Fielding. Sal, you also make time to go and see Honest John.'

'Really, sir?' Sal groaned.

'Really, DC Ahmed,' Ted said dryly. 'We know it's not him, of course. But if someone is so desperate for human contact they resort to confessing to crimes, it would be a sad world if we couldn't give them ten minutes now and again. Don't go out of your way, but when you're passing in his direction, call in. He's always there. Ask him a question only the killer could answer, then tell him he's eliminated from our enquiries. It will make his week, probably make his year. Look on it as community service.

'Rob, go and have another chat with the ex-boyfriend. I can't see it being him, not for a moment. He's short of money, so I can't see him affording to pay a girl, but maybe he got money from somewhere and maybe a bit of what Maggie was offering is the most he can manage these days. Check it out.

'Since that hatchet job in the local paper, I'm really concerned about the possibility of copycat crimes. Steve, no one is better at research than you are. I want you to go through the press articles and find out twice as much as they found out about historical killings in this area. I'm worried some sick joker will try to mimic one of those. We can't prevent it, but at least if we have all the information we can find, it puts us in a stronger position.

'Right, you all know what you have to do. Now go do that voodoo that you do so well.'

Mike Hallam looked thoroughly confused. The rest of the team knew that one of the boss's favourite films of all time was Blazing Saddles, from which he would sometimes trot out quotes.

Ted headed for the DCI's office. Since Mike had mentioned the dreaded 'psychological profiling' phrase, Ted thought he'd best pre-empt that idea just in case Jim Baker was having the same thoughts.

Ted was not averse to taking help from anyone when working a difficult case. It's just that he liked to go with things which had some scientific basis or proven track record, and he had yet to be convinced of either in the case of psychological profiling.

He knew the DCI had tried every method known in trying to find his missing daughter, including contacting a so-called medium. She had taken a lot of his money and fed him a load of mumbo-jumbo, raising his hopes only to dash them again when nothing she said was borne out on investigation.

The DCI was a good, solid copper with an impressive conviction rate of his own, but something of a steady-Eddie plodder. He and Ted made a good double act for bouncing ideas off each other, and Ted wanted to bring him up to speed as well as exchanging ideas, in case there was anything he was missing that was staring him in the face.

He filled in the DCI on the identification of Maggie

Fielding. It was always acutely painful for both men to talk
about runaways. Maggie's leaving home had been
understandable. Rosalie's was much more complex. She had
hated the way her mother treated her father and wanted him to
leave her, or preferably to throw her out. But the DCI was a
religious man who took his 'till death do us part' vow
seriously. Rosalie was effectively asking him to choose
between his daughter and his wife and it nearly broke him. He
was now left with no daughter and a wife he only saw
occasionally when she wasn't out sleeping around.

Ted mentioned the profiling idea and was relieved when
the DCI agreed that it was too early to consider any such thing
at the moment.

'Coming up to Christmas, Ted,' the DCI said
conversationally. 'Got any plans?'

'Get this bastard behind bars first,' came the swift
response. 'Then if that's done and dusted, Trev will be cooking
something fabulous as usual. You're very welcome to come
and join us, Jim, if you want to. I know Trev is thinking of
asking Hard G's ex, Willow – they've become quite good
friends.'

'That's kind, Ted, but I'll be spending Christmas with my
wife, of course,' the DCI said, although both men knew he
probably wouldn't.

'Well, the offer's there, if your plans fall through,' Ted told
him. 'Right, I'd better get on. We have a killer to catch.'

Chapter Twenty-one

DC Dennis 'Virgil' Tibbs really enjoyed undercover work on the streets. He loved getting into a role; it gave free rein to his vivid imagination. This evening he had taken the boss at his word and gone for shiny suit and bling, for the perfect pimp look.

His car didn't quite match the image. It wasn't new or polished chrome enough, but at least it was a Beemer and at least it was black. He had the car's sound system cranked up to the max, belting out rap tracks that he would never normally listen to. It wouldn't really work with his undercover image to be cruising the streets talking to prostitutes with the soft tones of his preferred Michael Bublé discs issuing forth from his car speakers.

Virgil was drenched in aftershave which smelled expensive but was actually a cheap copy from the market. Not a counterfeit, of course, or the boss would have had his guts for garters. He looked the part, especially with his carefully honed figure, the result of his passion for body building.

He was so enthusiastic about throwing himself into the role that he was actually out on the streets a little earlier than he had intended, although on these wintry days, darkness fell even before late afternoon. So he knew some of the girls would already be stirring.

As well as being a good detective, Virgil was known as a bit of a joker on the team. He could never resist the chance of a laugh. When he saw the pool car ahead of him, cruising slowly along the kerb, he couldn't help himself from tucking in behind it and waiting for his chance.

As DS Hallam slowed the pool car to a crawl, having spotted a girl lurking on a street corner, Virgil was out of his car and round to its passenger door in a flash. It was unlocked, as he'd expected in the circumstances. He slid in and drawled a 'Yo, dude.'

The DS went ashen-faced and nearly leapt out of his seat, a hand that was visibly shaking flying up instinctively to steady his heart, which had suddenly gone into overdrive.

'Whoa, sorry, Sarge,' Virgil said contritely, 'didn't mean to scare you. I just couldn't resist.'

'You nearly gave me a heart attack,' Hallam told him, his voice sounding a little unsteady. 'These bloody pills they've got me on make me a bit twitchy as it is. Just as well they don't let us out armed. And you could have blown both our covers.'

'Sorry, Sarge,' Virgil said again, 'but no danger of that. What could be more natural than a pimp having a word with a john who's maybe not paid his dues in full? You got anything?'

'Some very interesting offers,' the DS smiled, more relaxed now that his heart-rate was coming back down nearer to normal. 'Talked to a couple of the girls who knew Maggie slightly. Seems her style was always a quickie for cash. She was more interested in having money for the next fix than saving into a personal pension fund, so she didn't work as much as some of the girls, too off her face a lot of the time.'

'Poor kid,' Virgil said with feeling. 'Sad way for her to end up. Anyone know where she hung out?'

Hallam shook his head. 'One of the girls thinks she sometimes squatted in an empty house round the back of Wellington Road somewhere, but nobody I've spoken to yet knew for sure. They don't think she had a pimp, but you'll be able to find out more on that score.'

He turned and looked at Virgil from head to toe. 'I must say you look, and smell, the part. I'm glad this is a pool car, would hate to have mine stinking like that for days.'

'Hard to see what she had in common with Vicki Carr, so far,' Virgil mused. 'No doubt that Maggie would have got into a car with anyone flashing the cash, but would Vicki? Doesn't really seem to fit what we know of her. Although I suppose she'd have accepted a lift from someone she knew or at least recognised. But the two didn't exactly move in the same social circles.'

'Don't be too sure of that,' the DS laughed. 'You'd be amazed at the types that do go with the girls for a quick knee-trembler up an alleyway. I was gobsmacked when one of them asked after a copper from our nick when they realised I wasn't just another punter. Not one of our team, but still someone you'd be shocked about.'

'Really?' Virgil said. 'You have to tell me now, Sarge, you can't leave me in suspense.'

'If I tell you, I'll have to kill you,' the DS smiled. 'And talking of being killed, my missus will kill me if I don't get back home pretty sharpish. I'm supposed to be taking my lad to a sports club tonight to get him signed up for some baseball training. That should at least spare me from any more bruises or cracked ribs. Do you have kids, Virgil?'

'No, Sarge,' Virgil shook his head, 'and the way things are going with me and my wife at the moment, it's not likely to happen. I'm on restricted privileges – very restricted, if you get my meaning – because we keep having big rows over my hours. I did try to warn her that being a copper was not a nine to five job. And she hates it when I'm out doing stuff like this.'

'My wife isn't wild about it either,' the DS said, 'although she's got used to it over the years.'

'We usually have a few drinks with the boss for Christmas, with partners invited,' Virgil told him. 'Maybe yours could have a word with mine, explain things a bit. Otherwise, if I get any interesting offers tonight, I might just be inclined to take them up!'

'I'll pretend I didn't hear that, Detective Constable,' the DS smiled. 'Right, take care out there, go and see what you can find out. What's that bit about the voodoo the boss said?'

Virgil laughed. 'If you want to get on the good side of the boss, learn a few quotes from Blazing Saddles, Sarge. It's his favourite film, he knows the sound track by heart.'

'I'll see you tomorrow,' Hallam said, as Virgil got out of the car. 'I'm going to take this car in to be fumigated so the next poor user doesn't choke to death on your aftershave fumes.'

As soon as Virgil got out of the car and into the gathering night, he slipped effortlessly into his new persona. He was hard to spot as a cop to anyone who didn't already know him. If he was careful how he approached the girls and pimps alike, he should turn up some leads, without putting himself at any risk.

Like the rest of the team from the boss on down, he was worried that their killer may be someone just randomly snatching his victims with no pre-planning, always the hardest to track down. He knew the girls on the streets did their best to keep an eye on one another and that the older ones in particular kept a motherly eye on the younger ones, especially those without pimps to protect them.

His gut feeling was that Maggie had been operating alone with no pimp to keep an eye on her, but he needed to find out if his instincts were correct.

Virgil had good contacts on his patch. He was liked and respected by most as a good, fair copper, doing his job without excessive zeal. It paid off when he needed information in exchange. What earned him most respect was that he investigated crimes against, as well as by, people of all races equally.

By the time he'd finished his shift, he had a lot of information about Maggie. He knew the precise location of the derelict house where she usually took shelter. He knew her method of working and knew with certainty that she would get into any car with anyone, the flashier the motor the better, because it smacked of more money. And he knew she definitely didn't have a pimp.

The trouble was, spending so much time on the streets on a cold winter's evening, delving into the murky side of the sex trade had left him largely feeling cold but also feeling extremely horny. There was one part of his body which was far from feeling the cold.

Hoping to bring warmth where it was needed and take the heat out of other parts, he peeled off his pimp's threads and bling as soon as he got home and slid quietly between the sheets next to his already sleeping wife. Eagerly he moved close up against her, pressing the most optimistic part of his anatomy against the soft curve of her buttocks.

At the contact, his wife shot bolt upright in bed and shrieked harshly, 'Jesus Christ, Dennis,' as she refused to use his work nickname. 'You're freezing and you stink like a whore's boudoir. For God's sake go and get a shower and make sure you scrub every bit of you before you come anywhere near me. I dread to think what you've been up to tonight.'

Virgil slunk obediently away to do as she said. By the time he returned, freshly showered and smelling of ginseng and cinnamon instead of like a Haitian pimp, his wife was sleeping the sleep of She Who Must Not Be Disturbed.

Chapter Twenty-two

Ted was in early, ahead of his team, but his DS was not far behind him, both eager to dissimulate the information from the previous night's work, to push the enquiry forward.

'Blimey, Mike, you look even worse today,' the DI commented as Hallam came slowly and stiffly in through the door, every movement clearly causing him a lot of pain.

The DS tried to laugh it off but gave up the attempt, which clearly hurt too much. 'This is you trying to be encouraging, is it, sir? I am actually getting better, slowly. I just stopped taking the painkillers. They were knocking me out and I can't really drive much when I take them.'

'Well, clearly you know your own body best but for goodness sake take some time off if you need to,' Ted told him. 'If you push yourself too hard now you're not going to hold out for the rest of the enquiry.'

Hallam nodded, with gritted teeth, and eased himself down into his seat.

The rest of the team were in on time as usual. Maurice Brown stunned everyone by producing a big bag of clementines instead of his usual sticky buns. He laughed at the DI's surprised look and patted his not inconsiderable girth.

'Early New Year's resolution, boss,' he said. 'Hopefully we'll not be long before we're collaring this bastard. I want to be able to do something more useful for the team than just squashing him into submission.'

With the information feeding in, their white board was getting fleshed out. One thing it was showing was that there were almost no similarities between the two victims but plenty of differences, pointing more and more to random selection.

There had been hardly any response to the appeal for information on Maggie Fielding, the second victim, but Ted was not surprised at that. The only people who were likely to be able to identify her were those who paid for her services and those who sold her drugs, neither of which group was likely to contact the police willingly.

Then Rob O'Connell took a call, put his hand over the mouthpiece and called across to the DI. 'Sir, got someone on the line who says he has some information, but he'll only talk to you.'

Ted headed for his own office, calling, 'Put him through,' as he went. He hoped it wasn't going to be Honest John or Oliver Burdon, calling for a chat.

'Is that Detective Inspector Darling?' a voice asked, as soon as Ted picked up the phone and said, 'Hello.'

'Speaking,' Ted replied.

'I saw your appeal on the television. I have some information about the second victim. I'm willing to come to the station to talk, but only to you in person and only on the assurance that what I tell you is in confidence,' the voice continued.

'Sir, I'm conducting a murder enquiry,' Ted said sharply. 'If you are in possession of any information, it is your duty to disclose it and there are no pre-conditions possible. Bearing in mind that my team can and will trace you, I strongly suggest you come in to the station of your own free will for me to interview you and hopefully, from your point of view, eliminate you from our enquiries.'

There was a long pause. 'Very well, Detective Inspector,' came the terse response. 'I will be at the station in approximately half an hour.'

'Thank you, Mr ...?' but the caller had already rung off.

Ted went back out to his team.

'Interesting,' he told them. 'We have an as yet unidentified male coming in shortly, who says he has information on our Victim Number Two. He wants anonymity, so I think we can make an educated guess at what his relationship may have been with Maggie.'

He looked round the room at the expectant faces.

'Who wants in on this one with me? Sal, what about you? Do you fancy a break from the fraud case? Pass that over to someone else for a bit?'

Sal let out a huge audible sigh and punched the air. 'I thought you would never ask, boss,' he said. 'Now, what am I bid for a lovely fraud case? One careful owner? Still lots of mileage? Form an orderly queue, don't all shout at once.'

When Ted and Sal got the call that the potential witness was in an interview room awaiting them, they went downstairs. As Ted went into the room, he was astonished to find that he knew the man, at least by sight. He was the manager of a bank in town.

Ted introduced himself and Sal, for the tape. The man identified himself as Leslie Jones and immediately reached out to shake Ted's hand. As soon as Ted felt the thumb pressure on his forefinger, he dropped the hand and sat down.

'Mr Jones,' he said, 'let me begin by saying I do not belong, and never have belonged, to any secret society, certainly not the Freemasons. So any funny handshakes or supposedly secret distress signals are wasted on me. If you have any information for us, I would like you simply to state it, clearly and slowly for the purposes of the tape.'

The man looked shocked and uncomfortable. 'I am well known socially to a number of your superior officers,' he said snippily.

'Then I congratulate you, sir,' Ted said, still just on the right side of open discourtesy, 'but my only interest is in the brutal murder of two young women and your claim, in a telephone call, to have information on at least one of them.'

Jones looked increasingly ill at ease, positively squirming in his seat.

'I do have information, but it could be very compromising for me to disclose it,' he said.

'All I can say to that, Mr Jones, is it will be much more compromising for you, in all probability, if I have to find out such information for myself,' Ted told him.

Sal was watching the exchange between the two men with silent fascination. He knew the boss played various racquet games like badminton and tennis. He made the the score so far definitely 'Advantage DI Darling'.

'Very well,' Jones sighed, after a pause for reflection. 'I, er, I paid the girl Maggie on a couple of occasions for her, er, for her services. My wife is very … she's a cold woman, not at all forthcoming …' He broke off, looking beseechingly at the two men for their comprehension.

'Go on, Mr Jones,' Ted said patiently. 'It is not my job to judge you.'

'The thing is … ' again the hesitation. 'The girl was in my car on Tuesday evening, and I think that is the day you were asking about.'

Ted and Sal exchanged loaded glances.

'Mr Jones, I think at this stage you should consider having a solicitor present, before you make any further statement or answer any further questions,' Ted told him.

'Am I under arrest?' Jones asked indignantly. 'The girl was alive when she left me. I just wanted to come in because she was in my car and we, well you know, we had a bit of business. I wanted to come in to clear it up, just in case anyone had seen us, though I am always very careful to avoid that.'

'Mr Jones,' Ted said patiently. 'This is a murder enquiry. Surely you must realise that I cannot simply take your word for anything. I need to check everything you tell me. What time were you with the girl?'

'I went out shortly after seven. I told my wife I was

popping back to work to pick up a folder I needed. She always watches East Enders, so I knew she wouldn't take much notice of my absence.

'I picked the girl up quite quickly and we drove round the corner to a patch of waste ground which is badly lit. We, er, we did the business. We stayed in the car, less chance of being seen like that. It didn't take very long. I don't last long these days, it's such a rare treat,' he said with evident distaste. 'I drove her back to where I'd picked her up, paid her, dropped her off and went home. That's all. I was back shortly after eight, my wife can confirm that.'

'Where is your car now, Mr Jones?' Ted asked.

'It's parked at the bank. Why?' Jones asked.

'We will need to get it forensically examined,' Ted told him.

'Why? I told you the girl was in it with me, clearly there will be traces of her there …' Jones broke off as light dawned on his face. He suddenly went deathly pale. 'Oh, my God, you want to check to see if she was killed in my car, is that it? But I didn't kill her!'

'Mr Jones, it would be very helpful indeed if you gave me the keys to your car so I can arrange for an officer to collect it and have it examined,' Ted said. 'I will want to ask you more questions but I suggest we take a break for now to allow you to contact your solicitor, and I strongly advise you to do so.'

'Am I under arrest?' Jones asked again, blustering.

'Not at this stage, Mr Jones, you are merely voluntarily helping us with our enquiries,' Ted told him. 'But I have to inform you that I cannot rule out that becoming the case in the near future.'

Chapter Twenty-three

'Got a possible suspect, Jim,' Ted said, as he walked into the DCI's office. 'Came in of his own accord, which is strange, as he looks a strong contender. He admits having sex with Maggie in his car on the night she was killed.'

The DCI looked up, interested, hope sparking in his eyes. They badly needed a break on this one, and soon. 'Who is it?' he asked.

'Leslie Jones, the manager of that bank in town,' Ted told him. 'You might know him. I know him by sight.'

'Good God!' the DCI looked shocked. 'I know him too, through the Lodge. Has he confessed?'

'Not yet,' Ted replied. 'I've put him on ice while he sorts out a solicitor. I'm having his car brought in now so we can see if having sex was all he did to her in there.'

'I really can't believe it,' the DCI said. 'My wife and I have had dinner with him and his wife on several occasions. And you tell me he goes with prostitutes?'

'Not all marriages are quite what they seem from the outside, Jim,' Ted said gently, hoping he hadn't crossed a line.

'What's the plan now?' the DCI asked.

'I'll question him, while they're working on the car. He's only just come in so we've got nearly all of our initial twenty-four hours left to hold him, until I see if we have enough to charge him,' Ted said. 'Meanwhile I've got the team working on looking for any connections at all between him and Vicki Carr.'

'Leslie Jones, though?' the DCI said in bewilderment. 'I

just can't see him cutting off women's breasts and taking out their ovaries. I seem to remember he made a very poor show of carving the turkey when we had a Christmas meal with them one year. Keep me posted on this one, Ted, every step of the way.'

'Yes, of course,' Ted agreed as he made to leave. Then he turned back and added, awkwardly, 'Jim, I know you won't take this the wrong way but, in view of your social connections to a prime suspect, I just thought I ought to raise the question of keeping a lid on this.'

The Big Boss gave him a intensely long, hard look, which Ted held unwaveringly.

'You get away with a lot, Ted, because I know you're such a good copper,' he said eventually. 'And also because, in your position, I would have said exactly the same thing and would not have considered I'd done my job properly if I hadn't.'

As Ted headed back towards his own office, DS Hallam called out to him. 'Boss, young Steve's got something.'

'Yes, Steve?' Ted asked.

'Sir,' the TDC said, and Ted was pleased to see he was looking more at ease in speaking out. 'DS Hallam told me to start looking for any links between Jones and Vicki Carr.'

'And?' Ted prompted gently.

'She had an account at the bank where he works, sir,' Steve told him.

'Did she indeed?' Ted responded. 'Right, good work, keep digging. I want to know every link, no matter how small. If they even sat next to one another on a bus one time, I need to know about it. Sal, you're with me again. With Jones's Masonic connections, I bet his brief will be there before we even get back downstairs.'

He wasn't quite, but the solicitor did arrive in a remarkably short time. Huw Edwards and Ted knew each other slightly and had a grudging mutual respect. As soon as the two officers were sitting down opposite Edwards and his client and the tape was running, Edwards made it clear that he was not happy.

'For the record, is my client under arrest?' he began by asking.

'No, sir, as I have already explained to Mr Jones, twice, he is not,' Ted told him formally. 'Your client is currently helping us with our enquiries and came in of his own free will to do so. I am strongly suggesting that he remains here until we are satisfied we have all the information necessary to decide whether or not charges will be forthcoming.'

Turning to the new suspect, Ted asked, 'Mr Jones, does the name Vicki Carr mean anything to you?'

Jones looked thoroughly bewildered. 'Nothing at all,' he replied. 'Should it?'

'Ms Carr has an account at the bank in which you work,' Ted told him.

The solicitor scoffed. 'Oh, please, Detective Inspector. Have you any idea how many people do? Is my client supposed to know every person who banks in his branch?'

Ted watched Jones's face carefully whilst he told him, 'Vicki Carr was the first victim in our current murder enquiry. I'm presuming you saw either the press conference on the television, or the report of it in the newspapers, which is what led you to telephone me with information. I'm surprised, therefore, that you claim to be unfamiliar with the name.

'We are currently investigating any possible links between you and both of these two young women, Mr Jones.'

Jones's face went ashen. He looked totally shell-shocked. It was beginning to dawn on him that he had suddenly gone from being a respectable member of society, admitting to some dubious sexual activity, to being a prime suspect in a double murder enquiry.

Edwards also looked incredulous but was professional enough to cover it up quickly.

'In that case, Inspector, I insist on some time alone with my client, in order that I may advise him on how to respond to your questioning.'

'Of course, sir,' Ted said politely, as he and Sal stood up. 'DC Ahmed and I will leave you to it. I will arrange for some tea or coffee to be brought to you. Just inform the officer who will be outside the door when you're ready to resume questioning and we'll come back. But please, take as much time as you and your client need.'

As he and Sal headed back upstairs again, Ted asked him, 'What are your thoughts, Sal? Do you think he's our man?'

'Well, sir, if he is, he's taken one hell of a gamble, coming in here and telling us he'd been ...' he caught himself up short just in time before he said 'shagging', as he was not quite sure if the DI would approve '...if he'd been going with prostitutes and had Maggie in his car the day she was killed. The likelihood of us finding that out for ourselves was very slim and he must surely have known that.'

'I'm struggling to see where he got his surgical skills,' Ted admitted. 'It does seem somewhat unlikely for a bank manager. Although, of course, we can never tell what things people get up to in their own homes.

'We'll have to wait and see what forensics come up with on the car. He's admitted she was in it with him and that they were at it in the car, but I still don't see how we could make a murder charge stick on that alone. Especially if his wife confirms that he was home just after eight. I need to check the post-mortem report but I don't think that would tally with the time of death. Which reminds me ...'

They were back in the CID office by now and Ted looked around to see who was available.

'Tina, I need you to go round and get a statement from Mrs Jones on her husband's movements on the night in question. Mike, are you up to going along on this?'

'Not really, boss, if that's all right,' the DS said. 'Still a bit painful getting in an out of a car at the moment, even a pool car, but especially a Mini – no offence, Tina.'

'None taken, Sarge,' she smiled. 'You certainly do look pretty rough.'

'Steve, you go along,' Ted told him. 'You deserve to go out a bit, that was good work you did earlier on. Meanwhile we're just waiting for our Mr Jones to have a long talk with his solicitor to get his story straight before Sal and I go and talk to him again.

'I'm not convinced he is our man, at the moment,' he told the team. 'I can't for the life of me figure out why he would give himself up on a plate, yet without fully confessing, if he is the killer. Unless it's the most monumental bluff of all time.

'Keep digging, keep looking for links between Jones and both of the victims. Someone draw me up a time-line of Vicki Carr's last hours. I need to know exactly what times I need Jones to account for his movements, so he can talk himself in or out of the frame for both these killings.'

Chapter Twenty-four

Tina and Steve had driven round to Jones's house, Tina at the wheel of the Mini. Steve was impressed. He had a secret crush on the DC anyway and going anywhere alone with her was the stuff of his dreams. It took a lot of self control to stop it spilling over into fantasy, which would have had embarrassing consequences.

The Joneses lived in a modest semi, on the edge of Bramhall, which was probably an expensive piece of property because of its postcode alone. The front garden was neat and trim but definitely boring. Its only striking feature was an impressive monkey puzzle tree in one corner.

Both officers had their warrant cards in their hands when Mrs Jones came to the door, and Tina was quick to reassure her that there was no cause for alarm, they were just there to make routine enquiries.

They were shown into a fussy front room with rather too much Lladró around for Steve to feel comfortable. He was terrified that one false move on his part would bring a few porcelain figurines crashing down around him.

'Mrs Jones,' Tina began in her most business-like manner, 'your husband is fine, please don't worry. He may have been a witness to an incident we're investigating. We just wanted to check his movements and wondered if you could tell us what he was doing on Tuesday evening, please.'

The woman looked bored rather than remotely worried.

'Tuesday?' she asked. 'Let me see. We ate not long after he got in from work, about half past six, I would think. Do you need to know what we ate? I think it was haddock, it usually is on a Tuesday.'

'That's not necessary, Mrs Jones,' Tina assured her, 'but thank you for the information.'

'Tuesday is one of my East Enders nights, I never miss it,' she continued. 'My husband doesn't like it, but I do. He said he had to go back to work to pick something up. I don't remember what he said it was, so he went out as soon as he'd finished eating, probably just before seven. Is this right? Is this what you need to know?'

'Perfect, Mrs Jones,' Tina reassured her. 'Please do go on.'

'Do you want a cup of tea or anything?' the woman asked. 'I really should offer you something.'

Tina had a sudden mental image of Steve trying to cope with a bone china tea cup and saucer, and had to suppress a smile. 'That's very kind, Mrs Jones, but no thank you, we don't really have the time. Please go on.'

'East Enders was actually a bit disappointing,' she said rather wistfully. 'A lot of shouting, but not a lot of action.'

Tina wondered if soap operas were the most exciting thing in the woman's life, as she gently prompted her again to continue.

'I decided to watch Holby City afterwards. I don't always, it's a bit too gory for me, but I was bored so I left it switched on. My husband came back in when that had just got going, they'd done that recap bit at the beginning they always do and just got started with the story,' she said. 'I suppose that would make it about quarter past eight or so? I watched it till the end – such a nice man, that Sacha Levy – then I went to bed with my library book.'

'Did your husband go out again at any point, Mrs Jones?' Tina asked.

'I don't think so,' she said, 'but I wouldn't necessarily know for sure. We have separate rooms. Leslie gets so … ' she paused, looking at Steve and trying to find the right word, 'restless at night, it stops me sleeping.'

'You've been very helpful, Mrs Jones, thank you so much for your time,' Tina said as she rose. Steve blundered to his feet and she hoped he would managed to make it to the door without knocking anything over.

As they got back into the Mini, Steve said, 'Erm ...' because he was never quite sure how he was meant to address Tina. It was all very informal amongst the team but he still felt a bit uncomfortable addressing her by her first name. 'I've had an idea.'

Tina looked at him and grinned.

'You mucky little beggar,' she said teasingly, watching him go bright red as usual, then taking pity on him. 'Go on, Steve, you're on a winning streak with your ideas. What's this one?'

'If we make a quick detour through town, I think we could chase up another lead while we're at it,' then cringed in further embarrassment as she laughed at his choice of words.

'Okay,' she said, 'let's do it. Tell me where you want me to drive to.'

What a difference a short stay in a police station made. When Ted resumed his questioning of Jones, still with Sal sitting in, the man had lost all of his earlier bluster. He looked as if he had shrunk in size and was scared out of his wits.

His own clothes had now been taken for forensic testing so he was wearing an all-in-one white coverall. His solicitor was with him again and had clearly instructed him to say as little as possible for now.

Ted began with a formal caution. 'You do not have to say anything. But it may harm your defence if you do not mention when questioned something which you later rely on in court. Anything you do say may be given in evidence.

'Mr Jones, did you ever have occasion to meet Vicki Carr, who was a customer at your bank?'

'No,' Jones told him. 'But then there are hundreds of

customers I have never met.'

His solicitor gave him a warning look and shook his head slightly. He was obviously keen that Jones should restrict himself to answering questions in the simplest way possible, without sounding defensive.

'So when her name was released in the course of the press conference on the two cases, the name meant nothing to you?' Ted asked.

'Nothing at all,' Jones said, and this time resumed a tight-lipped silence.

'Tell me again about your movements on Tuesday evening,' Ted told him.

'I've told you already. There is nothing more I can add,' Jones said. 'I was in the mood for sex. My wife no longer obliges on demand. I made an excuse to leave the house and went looking for a girl, a prostitute. I saw the girl Maggie very quickly. I'd been with her before. She was … satisfactory.

'We drove round the corner, had very quick but for me very satisfying sex, in my car. I drove her back, paid her, dropped her off and drove away. She was alive and well when I left her. When I got home, my wife was watching that ridiculous hospital drama so I suppose it was shortly after eight o'clock.'

He was interrupted by a light knock at the door and Tina's head appeared. 'Sir, can I have a quick word?'

Ted left the room and found Tina and a very awkward-looking Steve, waiting outside.

'The wife's alibi for him checks out, boss, she says he got back about eight-fifteen,' Tina told him. 'I honestly doubt if she would have noticed if he'd got home still with his kecks around his ankles. Then Steve had one of his brainwaves.'

'You did?' Ted asked him.

Now red in the face, Steve said, 'Yes, sir. I thought while we were in town, we could call at the bistro and see if they knew Jones and if he had been in recently.'

'Did you have a photo of him to ID him by?' Ted asked in surprise.

'No, boss,' Tina told him, 'but this was Steve's bit of genius.' She gave the young TDC a friendly shove which nearly knocked him over. 'You tell him.'

Looking acutely embarrassed now, Steve muttered, 'We called in at the bank, sir, and I picked up some of their brochures. There was a picture of Mr Jones in it, part of their image of trying to be friendly and approachable.'

Tina cut in, clearly too excited to wait for Steve to stumble his way through the rest of the story. 'We took it to the bistro where Vicki Carr worked and hit the jackpot. Jones is well known there, he's a regular for meals and for drinks. So he could possibly have known Vicki Carr, at least by sight.'

Ted looked from one to the other, 'Steve,' he said, 'I think I love you.' Then added hastily at the young man's evident discomfort, 'in the best possible professional way, of course.'

He went back into the room and sat down.

'Mr Jones, in light of new information which I have just received, I have to tell you that you are now under suspicion of the murders of Vicki Carr and Maggie Fielding and will be held for further questioning. I would like to remind you again that you do not have to say anything. But it may harm your defence if you do not mention when questioned something which you later rely on in court. Anything you do say may be given in evidence.

'Is there anything you wish to say, Mr Jones?'

'I'm going to be sick,' Jones said, and promptly was, narrowly missing the desk and the voice recorder but still managing to splatter his solicitor's expensive Italian shoes.

Chapter Twenty-five

Trev was talking on his mobile phone in the kitchen when Ted got home. He put a hand over the mouthpiece and mouthed, 'Willow'.

Ted moved in close enough to plant a kiss on Trev's cheek and to say, 'Hi Willow,' into the phone as Trev moved his hand, then headed for the kettle and his green tea. Although they now had a suspect in custody, Ted was still far from convinced it was the right man. But it was a start, at least.

'We're both really looking forward to it,' Trev was saying into his phone. 'Come about twelve, time for drinky-poos before we eat. It's very informal, and no paper hats allowed.' He laughed. 'You too, sweetie, love you, bye.'

As he rang off, he moved over to Ted to return the kiss and to ask, 'Are you sure you don't mind about Willow coming on Christmas Day?'

'Of course not,' Ted assured him. 'It'll be nice and I promise not to feel like a gooseberry between you two new Best Friends Forever,' he added teasingly. Then he went on, 'We have a suspect in custody now. I'm not a hundred per cent convinced but it's a start. So do you fancy doing something at the weekend? Take the bike, take a picnic, go and blow a few cobwebs away?'

'Not Saddleworth,' Trev said emphatically. When difficult cases made him particularly maudlin, Ted would often go up to the moors and tramp about, acutely aware that one of the Moors Murders victims at least was still there and had never been brought home.

Little Keith Bennett's body had been up on that windswept and desolate landscape since 1964, possibly with other bodies of missing children. Ted would go from time to time to motivate himself to do his utmost to ensure that missing youngsters on his patch were returned safely to their homes.

'No, not Saddleworth,' Ted agreed, 'I was thinking more of Kinder Scout.'

Trev smiled and hugged him. 'Soppy thing,' he smiled.

Kinder Scout had been their first real date. The two had originally met when Trev was nineteen and joined the same judo club as Ted. He had his brown belt and was training hard for his black. As he wanted to work on technique and no one in the club had the edge on Ted for precision, Bernard teamed them up for training, week after week.

Trev was a diligent pupil, learning fast, a sponge for new knowledge, and Ted was a good teacher. From the first time he saw those incredible blue eyes, he was utterly smitten but remained detached and professional.

Every week after training, once they were showered and changed, Trev would pick Ted's brains on more and more detail, asking for further explanation of throws and holds, always eager to learn. Gaining his black belt should be a foregone conclusion but he also wanted to work his way up through the next levels to at least match Ted's black belt second dan. And always after their discussions, Ted would turn away and go home alone. Just occasionally, they'd both gone for a drink in a group of the other members.

After a few weeks, as Ted was turning to go, Trev said, 'Well, if you're not going to ask me, I'll just have to ask you. Will you come for a drink with me?'

Ted was staggered. His gaydar was accurate enough as a rule, but he couldn't imagine why such an attractive younger man was showing any interest in him. Ted had had a long succession of brief and unsatisfactory relationships. He'd recently ended one which seemed to be going nowhere. Ended it the first time he clapped eyes on Trev. He'd never found anyone who intrigued him as much as Trev did.

The drink together was excruciatingly uncomfortable. Ted was on pins the whole time, totally unable to relax. He felt as if an exotic bird had landed on the table in his garden and if he made the slightest wrong move, it would fly away, never to be seen again.

Before they parted, though, Ted plucked up the courage to ask Trev if he liked hill walking and if he fancied joining him at the weekend for the circular walk from Edale up Jacob's Ladder to Kinder Scout, with a picnic by the Kinder Downfall waterfall.

It had been a bitterly cold winter's day, cold enough to ensure that no one else was foolish enough to be out picnicking in the wind. As they sat huddled together, partly sheltered by rocks, they finally relaxed enough to share their life stories.

Trev's parents had been ultra-religious and utterly appalled when their brilliant, academically gifted son had come out as gay at the age of fifteen. They reacted by throwing him out and refusing ever to see him again.

Luckily, Trev had a far more relaxed arty, hippy aunt who took him in, looked after him, supported him in everything he did and loved him unquestioningly and unreservedly, until she was killed in a road accident just as Trev turned eighteen.

The aunt was not wealthy. Her house was rented, she had few savings, but what she had, she left to Trev. He used it to fund a gap year to the Far East, earning his keep by teaching English as a Foreign Language, and taking the opportunity to take up martial arts, flying effortlessly through gradings.

Trev had been accumulating A Levels since the age of twelve and had a frightening array of them in languages and sciences, all at the highest level. Both Oxford and Cambridge had already made overtures to him. He also told Ted that he had had an interesting visit from two men in suits, proposing a career which had not previously occurred to him.

By the time he returned home from his trip, at nineteen years old, Trev was still undecided in which direction his life and future career would take him. Then he met Ted.

If Trev had ever sat down to draw up a list of the least suitable future life partner he could imagine, he would have been hard put to outdo a short, much older copper with no dress sense and a shed-load of angst and self-doubt.

He was under no illusion about how difficult such a relationship would be, not just because of the hours involved in Ted's work, but also the considerable amount of homophobic prejudice which still existed in his profession.

But somehow here Trev was, sitting at the top of a thirty-metre waterfall, sharing green tea from a battered stainless steel flask, with this intensely complex man and somehow not wanting the moment to end.

They shared no more than one hesitant and tender kiss, on top of Kinder Scout, after which Ted pulled away as if terrified he had moved too fast.

They started to see a lot more of each other, not just at the dojo but going out for drinks or a meal, long walks in the Peak District, sometimes venturing further afield to Snowdonia, but never staying over.

Trev shared a flat with two students and Ted was renting the ground floor of a small house in Offerton. He had the advantage of rights to the back garden, in which his green-fingered skills were confined entirely to growing fragrant oriental lilies in pots.

Ted was a competent if not particularly inspired cook. They ate a lot of chilli con carne. Trev was a brilliant cook but he was so afraid of shaking Ted's already precarious confidence, that he never once offered to cook in the early days.

They spent a lot of time together, just getting to know one another. Ted learned to share Trev's enthusiasm for Queen and heard with surprise of his passion for cats. The aunt had owned a beloved Siamese cross and it was in fact the cat which had indirectly caused her death. She'd looked out of her front window to see a lifeless little chocolate point form lying in the road and rushed straight out, oblivious to her own safety and to the car coming towards her at slightly more than the speed limit.

Ted and Trev had several weeks of taking things so slowly it was driving Trev insane. After a slightly more adventurous meal of Thai green curry, Trev said, 'Before you show me your stamp collection or get your train set out, I just have one simple question to ask you. When are you going to take me to bed?'

So Ted did. And the rest, as they say, was history.

Chapter Twenty-six

'Roger, it's Ted.' Ted's first call of the day was to Hard G. 'I need your help.'

'But of course, dear boy, anything at all I can do,' the Professor said immediately.

'I've got a suspect in custody,' Ted told him and Hard G immediately interrupted.

'You have? But that's wonderful, well done.'

'I have links between him and both victims,' Ted went on. 'Very strong links with the second girl, Maggie Fielding. He's admitted picking her up off the street and having sex with her on the evening of her death.'

'Good gracious,' Hard G said. 'How very naughty of him.'

Ted thought that was a bit rich coming from a serial womaniser who admitted going dogging, but he let it pass. 'I have links between him and Vicki Carr whilst she was alive but at the moment, nothing at all to tie him in to her body. I'm having his car gone over with a fine-tooth comb now, to see what that comes up with. I just wondered if there was anything on the body, anything at all, that James could have missed on the post-mortem?'

'James is very thorough, he's like a beagle on a scent,' the Professor told him. 'I would be very surprised if he missed anything, no matter how seemingly insignificant. Would it help if I went through his report this morning, just to see? You do know the body has now been released for burial, so short of exhuming the poor girl, there's not much we can do, even if there is a chance James had missed anything, and I would be surprised if he had.'

'Anything would be helpful, Roger,' Ted told him. 'Thank you, that would be great.'

'I'll tell you what, old chap, why don't I take you to lunch afterwards and go over what I've found?' he suggested. 'I still feel very bad about how I behaved at the club; quite unforgivable of me. At least let me buy you lunch to make up in some small way.'

Ted hesitated. Lunch with Roger was low on his priority list. He had too much to do, including more interviews with their prime suspect. On the other hand, he did need to eat and if anyone could turn up anything at all that may have been missed on the initial report, the Professor was the person to do it, so he agreed.

'Splendid!' Hard G said. 'I'll come and pick you up, around twelve-thirty? Look forward to it.'

Ted's next port of call was the DCI. His team was flat out trying to establish any and all links between Jones and the two dead girls, particularly Vicki Carr, as he had already admitted to being with Maggie Fielding. There was a lot of leg work involved now to see if they could find any witnesses who had seen him with Vicki Carr on the day she died.

Ted would be spending much of his time interviewing Jones. So far he had only circumstantial evidence to link him and he wanted something much more concrete, preferably a confession. He still couldn't work out why Jones had come in with information yet stopped short of admitting the killings. Unless, of course, he really was innocent and just unlucky enough to have been one of the last people to be with Maggie Fielding before she was killed.

The forensic tests on the car would show if there was any blood. It was possible that Jones had taken the girl somewhere other than the waste ground he had mentioned and either killed her immediately or held her captive somewhere before going back to finish her off. His wife almost certainly would not have noticed. But Ted was uneasy about the time-frame because of the wife's testimony and also uncertain where Jones might have taken the girl.

He would possibly have asked the DCI to sit in on the interviews for an important case. His size and solid bulk made the perfect foil to Ted's slight build and mild way, but it would be completely inappropriate, given the boss's personal and social links to the suspect. He might settle for Maurice Brown instead, as he looked slightly menacing at the best of times.

'We've got to be absolutely certain of our ground on this one, Ted,' the DCI cautioned him. 'If we get this wrong, with his connections, Jones will have us hung out to dry and we'll both be singing soprano with the Vienna Boys' Choir.'

'I know, Jim, and I have to say, my gut feeling has been telling me all along that this is not our man,' Ted said. 'I've got Hard G going through the post-mortem report again, to see if there is anything that's been missed. I'm meeting him for lunch to discuss it.'

'Nice,' Jim Baker growled. 'If Roger's taking you, it will be somewhere expensive with very good food. The club?'

'Not sure but it's never exactly a pleasure dining with Hard G,' Ted smiled. 'The things I do for the job, eh? Right, Maurice and I will go and have another crack at Mr Jones. I think we should get a search warrant for his house and any other property he has, if you could set that up for me? I'll get someone to check with the wife if there's a lock-up or anything. I'm far from convinced but let's go with what we've got.'

Jones looked dreadful. He clearly hadn't slept at all, his eyes were red and shadowed underneath. His solicitor had been summoned again and was still playing the hand of disclosing nothing, letting the police do all the legwork and set out their stall.

Ted probed and questioned gently, going back over what

Jones had said before, checking facts and timings. Jones stuck to the same story throughout. He didn't know Vicki Carr and had merely had sex with Maggie Fielding who had been alive and well when he left her.

For once Ted found himself almost looking forward to some time with Hard G. At least it was time out of the office, with a decent meal. He still could not shake off the impression that they were wasting their time on an innocent but unlucky man while the real killer was still out there.

Despite the chilly day, Hard G swept up in the Jaguar with the top rolled down. It was a custom rebuild, so the top was cream to match the Italian leather of the seats. It was the first time Ted had had the occasion to ride in the car and he was looking forward to it.

He was surprised to find that the seats were protected by plastic slip-on covers and there was clean new paper in the passenger foot-well.

Hard G saw his look and laughed.

'Hand stitched Italian leather, dear boy,' he said. 'You don't think I allow mere mortals to park their arses on it, do you? Nothing personal. It's my favourite toy, I have my man give it a full valeting every day.'

Ted couldn't believe the power and thrust from the motor as Hard G pulled away from the curb, making him feel he was being pressed back into the seat. Although the Professor drove within the speed limit, just, he opened the Jag up whenever there was the slightest possibility.

'French food all right for you?' he asked as he overtook another car with scant inches to spare. 'I should have checked, rude of me.'

Ted knew Hard G had several holiday homes scattered about the globe, one of which was in the south of France.

'It's fine, Roger, whatever. It's very kind of you.'

'Nonsense, old boy, I behaved abominably the other day, it's the least I could do,' the Professor said, as the powerful car sprang away from traffic lights like a greyhound out of the trap. 'We're heading for a little place I know just the other side of Marple. Not far, it won't take us long in this old bus.'

Roaring up Dan Bank, Ted did briefly have the strange illusion that the car might actually take off and fly the rest of the journey. It was, he hated to admit to himself, one of the most exciting car rides he'd ever had, even at modest speeds. He also had to grudgingly concede that Hard G was an excellent driver.

Their destination was a small pub at the side of a country lane, with impressive views. It looked unprepossessing from the outside and there were not many cars in its car park. When he caught sight of the prices on the menu, Ted understood why. Even for a wealthy county like Cheshire, it was eye-watering.

'Have whatever you like, Ted,' the Professor reassured him, seeing his expression.' As I am in the company of the long arm of the law, I shall be very good and restrict myself to just one small glass of wine, and I seem to remember you don't drink.'

A deferential waiter appeared and took their order. As he disappeared, the Professor said, ' Shall we talk shop now whilst we wait? Then we can enjoy our meal in peace, without thinking about gory details. Although, in short, I'm afraid I have nothing at all new to offer you.

'The body was very thoroughly cleaned after death, inside and out, if you follow me. You're not going to find any trace of your killer from that source, I'm afraid. No semen, no blood, no pubic hairs, not even a nasal hair. The only thing the body tells us about your killer is that the fatal wound to the neck was made with the left hand, whereas the rest of the scalpel work was probably right-handed.

'Other than that, any other information you need to link your suspect in custody to the death of this young woman is going to have to come from your not inconsiderable detection skills. I'm sorry if that's not the news you were wanting.'

It wasn't, so Ted had to console himself with the meal, which was incredible, and another fast and exhilarating ride back in the Jag.

Chapter Twenty-seven

Pocket Billiards was lying in wait for Ted the minute he arrived at the station the next day. He spotted Ted's car and pounced as soon as the DI pulled up. Then, as Ted did his best to ignore him, he trotted next to him across the car park towards the entrance, left hand working away frenetically through his pocket lining.

'Is it true you have a suspect in custody, Detective Inspector?' he asked.

'Have you been through the correct channels to check out your information with the Press Office, Alastair?' Ted asked impatiently.

'I was just hoping you might be able to give me some information,' he said hopefully.

'Information?' Ted stopped and looked at him. 'Well, let's see. The longest gestation period known in mammals is that of the African elephant, at six hundred and sixty days. By contrast, the shortest animal gestation period is probably that of the opossum, at just twelve days.'

'Are you denying you have a suspect in custody?' the reporter asked, desperately trying for a quote he could use.

'I am neither confirming nor denying it,' Ted said shortly. 'I hope you will remember that when you write your piece. I would hate to have to come and find you to remind you of my exact words,' and he turned and disappeared inside.

After he'd touched base with the team and the DCI, Ted wanted to have another go at Jones. They'd applied for, and been granted, an extension to hold him for up to seventy-two hours for further investigations. After that time they were either going to have to charge him with the murders or let him go.

Without finding traces of blood in his car, or a secret cache of surgical instruments at his house, Ted didn't think they had a hope in hell of making charges stick, unless he could get a confession.

Jones looked so dreadful that Ted actually felt sorry for the man. He still didn't believe he was guilty. Jones had just done what he thought was his duty as a good citizen in coming forward with information, and he now found himself caught up in a nightmare. But Ted was a police officer and a good one. It was his job to do a thorough investigation, for the sake of the two young dead women and their families.

Ted and Sal took their seats opposite Jones and his solicitor and Ted took care of the formalities. Maurice was out doing legwork so he'd brought in Sal once more.

'Mr Jones, I appreciate this is all very difficult for you. But this is a serious murder enquiry and I have to ask you these questions in order either to charge you or to eliminate you from our enquiries,' Ted told him. 'I'm still waiting for the results of the forensic testing of your car and the search of your house. Do you have any other property anywhere that we should be aware of? An allotment, perhaps? A lock-up garage or storage unit?'

Jones looked exhausted, demoralised and utterly bewildered. 'An allotment?' he echoed. 'No, nothing remotely like that, I'm not interested in gardening at all. I'm just a very ordinary person. I go to work, the wife and I don't go out much. The only place I go to is the Lodge with ...'

He was clearly again about to mention the number of high ranking officers from the force with whom he was acquainted, but his solicitor laid a restraining hand on his arm and he stopped in mid sentence.

Before coming downstairs to question him, Ted and Sal had bounced a few ideas around to see if they could open up a new line of enquiry.

'Ask him about the eyes, boss,' Sal had suggested.

'The eyes?' Ted asked.

'Yes, sir,' Sal clarified. 'We know both victims had blue eyes, and Steve made that good point about it possibly being significant because the killer cut out Maggie's eyes. You could ask him if he knew what colour Maggie's eyes were.'

Ted looked dubious. 'Would any john know the colour of a prostitute's eyes anyway? It's not a road I've ever been down myself.'

Sal laughed. 'Me neither, sir, never had to pay for it in my life. But maybe just asking him about eyes in general may cause a reaction? The eye thing hasn't been leaked yet, has it, so only the killer would know there was anything significant about eyes. Worth a shot?'

'Anything is worth a shot at this stage, Sal' Ted said. 'At the moment my personal feeling is that we have diddly-squat and we are barking up entirely the wrong tree. Good idea, we can try it.'

'Mr Jones,' Ted asked him now. 'What colour eyes did Maggie Fielding have?'

Jones looked absolutely incredulous. 'Eyes?' he echoed blankly. 'I, er, I wasn't looking at her eyes, I was looking at the back of her head mostly.'

Ted and Sal exchanged a loaded look, both remembering the detail of the post-mortem report on Maggie Fielding.

'Mr Jones, are you saying you had anal intercourse with Maggie Fielding?' Ted asked.

'No!' Jones looked and sounded horrified at the suggestion. 'No, god, no, nothing like that. I was looking at the back of her head because she was ...' he was visibly squirming. '... her head was ...' he pointed towards his crotch, '... her head was in my lap.'

'I see,' Ted said neutrally. 'So what you are saying, Mr Jones, is that you had oral sex with Maggie Fielding. Did you also have any form of penetrative intercourse with her?'

Jones shook his head miserably.

'For the purposes of the tape, Mr Jones, could you please confirm aloud what you are saying?'

Jones cleared his throat a few times before he could manage to speak. 'We didn't have penetrative sex. We just had oral sex,' then, with clear revulsion in his voice, 'I paid her to give me a blow job.'

'Thank you, Mr Jones,' Ted said quietly, 'I appreciate this is very difficult for you. Your honesty is very helpful, both to our enquiries and to yourself. By the way, do you have any form of medical training?'

'Medical training?' Jones asked, astonished. 'None whatsoever. I can't stand the sight of blood. They wanted me to go on a first aid course for work but just the idea of it made me unwell. I couldn't do it.'

Ted went on, 'Mr Jones, do you have a particular preference for eye colour in women?'

The solicitor interrupted. 'Really, Inspector, what kind of a question is that? My client has been nothing but cooperative so far and you are asking him about his preference for eye colour? Can we please stick to basic facts, not speculation and fantasy.'

Ted had been watching Jones whilst the solicitor was speaking. He saw no signs of any reaction to the mention of eyes or eye colour from the man. It either had no significance for him or he was an extremely good actor.

Jones sighed wearily and his voice was resigned. 'I don't mind answering,' he said. 'I want to cooperate in any way I can, to bring an end to this total nightmare so I can get out of here. My wife has green eyes, very cold green eyes, so I like eyes that are warm and inviting. I don't recall what colour eyes that poor girl had, it wasn't that sort of a relationship. I just paid her to do the business. Whatever her eye colour, she was a lot kinder to me than my wife ever was. Above all, she didn't laugh at me.'

Ted felt his heart go out to the insignificant little man across the table from him. He sounded so dejected. He sincerely hoped he could find enough evidence to clear him as he doubted even more that he was guilty of killing anyone. But he wouldn't be doing his job properly if he didn't investigate each and every lead, and Jones wouldn't be the first seemingly mild-mannered and hen-pecked husband to turn out to be a murderer.

His evident self-loathing at going with prostitutes could well be motive enough to explain the killing of Maggie Fielding. How he fitted into the Vicki Carr case Ted was not yet sure, but he needed to keep him in custody until all the search and test results were in, at least.

'Mr Jones, I am hoping to have results back very shortly, when I will talk to you again. In the meantime I am afraid you are going to be held a little longer,' Ted told him, as he and Sal left the room.

The test results from Jones' car were waiting for him when he got back to his desk. They told him absolutely nothing he didn't know already. They backed up Jones's story of his brief encounter with Maggie Fielding in the car but there was no trace of blood at all and certainly not of the quantity which would have been left by her having her throat cut in the car.

The house search had thrown up nothing, either, certainly no trace of the girl's presence at the house either alive or dead.

He went in to see the DCI to bring him up to speed. 'We're going to have to let him go, Jim,' he said, 'we have absolutely nothing to justify keeping him any longer and his brief is already getting very twitchy. I think he really is what he appears to be, a sad little man whose wife doesn't put out, so he pays for what he can get on street corners but probably wouldn't hurt a fly.'

'Bad business, Ted,' the DCI shook his head. 'He came in of his own free will, trying to be helpful and he's been treated like a criminal.'

'We had to check out his story thoroughly, Jim,' Ted said, aware that the DCI felt compromised because of his links to Jones. 'I'll go and tell him the good news and I'll be as diplomatic as I possibly can. I suspect he will be so relieved to be off the hook he won't even think of making a fuss.

'But then we're back to square one, because if it's not Jones, then who the hell is it?'

Chapter Twenty-eight

Trev was sitting at the kitchen table, deeply absorbed in a technical motorcycle manual in Japanese, one of his languages, when Ted got home.

'Club tonight?' he asked, without looking up.

'Yes, club would be good,' Ted said, giving him a quick hug. 'And no out of control rough stuff tonight, promise. Interesting read?'

'I don't mind a bit of rough stuff,' Trev looked up with a wink. 'Fascinating manual this, the advances in technology are so rapid they're changing daily. You've got to keep running to stand still.'

Ted loved the way his blue eyes shone with enthusiasm whenever he talked about any of his passions. Trev noticed how tired Ted was looking and asked, 'Another rough day? No progress?'

'Only backwards,' Ted sighed, sitting down. 'Had to let the suspect go. I never did think it was him and we couldn't come up with anything at all to hang it on him. Just another poor guy paying hookers because his marriage is shit. We're all right though, aren't we?'

Trev immediately shut his manual, looked at Ted and took hold of one of his hands across the table. 'Of course we're all right,' he said. 'What's brought this on? What's worrying you?'

'Apart from two murders on my patch and I can't solve either of them?' Ted said ironically. 'I don't know, just humanity, I think. I see people all around us, suffering so much, sham marriages, loneliness, using drink and goodness knows what else to get through life. And here's us, just jogging along, still together.'

Trev looked shocked and a bit hurt. 'You say that as if it's not a good thing,' he said.

'Of course it is,' Ted hastened to reassure him. 'It's just I can't understand how I got so lucky. Look at Jim. We all know what his wife is like, and we know he spends most of his time waiting for a phone call which is likely to kill him when he gets the news we're all dreading. I asked him to join us for Christmas but he said he'd be with his wife. But he knows he won't, and he knows I know he won't.

'And then there's you. With me. You're so young, and brilliant, you could be with anyone, doing anything you choose. Yet you're here, with me, and I don't understand it and sometimes it just scares the hell out of me.'

'Whoa, this is all getting a bit intense,' Trev said, taking Ted's other hand as well. 'Where's it all coming from? I'm with you because I love you. Can't you just accept that, instead of over-analysing?'

Ted pulled his hands back and rubbed them over his face in a gesture of fatigue. 'Sorry,' he said. 'Sorry, you're right, I know. Just a crisis of self-confidence. Middle-aged angst. Some bloody thing. I don't know, just ignore me.'

'Can I help in some way?' Trev asked. 'Bounce some ideas around? Something? Anything? We've got half an hour before we need to leave for the club. Talk to me.'

They had a tacit agreement that they hardly ever talked about Ted's work, except superficially. Ted knew he could trust Trev implicitly and that anything they did discuss would go no further, but he always preferred to leave work stuff behind once he came home.

'I know,' Trev laughed, trying to lighten the mood, 'let's do some psychological profiling,' knowing how much Ted hated the concept.

Ted threw him a mock glare, then said, 'I hate bringing work home, you know that. But maybe you might spot something we've missed, because we're too close to it.'

'Try me,' Trev said. 'You know I'm quite good at mind games. What links your victims?'

'Not a lot, it seems,' Ted said. 'One was a respectable young woman, good family background, in work, not struggling financially, from what we've seen of her accounts. Sharing a flat, parents helping her out with the rent. Second one was a sad runaway, selling sex to buy the next fix.'

'Physical similarities?' Trev asked.

'Both had blue eyes. We're wondering if that's significant. Otherwise, the second victim was much shorter in height than the first, and had mousey hair, whereas the first was a blonde,' Ted said. 'Death by having their throats cut by a sharp implement, probably a surgical scalpel, a stroke made with the left hand. Mutilation of both bodies, done by someone who seemed to know what they were doing. We've been going on the basis of someone who didn't like women very much.'

'Or, of course, someone who wanted you to think that,' Trev said.

'It worries me a lot that the second body was dumped so close to here,' Ted confided. 'I can't help wondering if that was a personal message to me.'

'I wouldn't read too much into that too soon, it could just be a coincidence,' Trev said. 'So, scalpel skills – I imagine that gives us doctor, surgeon, vet, nurse, midwife,' then he laughed and added, 'pathologist, of course, as most of them seem to be as barking mad as Hard G.'

'The bodies were also kept somewhere cold before being dumped, though not in a domestic freezer or anything like that,' Ted added.

'Butcher? Butcher's cold store? What about a mortuary assistant? Would they have the necessary skills?' Trev asked. 'I'm assuming the killer is a man?

'In all probability,' Ted said, 'although Hard G did say something about strap-on dildos and a woman killer, but I think he was just being his usual provocatively crass self.'

Trev laughed, in spite of himself and in spite of the serious subject. 'He really is a piece of work, isn't he? And he does so love to wind you up.'

'I'm constantly amazed at the dubious stuff he knows about,' Ted told him. 'Although I'm a copper, he sometimes makes me feel I've led a very sheltered life. All this stuff about dogging and sex toys – it's a bit beyond me.'

'I don't like to add to your paranoia but if, and it's a whopping big if, your killer is sending a personal message to you,' Trev said, 'then is it possible he knows you have a thing about blue eyes? And that your biggest fear is of getting a phone call about dead missing runaways?'

Ted gave him a long look. 'Someone who knows me, you mean? Really knows me, rather than knows of me?'

'Knows you well enough to know where you live, perhaps,' Trev said. 'How many scalpel-wielding woman-hating maniacs do you know? The woman-hating angle would surely rule out Hard G? What about Tim Elliott? Could he ever stop sneezing long enough to kill anyone? How about a disgruntled ex-policeman you scared once too often with the kick-trick? Someone who'd watched enough autopsies to know how to handle a scalpel?'

He saw that Ted was at least grinning broadly by now and laughed, 'I'm not much use, am I?'

'You'll never know how much,' Ted said with feeling. 'You've cheered me up at least, even if you haven't solved the case for me, Miss Marple. Come on, let's go and make the next generation of kids into nicer people, lighten the workload for the coppers of the future.'

'Give me two minutes to brush my teeth and grab my kit-bag. Yours is in the hall,' Trev said then went up the stairs two at a time, singing Barcelona at the top of his voice.

Trev had many incredible talents. Sadly, singing was not one of them. He was completely unable to carry a tune, despite a lot of enthusiasm. Ted chuckled to himself at the thought of Freddie Mercury turning in his grave as Trev systematically slaughtered every note, not just the top ones.

Chapter Twenty-nine

'I had this perfect dream.'

This time it was the unmistakable voice of Freddie Mercury himself which woke Ted from what had been a surprisingly pleasant dream. He reached for his mobile phone and checked the time as he took the call. Just before six-thirty, when his alarm would have woken him anyway, so hopefully this time it was some good news. Maybe someone other than Honest John had come into the station with a confession.

The gravity of the duty sergeant's voice as he began to speak immediately let him know that that was misguided optimism.

'Sorry, Ted,' he said, 'yet another one for you. Just inside Woodbank Park. Doctor and SOCO on their way, so are Virgil and Sal. Want me to ring round the rest of your team while you head off to the scene?'

'Thanks, Bill, that would be a big help,' Ted said. 'I'll be there very shortly. This is turning into a bloody recurring nightmare.'

Trev rolled over and opened his eyes. 'Another one?' he asked. 'Not Rosalie though?'

Ted shook his head. 'No, Bill would have said if it was. Goodness knows what time I'll be back tonight. I'll text you.'

'It's fine,' Trev said. 'We really are all right, you know. Go catch a killer.'

It was with a sense of déjà-vu that Ted parked the Renault close to the gates of Woodbank Park, just near its boundary with Vernon Park. The scene was already taped off and there were signs of activity everywhere.

Virgil and Sal saw him arrive and joined him as he followed the sound of sneezing and headed towards the tent. Ted was already opening a new packet of Fisherman's Friend.

'You're not going to like this one, sir,' Sal told him.

'I don't like any of them, Sal,' Ted said dryly. 'What's different about this one?

'A personal message to you, boss,' Sal told him.

The three of them ducked into the tent. The doctor was just preparing to leave.

'Death certified,' he told Ted. 'Same MO, throat slit, but not here. I phoned the senior coroner, he's sending Professor Gillingham here directly. I thought he might prefer to do his first examination on site, given the circumstances.'

Ted glanced beyond him to the victim's body. Lights had already been rigged up and he could see that it was once again a young woman, naked and with no signs of any personal possessions nearby. At first glance Ted thought there was no mutilation this time. Then he saw that a sharp implement had been used to carve out letters on the victim's abdomen.

'To save you going any closer,' Dr Elliott told him, 'I can tell you that what has been carved on her says, "She's dead Ted". I think that makes it abundantly clear that this is personal.'

'Shit,' Ted said emphatically, and Sal and Virgil looked shocked. They weren't used to hearing the boss use any strong language outside the office, except between him and his team.

He turned to them. 'Right, any CCTV around? Probably not just here but anything nearer the museum? Find out, get it checked out, if there is. Too early to knock doors yet, probably, but keep an eye out for anyone leaving for work, see if you can find anyone who saw anything at all. I'll have this sick joker, if it's the last thing I do.'

Ted didn't have long to wait for Hard G to appear. The Professor had to duck into the tent. He stood back and surveyed the scene with a practised eye before approaching. He was already wearing protective coveralls from top to toe, to avoid any contamination of the crime scene.

'I'm just going to do the preliminaries here, Ted,' he told him, 'then I'll get her taken in and I'll crack on with the post-mortem for you straight away. I know you're up against it with this one, so I'll do all I can to help, to get you some information as soon as possible.'

He pointed to the lettering on the victim's body. 'This is interesting, not just because it mentions you by name. It was also done before death, evident because of the amount of bleeding around the incisions. I'll know better when I get her back, and I stress that I am no handwriting expert, but I would hazard a guess that this writing was done with the right hand, whilst the wound to the throat again looks like a left-handed cut.'

'Christ,' Ted said, 'I hope to heaven the poor girl was at least unconscious when someone did that to her. Any signs of any restraints?'

Hard G carefully examined wrists and ankles. 'Nothing obvious at all,' he replied. 'If there was restraint, I would say it was of the chemical kind, but as the body appears to have been dead for perhaps forty-eight hours, once again I would say there is very little chance of finding anything on a blood test.

'Which brings us to something else rather interesting. If this young woman has been dead that long, that means she was already dead whilst you had your latest suspect in custody, from what I heard on the grapevine, doesn't it? So if you had any lingering doubts at all of his guilt, I would say this effectively destroys them.'

'Anything else? Ted asked him.

'Well, as you can see, a young woman, early twenties, long fair hair, blue eyes like the first victim, I believe – is that significant or coincidence, I wonder? Underweight for her height, I would say – voluntarily, or not able to afford to eat well? There's a small but noticeable septal perforation, so our young lady was no stranger to cocaine,' Hard G mused aloud.

'Pubic hair missing again, recently removed, but that's quite fashionable amongst women these days so it may not be related. It can make my job harder, we often get lucky in finding a killer's hair when two sets of pubic hair meet in intimate circumstances.'

He manoeuvred the body skilfully and continued, 'Again, signs of recent sexual activity, quite rough once again; I'll know more when I've had the time to examine her fully. Overall the body looks scrupulously clean, so once again it's possible that our man cleaned her up when he had finished, which means that yet again we're unlikely to find any of his DNA. The most we're likely to find is some of Elliott's if he has been careless enough to sneeze all over her before he put his mask on.

'She's been brought here and dumped. There would have been considerable blood loss when her throat was cut and there's none visible here. Killed elsewhere, cleaned up, stored for some strange reason then brought here and dumped. First thoughts on storing her would be to allow time for any drugs in her system to become undetectable and to allow rigor mortis to pass, so that the body would be much easier to manoeuvre.'

'I still struggle to see how anyone can park a car next to a busy road then carry a dead body any distance at all to dump it,' Ted said. 'It's like something from a very bad crime series on television.'

'Oh my dear boy,' Hard G laughed, 'what a very sheltered life you have led! If I had a fiver for every extremely inebriated young lady I've half carried back to halls, or to her parents' house or elsewhere, without anyone noticing, I would be even more well off than I already am.

'This isn't a known dogging site, so far as I am aware, but I suspect many a young man has dragged his girlfriend in here for a bit of fun in the bushes, away from watching eyes, when she'd had enough drink to make her more amenable. In fact, it would be rather fun, I might be tempted to try it,' and he gave Ted a lewd wink.

'Right, I'll arrange to get her taken in and I'll make a start as soon as I can. I'll phone you before I do and you can join me as soon as you are free,' he said. 'I imagine you'll be going into the station first to bring your big chief up to date?'

'Yes, and he's not going to be best pleased,' Ted admitted. 'He knew the suspect we had in so it was delicate enough when we thought he might be our man.'

'Well, I'll see you later and I promise to try to find something for you this time, dear boy.'

Ted was right about the DCI. He hadn't often seen him in such a bad mood, not since Rosalie first went missing, in fact.

'You wouldn't believe the crap I'm getting from the top, Ted,' he growled, banging two mugs of his version of coffee on the desk in front of them. 'The Chief Super is going ballistic; he's in the same Lodge as Jones. He's really furious about the whole thing, ranting about waste of manpower and resources. I need something to give him to get him off my back, then I don't need to jump on yours.'

'We're doing everything we can, boss,' Ted told him. He almost never called him 'sir'. 'Boss' was as formal as he got when the occasion warranted it. The two men went back too far together. It was on Ted's shoulder that the DCI had cried, literally, on many a long evening as he tried to come to terms with the loss of his daughter and the behaviour of his wife.

'Hard G is going to give me a call when he starts the post-mortem and I'll go along. I'm getting the team to widen the search for anyone with previous form involving blades, pull a few in, check their movements.

'So far the killer's been lucky and we haven't. But he is going to slip up, before too long. There'll be something, some trace, that he's overlooked, and we will find it. We need to keep believing that.'

Chapter Thirty

On his way from the nick to the hospital for the post-mortem, Ted pulled over and stopped to get his mobile phone out. He felt a sudden irresistible urge to talk to Trev, to touch base with a bit of normality.

He hardly ever phoned Trev at his workplace. Not that Trev's boss would have minded. He thought Trev was so much the dog's bollocks, he would let him get away with anything. He simply could not believe that he had landed someone as skilled and brilliant as Trev, someone with more than twice as many A Levels as he had CSEs, who was blissfully happy to work for him at a fraction of what he was capable of earning.

'It's me,' he told him when Trev answered, although clearly Trev would know that. Ted's name would display on the screen and, unlike his technologically-challenged partner, Trev knew his way round a mobile phone, so he had different ring tones for different people.

It was Trev who had sorted out hi-tech bike helmets with intercoms and Bluetooth, so Ted could use his mobile phone hands free from the bike when he needed to. Ted wouldn't have known where to begin.

'Are you all right?' Trev asked anxiously. It was so rare for Ted to phone him at work.

'Yes,' Ted said, then, 'No, not really. I just needed to make contact with the clean world. I'm just on my way to another PM with Hard G.'

'It will get better,' Trev told him. 'I'll see you later.'

Ted had left the team yet again checking records for

missing persons who might correspond to their latest victim. Hard G had given him her height and weight. Ted had also put Maurice and Steve onto double-checking the records of anyone in their area with previous convictions for knife-related crime, although he wasn't holding out much hope on that line of enquiry. They were more likely to turn up gang members with scores to settle or drunken pub brawlers with short fuses. This killer was obviously coldly calculating. Ted's gut feeling was that he did not yet have any convictions.

Ted slipped into coveralls before joining the Professor as he started the first incisions for the post-mortem. He crunched furiously on his menthol sweets and looked anywhere but at the victim's body. He should be used to it by now, but that first cut always seemed so intrusive, so impersonal, that he had difficulty watching.

Hard G kept up a running commentary as he worked, for his tape, noting any significant details, but interspersing his professional observations with social chit-chat to Ted.

'What are your plans for Christmas this year?' he asked.

'Dear Santa, all I want for Christmas it to catch a killer,' Ted said ironically. 'If we do, Trev and I are going to have a quiet day at home, with some of Trev's fabulous cooking and probably some rubbish films on TV or DVD. Trev's invited Willow.'

'How adorable,' Hard G said mockingly. 'They do make the most beautiful couple. Doesn't it worry you?'

'No,' Ted said emphatically.

'This one's a sniffer, not a needle user,' the Professor told him, switching back into professional mode. 'You can clearly see the early signs of damage to the nasal septum here,' he indicated. 'It's possible she's another street girl, funding a habit. I take it you've no clue yet as to identity?'

'Nothing found at the scene again, not that I'm aware of. The team are trawling MissPers for any likely matches,' Ted replied.

'Your killer is not making it very easy for you, is he?' the Professor said. 'Let's see if we can't find something more helpful on this body. I read an intriguing crime novel recently where the killer was identified by a single nasal hair found in a bath tub. Ah, if only reality were like fiction.'

Ted knew that the Professor loved to read crime novels and watch police and forensic science dramas on television, just so he could dissect every error and laugh uproariously at any basic mistakes in procedure. Ted had heard that Hard G was once asked to act as a consultant for a drama series about the work of forensic pathologists but had refused saying, in his typical fashion, 'It's so much more fun when they make such basic mistakes.'

'I'll run full tox screens on her blood again for you,' the Professor was saying, 'with the caveat of what I mentioned before about the length of time since death. The same applies to stomach contents but I really am testing everything I can think of, Ted. I want to give you the breakthrough you need, old boy.

'By the way, if you and the gorgeous Trev want to take a break at any time, I have a chalet at Serre Chevalier which I hardly ever use. You would be most welcome to go there.'

Ted was taken aback. He'd known Hard G for a number of years, but this was the first time he had made such an offer.

'Thank you, Roger, that's extremely generous,' he said. 'Will you not be using it yourself over the festivities?'

'Oh, my dear boy, no,' Hard G said, as if the idea were unthinkable. 'The current blonde job and I will be flying off to St Moritz for some snow and some very lively après-ski, then possibly to the Riviera for some winter sun. I have small houses in both places.'

Ted had a sneaking suspicion that his and Hard G's definition of a small house might differ considerably.

'How's it going with Willow's replacement?' Ted asked, intrigued in spite of himself.

'Very well,' the Professor said with a suggestive chuckle. 'Handles very well, high performance, starts on the button every time. A little less temperamental than dear Willow, knows which side her bread is buttered.'

'Do you even know this one's name?' Ted asked.

'Luckily, I call them all God in the sack, so there's no chance of a mistake,' Hard G said, spreading his feet apart and making suggestive pelvic thrusts. 'You know, oh God, oh God!'

Even Ted had to smile at that. Just as quickly again, the Professor was back to professionalism. 'Talking of sex, as we were, there is evidence of recent sexual activity and yet again it's been rather rough. There are signs of bruising and some tearing. As I've said before, this may be normal activity between some couples, so it could be consensual.

'Not wishing to be boastful but I've inflicted the same, and probably worse, on more than one occasion, just by over-enthusiasm. There was one unforgettable occasion when the young lady in question needed medical treatment. Thank goodness for private hospitals.'

Ted always got uncomfortable talking to Hard G about sex. The Professor insisted on telling him far more than he wanted or needed to know. Ted's view was that what happened in the bedroom stayed in the bedroom.

To lighten the mood and change the subject, he asked, 'Will you be gone for Christmas?'

'No, the blonde job and I will have a small and intimate dinner at the pile on the Edge,' Hard G replied, referring to his house at Alderley Edge. 'We fly out on Boxing Day. Luckily I can use the family Gulfstream. Commercial flights are so tedious over the holiday period. So handy when I want to pop off for a weekend's jollies somewhere'

Ted knew that the Professor's family had made obscene wealth in the pharmaceutical industry. Hard G had chosen not to go into the family firm, but he still enjoyed the privileges of belonging to such a wealthy family and was a major shareholder in the family's companies.

'Small and intimate?' Ted queried, knowing that it would translate into having an extremely expensive outside caterer come in and provide everything, as was always the case whenever he had eaten there.

'Very intimate,' the Professor smirked. 'The staff will have the night off and I've ordered plenty of messy food which needs to be eaten with fingers, which will need licking and sucking afterwards.'

'Going to have to stop you there, Roger, definitely too much information,' Ted said. 'Can we stick to the task in hand?'

The Professor laughed at his obvious discomfort. 'Now this is also interesting,' he said, peering more closely at the body in front of him. 'Do you see here, near her right hip? She wasn't very fleshy at all, poor thing, but just here on the gluteus maximus. A little scratching, very fine. I would almost say from a hypodemic nerdle.' The Professor could never resist his own jokey little Spoonerism. Ted found very little to laugh at at all during post-mortems.

'It's strange because she has no other evidence of injected drug use and that would be an odd place to do so,' he continued. 'I doubt it was insulin, no signs of any other previous use. I wonder if we have finally found how your man keeps his girls still long enough to have his wicked way with them? It would certainly explain how this poor young lady lay still for him to carve out his message.

'A vet might administer an intramuscular injection of something like ketamine for pain relief and light sedation in horses, for instance, although I believe it's less effective in bovines. And the very good news for us, Ted, my dear boy, is that ketamine is obligingly detectable post-mortem. We may just be on the brink of our first breakthrough.'

Chapter Thirty-one

'Right team,' Ted addressed them when he got back from the latest post-mortem. 'First the bad news. If any of you are planning last-minute shopping trips with the family on Christmas Eve, please revise your plans. We're up to the wire on this, the top brass are complaining about overtime so there won't be any. As you know, I always try to let you all go early on Christmas Eve. This year that's not likely to be possible.

'So warn your other halves, mail order the kids' toys, arrange home delivery for the turkey, do what you need to do, but be advised I need everyone in right up to the end of play that day come what may. Unless we suddenly get a confession out of someone, which is looking like a slim chance.

'The good news. Because I'll be keeping you back, you're all invited to The Grapes as soon as we finish for Christmas, as usual. My shout, and Trev will make nibbles. Bring your other halves.'

A cheer went up from all the team except DS Hallam and the TDC, who'd not yet experienced either the boss's Christmas tradition, or Trev's incredible cooking.

'Will Trev be making mince pies, boss?' Tina asked dreamily.

Ted had often told Trev if he'd made pastry earlier on in their relationship, they would have ended up in bed together far sooner. It was so good it was sinful.

'If he doesn't, I'll arrest him,' Ted grinned, wanting to raise a few smiles before they needed to return to the serious business, now with three murders on their books.

He filled the team in on what little the post-mortem had revealed, then asked for progress reports.

'We're going to start out round known dealers, sir,' DS Hallam told him. 'Everyone will be out shortly, checking with their sources, see if she's known on our patch. Then there are a few from MissPers we need to check up on. We'll try the street girls again, too, in case she was a regular tom.

'But Steve and Maurice have something for you, boss. A possible suspect from offenders in the area.' He nodded to Maurice to take up the story.

'Boss, you're going to love this one,' Maurice Brown said confidently. 'How about a former medical student who once carved his name on his girlfriend's thigh with a scalpel? Steve found it, as usual. We've been checking on said potential suspect. He was out of the area for a time but he's been back on our patch a few months now.'

Ted looked from Maurice to Steve and back again. 'This had better not be a wind-up,' he said. 'It sounds too good to be true. Tell me.'

Maurice looked at his notebook, knowing it would be quicker for him to fill the boss in than waiting for Steve to stammer his way nervously through their findings.

'Nigel Foden, boss, twenty-four. Was studying medicine at Leeds and doing quite well but was always a bit of a party animal,' Maurice Brown told him. 'His tutors had a few words with him about his drinking, and there were suspicions of recreational drug use. But his grades were very good so he got away with it for a while.

'About eighteen months ago there was an unfortunate incident. He finished up having to haul the girlfriend off to casualty when they were both pretty well tanked up and he'd taken a scalpel to her leg to carve his name. In isolation, it may well have been overlooked as it was not a serious injury, though messy enough. Coming on top of everything else, his tutors were a bit worried about his suitability and had a discreet word with him about re-evaluating his direction.

'He left and took himself off to South America, doing voluntary work as some sort of medical auxiliary. Now he's back and not far away. Last known address was a flat in Hazel Grove. Do you want us to bring him in, boss?'

'Can you think of any good reason why not, Maurice?' Ted asked ironically.

Maurice laughed. 'None, boss, I'm on it now.'

'Take Steve with you,' Ted told him. 'Good work, again. Just one thing, though, and I'm not niggling. How has this only just come to light? I thought you'd been checking on knife crime before this?'

'Nothing ever came of it, boss,' Maurice Brown told him. 'The file went to the CPS as an advice file, but the Chief Crown Prosecutor advised against proceeding. The girlfriend was an unreliable witness, kept changing her story. They were both off their faces so much she couldn't remember if she'd given him permission to do it or even if she had asked him to. So it was a bit of a dicey case to take to court.'

'Even more impressive work, in that case, Steve, can't have been easy to track that one down,' Ted told him. 'Extra mince pies for you on Christmas Eve.

'I suppose it's too much to hope for that there are any connections between this Foden and our first two victims but do some cross-checking, just in case. Let me know when you've got him. I'm very much looking forward to talking to our scalpel artist friend. Oh, and Maurice, take a pool car. Don't subject him to yours.'

Whilst Ted was waiting to see if Maurice and Steve could find their potential latest suspect, Ted turned his attention to the white board that was taking shape. Their latest unidentified victim – Tina had christened her Alison – was up there.

'There's something else we need to map onto here,' Ted said to Tina who was sitting close by, working. She was the only one left in the main office now.

165

'What's that, boss?' Tina looked up.

'Me,' Ted replied. He picked up a marker pen and started to scribble. Tina got up and came across.

'The third victim makes it clear that there is a personal message here to me,' Ted said, drawing a line to connect Alison's name to where he had written his own. 'Maybe I knew this young woman in some way. I'll know more when we get a positive ID on her.

'Vicki Carr. Victim number one. Trev and I have eaten in the bistro a few times. I didn't recognise her but it's possible she served us there.' He drew another connecting line.

'Maggie Fielding. I have never been with a prostitute in my life but anyone who knows anything about me knows how I feel about runaways and she was one. That's pretty much public knowledge, from the press conferences I've sat in on.'

He had Tina's full attention now. She was watching the boss, fascinated. He perched on the edge of the nearest desk as his mind went into overdrive.

'We've been going on the basis that this is a woman-hating random killer,' he said. 'But what if we've been wrong all along? What if it's me they hate and they just see the victims as collateral damage, necessary to get their message across to me? That I'm somehow not doing enough to protect runaways?

'Perhaps we need to be looking at runaway cases I've worked on. Ones with a tragic outcome, like the girl down Otterspool, found dead in a field two weeks after she was reported missing. Someone in her family? Check that out.'

'Sounds a bit drastic, boss,' Tina said. 'Why would someone who had been through something like that themselves want to inflict it on other sets of parents?'

'Grief can do terrible things to people.' Ted replied. 'Grief, guilt, if they felt to blame for their child going missing in the first place. What about cases I've worked on where there's been no outcome, good or bad?'

Ted's team had been working with Uniform branch officers

on a Crime Prevention Initiative involving runaways. The theory was that keeping youngsters off the streets would help reduce crimes like drug dealing and prostitution on their patch.

Tina was staring hard at him at the same moment as Ted realised what he had just said. He shook his head emphatically.

'No, Tina, you're completely wrong,' he said adamantly. 'Look further afield.'

'Sir, you always told me that to do a proper job we need to look at all angles,' Tina said determinedly. 'You've been steering the search for the DCI's daughter for, how many years now? And there's still no sign of her. That kind of grief and stress could drive anyone to do crazy things.'

'No,' Ted shook his head. 'I know him too well. It can't be him. Look into other similar cases.'

'Sir, if you want me to work this up the right way, the way you taught me, I'm going to have to look at the Rosalie case as well,' Tina said stubbornly. Her being formal with him told her how serious she was about what she was saying.

There was a long pause. Then, grudgingly, Ted said, 'All right. Work up your notes on all the runaway cases I've worked on. One copy, my eyes only. No hard copies, wipe anything from your computer.

'And I hope I don't have to say, DC Bailey, that you talk to no one about this, other than me. No one at all. Is that clear?'

Chapter Thirty-two

Ted wasn't sure what he had expected the ex-medical student to be like, but he was certainly surprised by the young man Maurice and Steve had brought in, as he and Tina sat down opposite him in the interview room.

Tall, rather gaunt-looking, with a neatly-trimmed beard and dark hair, his skin still had the weathered look and darker tint which spoke of time spent in warmer climates than south Manchester in December.

'Thank you for coming in, Mr Foden,' he began. 'I'll try not to take up too much of your time. I'm hoping you can answer a few questions for me that would help us in our enquiries. You're not under arrest and you're not obliged to answer my questions.'

'So, from what I've seen on television and read in the papers, I'm guessing this has something to do with the use of a scalpel?' the man asked calmly. 'You have a slasher on the loose, so naturally enough you're talking to anyone with an unfortunate history of wielding a scalpel and I fit that profile.'

Ted said nothing. He often found it was useful to leave a pause for a suspect to fill with their own words.

'Well, Inspector,' Foden continued. 'You did say Inspector, didn't you? I carried out one random act on a very drunken night, when Joanna and I had both had far too much to drink, mixed with some rather silly stuff. It's something I bitterly regret – we both do. Joanna and I are still very good friends, by the way. I'm paying her as much as I can towards surgery to remove my pathetic effort, which left a scar.

'I've never done anything remotely like it before or since, and I paid a heavy price for my stupidity. I think the fact that I was never charged with anything should indicate to you that it was exactly as I said – a very stupid and infantile prank that got totally out of hand.

'Does that help you with your enquiries, Inspector?'

'It's a start, Mr Foden,' Ted replied, 'thank you for that. But given that previous history, I hope you will understand why you have been asked to come in?'

'Oh, yes,' Foden said bitterly. 'At least Joanna's scars will soon be gone completely. Mine have a habit of following me round and probably will for the rest of my life.'

'Would you mind telling me where you were on Wednesday evening, Mr Foden?'

'I would be delighted to, Inspector, as I can offer you an impressive roomful of witnesses for that evening,' Foden said, smiling with something like relief. 'Believe it or not, I am determined to get back into medicine one day. But a blot like that on your copy book takes a lot of erasing. I've been doing voluntary work overseas, partly as penance, partly to have something worthwhile to put on my CV other than "kicked out of uni for carving up girlfriend with a scalpel".

'On Wednesday evening, I was on a training course for volunteers being sent into areas affected by Ebola. There were about twenty of us, plus the training staff. I'll give you full details so you can check.'

Ted sat back in his chair, stunned. They had the wrong man, again, it seemed and this time spectacularly so. Still, he was determined to get something out of the interview.

He pushed a sheet of paper and a pen across the desk to Foden and said, 'Would you mind writing your name on that for me, in block capitals?'

'Ah, subtle,' Foden said, mockingly. 'Happy to do so, but to save you time, I am left-handed, if that is relevant to your case. However, like many medical students, I learned to use a scalpel, amongst other things, with both hands. It's incredibly difficult to get hold of left-handed surgical instruments, so we quickly learn to become ambidextrous. I take it that is significant?'

He was writing as he spoke, then pushed the paper back towards Ted. 'If you want to see the results of my handiwork, I'm sure Joanna wouldn't mind. As I said, we are still very good friends. We were both young, very stupid and very out of it.'

'Thank you, Mr Foden,' Ted said, 'I appreciate your frankness. I'm sorry to have taken up your time. It would be most helpful to our enquiries if you did not mention to anyone the line my questioning has taken. Certain elements of the case have not yet been made public.'

Foden laughed shortly. 'I might just have to say something to Joanna, Inspector. Otherwise it would seem a little strange asking her to come into a police station and show an officer her thigh.

'I imagine you have access to the file on me from the time, though, and I know a lot of photographs were taken then. I just thought it might be helpful to you to have a chat with Jo and then she could confirm what the incident was all about, that it was not some bungled murderous attempt on her life by me.'

'Another one bites the dust, boss,' Tina said, as they made their way back upstairs. 'I'll start on what we talked about before, at least start looking, doing a bit of a feasibility study to see if it's an idea worth running with.'

'It's not,' Ted said, more shortly than he intended. 'But you're right. We need to look at every angle. Just keep a tight lid on it, whatever you do, and remember – I don't want a paper trail at this stage.'

Maurice Brown was working at his desk when they got back upstairs. He looked surprised to see them returning so soon. Ted went across to his desk.

'Maurice, did you think to ask Foden for his whereabouts

on Wednesday evening, before you brought him in?' he asked.

'You said bring him in, boss. I brought him in,' he beamed with apparent pride.

Ted sighed. Maurice could be a bit dull at times. 'Right, well, DC Bailey has details of his alibi for that evening and on paper, it looks watertight. Go and check it out, and take young Steve with you. Where is he, by the way?'

'Little boys' room, boss,' Brown said cheerfully, standing up and getting his scruffy parka jacket.

'Right, pick him up and get going,' Ted told him. 'Next time, just ask first, then call me if you think there might be a tight alibi.'

He headed for his office. He was in need of green tea.

There was a knock on his door shortly after and Tina came in. He nodded at the spare chair and offered her green tea. To his surprise, she accepted.

'I've been having an initial look, boss,' she told him. 'Rosalie is now the only runaway case you've handled where there has been no outcome. In all other cases, the runaway has either gone home willingly or been found and returned, alive or dead.

'Of those missing from our patch over the years you've been here, five have been found dead; only the Otterspool one was a homicide. Two were drugs overdoses, one was a road accident, one was a young lass who died from the cold because she was sleeping rough.'

A shadow passed over Ted's face. 'I remember her,' he said, 'she was only a kid. What a way to end up. I could see a parent of one of those having a major axe to grind with me, not finding their child in time to stop something as dreadful as that from happening.

'But the Big Boss? Never. It's just too far-fetched. He's my boss. If he didn't think I was doing the job right, and he was the vengeful sort, he could have me up on a disciplinary, make my life very uncomfortable.'

'You said yourself, boss, that grief can do terrible things to people,' Tina said. 'Does he think Rosalie is still alive, or has he given up all hope and is he mourning her loss like a death now?'

Ted shook his head. 'I'm not buying it, not for a moment,' he said. 'Look into the others for now, but keep it quiet. I remember the father of the kid who died from the cold. He was quite abusive at the inquest, mouthing off a lot of threats at everyone. I didn't take him seriously at the time, I could see how much he was hurting.

'But that's a much more probable angle. Wanting revenge on the people he saw as letting his daughter down. Trying to discredit me by a series of murders I'm struggling to solve.

'It still seems totally far-fetched but I'd have a much easier time believing that than believing it was the Big Boss.'

Chapter Thirty-three

Ted sensed his team members were as thoroughly demoralised as he was with the current lack of progress on the case. Three victims, no leads going anywhere and still a lot of legwork to be done.

He made it a point every year to have a little get-together and he was more determined than ever this year to show his team they were appreciated and try to lift their spirits. A combination of an open bar at his expense and a spread cooked by Trev should hopefully go some way to easing tensions and uniting them.

It was an occasion for a bit of socialising, and was the reason he threw the invitation open to Significant Others every year. He was interested to meet his new DS's wife, to see if she was as dour in the flesh as she sounded on the two occasions when he had spoken to her by phone.

Dave, the landlord of The Grapes, made a small rear room available to them and Ted knew Trev would have been in from early on, sorting out his spread of food. Despite all the stresses and anxieties, Ted was at least looking forward to some festive food.

The get-together was reserved for Ted's immediate team but he had, as ever, invited the DCI to pop in for a quick drink and something to eat with them. He knew how badly he suffered, every Christmas, always optimistically hoping for news of Rosalie, inevitably going home to an empty house, keeping up the pretence that his wife would be there and they would be spending Christmas together as a couple.

Every year, in the run-up to Christmas, Ted redoubled his efforts to find a trace, any kind of a trace, of Rosalie. This year, to his shame, he had done less than usual because of how busy he had been with the killings on his patch.

Maurice Brown was the first through the door, on his own, and headed straight for the buffet, almost before he had a drink in his hand. Rob and Sal brought girlfriends, Virgil was with his wife, young Steve was on his own and looking more timid than usual at mingling in a social setting with his work colleagues.

Tina also came on her own, although Ted knew she had a steady boyfriend. 'I'm on my way to my parents' tonight, boss, spending Christmas with them. Midnight mass, Christmas dinner, the Queen's speech, paper hats, the whole works,' she told him. 'I've got the Cooper round the corner so I won't be drinking. Perhaps I'll try one of your Gunners.'

'They're an acquired taste, Tina,' Ted warned her. 'Some might say a bit dry.'

'Very appropriate for you, boss,' Tina laughed, able to relax in his company away from the work setting.

The DS was the last of the team to appear as he'd been home to collect his wife. Hallam headed straight towards Ted with her, to introduce her. He looked decidedly awkward. Ted put on his best welcoming smile and shook her hand.

The expression on her face was perfectly summed up by the saying 'bulldog chewing a wasp'. She was short, on the dumpy side, with hair cut in a severe bob and coloured an improbable shade of henna red. She took Ted's hand with an expression of barely concealed distaste as DS Hallam said, 'This is my wife, sir, Joan.'

'It's nice to meet you, Mrs Hallam,' Ted said, and wished he meant it. He called Trev over and said, 'This is my partner, Trevor. Trev, my new DS, Mike Hallam, and his wife Joan. Trev did all the cooking. Please, help yourself.'

Trev could normally charm the birds from the trees with a

quick flash of his blue eyes. The expression on the DS's wife's face told him that look was going to have no effect on her.

'I'm sorry I've been giving your husband rather long hours since he joined us, Mrs Hallam,' Ted said. 'I'm afraid he arrived at a rather difficult time. How is your mother doing, by the way? Not easy, I know.'

'Yes, Michael told me your father was a cripple,' she said.

DS Hallam looked mortified and said, 'I'll go and get you something to eat, love. I won't be long.'

Trev was standing just behind the DS's wife, out of her line of sight. He made a face at Ted and said, 'Do please excuse me, Mrs Hallam, I must just go and check on the food.'

Ted scowled at him for abandoning him but did his best to make conversation. 'So do you work, Mrs Hallam?'

'I did, until my mother had this accident of hers,' the woman said, and her tone made it sound as if her mother's serious injury was a major inconvenience, done just to annoy her. 'I was a midwife, and a theatre sister before that, but I've had to give my career up to look after her,' then added, 'Your boyfriend is a lot younger than you, isn't he?'

Ted was taken aback at her directness but was saved from a reply by the return of DS Hallam with a plate laden with food, which he handed to his wife. She scowled at it, and at him and said, 'Are those mince pies, Michael? Why did you get me those? You know how much I hate dried fruit.'

Ted hastily excused himself and hurried across the room in pursuit of Trev, who grinned at him, his eyes twinkling.

'What a charmer she is,' he said, keeping his voice low.

Ted was forced to agree. 'I'm surprised the DS doesn't put in for all the extra hours going, just to get away from her.'

'Good to see the team relaxing a bit,' Trev said. 'I know it's not easy for any of you.'

'This case is wearing us all down,' Ted said sombrely. 'We're really clutching at straws, it means we're coming up with some incredibly far-fetched theories. I'll tell you about

Tina's latest, when we get home.'

Trev glanced towards the door. 'O.M.G, look who's just walked in,' he said. 'Surely you didn't invite Hard G?'

'Certainly not,' Ted said, spinning round on the balls of his feet.

The Professor was making his way across the room. He knew most of Ted's team by sight, through court appearances and previous social gatherings. He shook hands with the men and kissed any women he came across, although Ted noticed that Mrs Hallam skilfully resisted.

'Ted!' Hard G said, clapping him on the shoulder, and insisting on kissing Trev on both cheeks in the French way. 'So sorry to gatecrash your party, dear boy, and I'm not stopping. I just wanted to pop in to give you a little something for tomorrow.'

Ted was completely taken aback when the Professor handed him a Fortnum and Mason's hamper. 'I can't possibly …' he started to say but Hard G waved away his objections.

'Nonsense, my dear fellow, it's just a little something,' the Professor said breezily. 'If you think it leaves you professionally compromised in some way to accept it, please give it to Willow, from me, and tell her to share it with you. It's just a few little treats you may not have indulged in yourself. I do hope you like Tokaji Aszu, I think it's a particular favourite of Willow's.'

Ted had no idea if it was something to eat, to drink or one of the Professor's sex toys. 'Roger, this is far too generous of you.'

'Not at all, dear chap, I haven't been able to give you your murderer for a Christmas present so I thought this may go some way towards compensating,' he said. 'I'll be flying off early on Boxing Day so I won't see you again until the New Year. Have as good a time as you can in the circumstances, and I hope you catch your killer.'

'Do have something to eat before you leave, Roger,' Ted

indicated the buffet table. 'Trev's made his famous mince pies.'

'Sounds delightful,' the Professor said, 'but I have the blonde job in the Jag outside and I think she has other ideas. I may be unwrapping my Christmas stockings early.'

Trev draped an arm around Ted's shoulders and forced a fixed grin onto his face as they waved the Professor off. 'He really is the most loathsome creature ever, isn't he?' he said through gritted teeth. 'But can you just imagine how much that hamper cost? Bit outside our usual shopping style.'

'Just unfortunate I have to work with him,' Ted agreed. 'He's an utterly brilliant forensic pathologist, whatever his other peculiarities. If anyone can find me the opening I need on this case, it's Hard G.'

Chapter Thirty-four

Shop talk was banned for the evening. The team knew they still had a killer to catch but the mood was as relaxed as it could be. Ted was standing the team down for Christmas Day. He knew everyone needed a break to recharge batteries and they would be be refreshed and more focused after some time away.

Trev was in his element. Always hugely sociable, he charmed the girlfriends and mingled effortlessly with everyone on the team, although Ted noticed he was giving the Hallams a bit of a wide berth. Ted smiled fondly as he watched his partner talking big bikes with Rob and Sal, his blue eyes showing his passion, the girlfriends hanging onto his every word.

Ted was the perfect host, circulating amongst his team, making sure everyone had all the food and drink they needed and felt at ease. Things were informal, he'd slipped from 'sir' to 'boss' all the time to everyone except young Steve, who was clearly still totally in awe of him.

He discovered the TDC was a Star Wars enthusiast. Ted had never seen any of the films but once the young man got started on them, he talked with such intense enthusiasm that Ted found himself curious about the whole phenomenon and made a New Year's resolution to watch at least one.

As he moved away, Tina came over and joined him. 'Boss, if ever you and Trev split up, can I have him?' she said. 'With the pastry he makes, I can't understand why you're not twice the size of Maurice.'

Ted laughed, in spite of himself. It was good to see the

team relaxing and letting their hair down. Only the Hallams continued to look stiff and ill at ease. He was just about to go over and have another go at breaking the ice with the formidable Mrs Hallam when the DCI walked in, giving him an excuse to abandon the idea and go and welcome him.

'Really good idea this, Ted,' Jim Baker said, taking off his raincoat and draping it on the nearest chair. 'Just what you and the team need. Now, where are Trev's mince pies? Lead me to them!'

'I'm afraid you have to sing for your supper first, Jim,' Ted told him. 'Come and meet the DS's wife. If I tell you that even Trev didn't manage to charm her, you'll get the picture. She might be more impressed by rank.'

He steered his boss deftly over to where the Hallams were standing in isolation. From a distance away, Ted could see that the DS was saying nothing. He didn't have chance to get a word in edgeways in the face of the non-stop monologue from his wife, who kept the same disagreeable expression on her face the whole time.

'Mrs Hallam, let me introduce you to the Big Boss,' Ted said. 'DCI Jim Baker, this is DS Hallam's wife, Joan. Mike, can I just borrow you for two minutes, please?'

He left the DCI to see what he could achieve with the formidably unpleasant woman and steered Mike away to the other side of the room.

'How's it going, Mike?' he asked. 'You've had a real baptism of fire, I'm afraid. I just wanted to make sure you were all right, feeling settled in and a part of the team. How are the ribs doing?'

'Sorry about the missus, boss,' Mike said with a rueful smile. 'She's not very happy about the changes in our lifestyle since the accident. She loved her work, she's not taken very well at all to being at home with her mother. It's hard.'

'Must be hard on you too and it's your welfare which concerns me,' Ted said dryly. 'How are the injuries? You still

179

look in a lot of pain.'

The DS laughed it off. 'Oh, I'm fine, honestly. Getting there. My New Year's resolution is to be less clumsy!'

Ted let him drift off back to his wife. He noticed that Tina had sidled up to the DCI and was chatting away to him, steering him towards the buffet table and making sure he had everything he needed.

Ted followed them over and gave Tina a loaded look. 'I do hope DC Bailey is looking after you properly and not pestering you for a promotion,' he said.

The DCI laughed. 'Not at all, Ted,' he replied, 'she's being very kind and helpful. It's rather nice to be so well looked after.'

The hint of wistfulness in his voice was not lost on Ted. Tina had to be wrong in her latest theory. No matter how he tried, Ted could not see his boss committing acts of violence on young women, however vengeful he was feeling.

The Hallams were the first to leave. Neither had relaxed much nor mingled. Ted noticed that the DS had eaten very little and drunk nothing. He came over to make their excuses, whilst his wife went and stood pointedly by the door, not saying goodbye to anyone.

'Sorry, sir,' the DS had returned to formalities. 'We're going to have to make a move. We left the kids and the mother-in-law baby-sitting one another and my wife is worried about both. Thank you for a nice evening, I'll see you back at the office after Christmas.'

The DCI was next to go. He looked much more relaxed than Ted had seen him look in a long time. Ted hoped he was going home by taxi, as he'd had plenty to drink.

He patted Ted fondly on the shoulder. 'What a nice young woman Tina Bailey is, Ted. Bright young thing. We chatted about all sorts. She was asking me what I like to watch on television. Turns out we have quite similar taste. We like the same characters in East Enders. I'm not sure if that will have dented my street cred, but I really enjoyed chatting to her. Happy Christmas, Ted.'

'And to you, Jim,' Ted replied. 'Don't forget, it's open house with us tomorrow, if you want to come over at any time, just for a drink or some more mince pies. You know where we are.'

Ted strode across the room towards Tina and steered her over to a quiet corner of the room. His eyes were flashing green daggers of warning.

'Please tell me you have not just been checking out the DCI's alibis for the nights in question by asking him about his television choices?' he said, his tone measured but with a warning edge to it.

'I was just chatting, boss, honestly,' Tina was all wide-eyed innocence. 'Television was a safe subject to talk about.'

'It's not even reliable. He could have been talking about things he'd caught up with on i-Player,' Ted told her. 'Or he could have recorded them on his box or something.'

'He's a worse technophobe than you are, boss,' Tina laughed triumphantly. 'He has no idea about any of that stuff, I asked him.'

'It's bad enough to suspect him in the first place,' he growled. 'To use a social setting to check out his alibis is just not on. I think you're going in completely the wrong direction here.'

Tina looked stubborn. 'It's an angle we have to consider, boss,' she insisted. 'I wasn't doing anything underhand, I was just chatting to him. I'm just doing my job, boss, like you taught me to.'

They locked eyes for a long moment, then Ted sighed.

'All right,' he said. 'But just be careful. Have you considered that if you start fishing and asking questions like that, if the DCI really was our man and he got the slightest hint of what you were doing, you could be putting yourself in danger? Remember that the Big Boss is not just a pen-pusher, he is first and foremost a copper and a damn good one, at that.

'Let's keep it by the book until we have considerably more to go on. And let's keep any and all interviews formal, recorded and inside the nick.

'Good night, Tina, and Happy Christmas.'

Tina followed her Christmas tradition and kissed him on the cheek. 'Night boss. Happy Christmas to you too and thanks for being the best boss I've ever had.'

Chapter Thirty-five

No golden tones of Freddie Mercury. Just an insistent, muted buzzing of a mobile phone on silent, its lights flashing the news of an incoming call.

With a sickening feeling in his stomach, Ted reached out an arm and picked up the phone.

Bill, once again the sergeant on duty, his gravelly voice thick with emotion.

'It's bad, Ted,' he said, clearly having difficulty speaking.

Ted shot upright in bed. 'Rosalie?' he asked.

'No, Ted,' there was a pause, while Bill cleared his throat several times before he could speak again. 'It's Tina. It's DC Bailey, Ted. Her body was found dumped just near the nick.'

Ted killed the call. He was totally unable to speak. Words seemed so futile. He turned to Trev, who was awake.

Trev seldom saw Ted in tears. It broke his heart when he did. Silently he sat up and folded his arms round his partner, holding him close.

'Rosalie?' he asked softly.

Ted shook his head, still not sufficiently in control of his voice to say anything. He was shaking.

With a supreme effort, he said thickly, 'It's Tina. They've found Tina's body near the nick.'

He pulled free and looked at Trev, tears rolling unashamedly down his face. 'How can I go in, Trev? How can I go and face the team when I've let them down? When I've let this happen to Tina?'

Trev reached for him again and hugged him fiercely. 'You

can do it, my love,' he said. 'You can put on your work face and go in there and get things rolling. You are going to get this sick piece of shit. You're going to do it for the team, and for Tina. Go and get a shower, I'll put the kettle on.'

'I've no idea what time I'll get back tonight, if at all,' Ted told him.

'I'll phone Willow, tell her what's happened and put her off,' Trev replied.

'No, please don't do that,' Ted said. 'You know Tina wouldn't have wanted you to. Have as nice a day as you can together. Save me some food for whenever I can eat it. The best thing you can do now for Tina, and for me, is to have the Christmas Day we can't have.

'Ring Willow and tell her she's staying over, then you can both drink as much as you like without worrying. Don't let her drive, and don't let her get in a taxi, not after this, when we still don't know who's out there doing this.'

Ted didn't feel any better after his shower and green tea. He was starting to doubt if he would ever feel better again. But he was at least functioning when he arrived at the station.

He went straight to the CID office, not yet ready to face the sight of Tina's body.

Bill had read his mind and called in the whole team, who were just arriving. They looked shocked rigid, any effects of drinking the night before gone in the face of such news. Young Steve's cheeks were wet, his eyes red-rimmed. Maurice kept blowing his nose noisily.

DS Hallam arrived just after Ted did. There was a rough bandage on his right hand, fresh blood showing through.

Ted had to struggle again before he trusted himself to address his team.

'We all know this is as bad as it gets. One of our own, and one of the best,' he began. 'That's why we're all in today. I'm sorry about your ruined Christmases but we won't rest now until we have this killer. It just got seriously personal to all of us.'

He took a moment to clear his throat again and needed a few deep breaths before he could continue. Tears were now running down young Steve's cheeks. He made no move to wipe them away.

'But I want you to remember something. Tina was one of ours, but we also have three other young women to consider. Especially Number Three, whose identity we still don't know. They may not have been police officers, two of them may have been "only" homeless street girls – but don't let me catch any of you voicing that thought – but they also deserve our respect and consideration.

'I need to go and talk to Doc Elliott now, get some detail. Clear your heads in the meantime, drink lots of coffee. I want you all at your sharpest.

'I'm going on the assumption that Tina never made it to her parents' house last night so I'll need to go and inform them, get them in for formal identification. I'll take ...'

He looked instinctively round the room for Tina to take with him, to help break the worst kind of news to grieving parents, then caught himself up short.

'I'll take an officer from Uniform with me. The rest of you, normal routine. Check all her last known movements. Where's her car? She told me it was parked near The Grapes. Is it still there? If not, where is it? Find it.

'You know what you need to do. Get it done. Mike, I want two people exclusively on victim number three today, too. We mustn't lose sight of the fact that she is still unidentified and we still have work to do on her case.'

He somehow couldn't bring himself to use the name Tina had given to the last victim before she became one herself.

'Maurice, Virgil, come with me and work the scene. See if you can spot anything, check out CCTV camera location. Perhaps this time we may just get lucky.'

He headed to the furthest corner of the car park where the

familiar sight of an incident tent and taping showed him Tina's last resting place. He stuffed a small handful of Fisherman's Friends into his mouth and took several deep breaths before he was able to go into the tent.

Tim Elliott came over, surprisingly shaken and sombre. He wasn't even sneezing.

'Bad business, Ted, a very bad business. My condolences,' he said. 'Death certified, not killed here. Same type of cut to the throat, again with a very thin blade. On a first and superficial examination, no sign of any mutilation, but the full post-mortem will reveal more. This time death is very recent, a matter of less than twelve hours, I would say.'

'Barely that,' Ted him. 'The whole team was together in The Grapes last night. Tina left just before eight o'clock.'

'I've informed the coroner, of course. He's left a message for Professor Gillingham but so far we've not been able to speak to him. It is Christmas Day, after all. I'm so sorry, Ted. A great loss,' Dr Elliott continued.

'Oh, and this time, it really is personal.'

He held up something in a clear plastic evidence bag, for Ted to see. It was a computer print-out, a single sheet, the edges adorned with festive symbols, holly, snowmen, reindeer and little Santas. In the centre, in Comic Sans capitals, was typed, 'Merry Christmas Ted. Hope you like your present.'

'Just give me a couple of moments alone with her, will you please, Doc,' Ted said.

The police surgeon hesitated. 'Erm, I'm sure I don't have to remind you about not getting too close … ' He dried up under Ted's glare and slipped out of the tent.

Ted took a hesitant step nearer to Tina's naked body. He felt extremely uncomfortable at the sight of her lying there like that and had to fight down an urge to cover her to protect her modesty and stop her from feeling the cold of the frosty morning.

'Tina, I'm so sorry,' he said. 'I let you down. I may have

put your life in danger and I didn't do enough to protect you. You were an excellent officer, you would have gone a long way. I'm sorry.'

Dr Elliott was still waiting, just outside the tent, when Ted came out.

'I'll wait with her, Ted, until they come to collect her. I'll make sure she is treated with dignity every step of the way.' He held out an awkward hand to shake Ted's. 'It's a dreadful business, really dreadful.'

Ted nodded. 'I'm just going to tell her parents that their daughter hasn't turned up for Christmas not because she was working late but because she has become our latest victim.'

Chapter Thirty-six

When Ted went back upstairs, DS Hallam told him, 'Sir, the DCI is in, he wants to see you in his office as soon as possible.'

Ted asked him, 'What happened to your hand?'

The DS looked embarrassed. 'I dropped a glass when I heard the news,' he said. 'Cut myself picking up the pieces so the kids wouldn't stand on them.'

Ted nodded and headed over to the DCI's office. He knocked briefly and went in. Jim Baker looked as bad as he felt, although he had clearly not started the day with a shower, nor a change of clothes, by the look of it. He smelt strongly of stale alcohol. Ted was worried by the idea that he might have driven in.

'That poor young lass, Ted,' the DCI said, pouring two mugs of his special brew. 'Why her? What are we missing in this investigation?'

'If I knew that, Jim, I would have prevented this from happening,' Ted said shortly.

'Sorry, yes, of course,' the DCI said hastily. 'I put that badly. Have the parents been informed?'

'I'm on my way over there next,' Ted told him.

'Are you sure you're up to it?' the DCI asked.

'How do you get up to it?' Ted asked ironically. 'It's bad enough telling any parent news like this. Where do you get the strength from to do it when it's one of your own team, and one of the best?'

'Would you prefer me to go?' the DCI offered.

Ted gave him a long look. 'With respect, Jim, you don't

exactly look the part.'

'So what's your starting point?' the DCI asked.

'I'm going to play it by the book,' Ted told him. 'Basic police work, forget the victim was one of ours, do it like I would do it for anyone else. First off, all of us were amongst the last people to see Tina alive last night. So I'm going to begin by checking alibis of all of us, where we were last night after we all left The Grapes, who we were with. Starting with you, Jim.'

The DCI stared at him. 'My movements?' he asked in astonishment. 'Am I a suspect suddenly? How and when did that happen?'

'You know that it's standard police procedure, Jim,' Ted said. 'I'll be giving a statement myself. It doesn't mean either of us is under suspicion.'

The DCI leant back in his chair. 'My God,' he said, as the realisation hit him. 'That's what last night was all about, isn't it? You really do suspect me. That's why Tina was asking me about my television habits. Where in hell has that come from? Ted, for God's sake, talk to me!'

'It's routine, Jim, a routine witness statement, nothing more,' Ted repeated obstinately.

'Bullshit it is!' the DCI roared, standing up. 'Tina was checking my alibis for all three killings, not just interested in whether I watch East Enders or Coro-fucking-nation Street! And now she's dead you clearly think I killed her, because I got wind that she was onto me.'

He was pacing up and down in the tight confines of his office, his voice getting louder as he got more angry.

'But just tell me why, Ted,' he said, trying to regain control of himself. 'Why in the name of God would you think me capable of such a thing?'

They were interrupted by Freddie Mercury. Ted's mobile phone was going off. He glanced at the screen and said, 'I need to take this, it's Hard G.'

The DCI slumped back into his seat. He looked utterly beaten and bewildered.

'Roger, hi, thanks for calling,' Ted said.

'My dear boy, I've been informed, of course. I am so very sorry,' the Professor said and actually sounded it. 'I will, rest assured, be carrying out the post-mortem myself on this one, I wouldn't dream of putting anyone else on it. I'm afraid I'm not really up to the task today after slightly too much festive spirit last night, but I will start on it first thing in the morning, early. I'll phone you when I'm beginning.'

'That's very kind, Roger, I appreciate that,' Ted said. 'I thought you were flying out first thing, though?'

'Absolutely out of the question now,' Hard G said firmly. 'I'll send the blonde job on ahead then catch her up when I can. It's the least I can do for you and for such a promising young officer.'

'Hard G,' Ted told the DCI as he disconnected the call. 'He's going to do the PM himself. He was meant to be flying out to Switzerland tomorrow but he's cancelling to do it.'

The DCI looked more weary than Ted had ever seen him, even on his darkest days after Rosalie went. 'Ted, please, we've been friends a long time. Tell me how you could possibly even think I might be behind any of this. Please.'

'I never thought that, Jim. Never,' he said. 'Tina was looking at a completely new angle. I didn't agree with it. But she was right, we wouldn't have been doing our job properly if we hadn't looked at everything, no matter how far-fetched.

'We'd been going on the theory that our killer was a woman-hater, then it got personal to me, so Tina started looking at people who could have a grudge against me. She came up with the idea of parents of missing children.'

'So as Rosalie was never found …' the DCI trailed off, then nodded. 'All right, I see. It's plausible, just. But it's not me, Ted.'

'I know that,' Ted assured him. 'But now can you see how

important your witness statement is about what you did after you left The Grapes last night?'

The DCI nodded. 'All right. I took a taxi home, because I'd been drinking. I had to get one to come back in this morning, my car was still on the car park. I can give you the details of the taxi firm for both times.

'When I got home, there was no sign of Margery. She never came home. I sat and watched a porn channel, with all the sordid details that implies. I got very well acquainted with a bottle of Glenfiddich. I must have fallen asleep in my chair at some point, because I was still there when I got the call from the station this morning. I came straight in, as I was.'

'There you have it. The full details of my pathetic life. And no alibi.'

Ted looked at his boss and friend, with sadness in his eyes.

'Thank you,' was all he could manage to say.

When Ted went back into the main office, there was a feeling of high tension.

'Some news, sir,' the DS told him. 'Virgil worked his way out from the car park towards The Grapes. He found the Cooper. Both the nearside tyres had been slashed, with a very sharp blade.'

'Bastard,' Ted spat between gritted teeth. 'So he made sure she was stranded then just came along and picked her up? Would she have got into a vehicle with someone she didn't know?'

The others shook their heads. Rob spoke up. 'No way, sir, Tina was far too streetwise. Why didn't she just call her breakdown cover? She was with the AA.'

'Perhaps she did call them, and that's who took her?' Maurice suggested.

'Maurice, get onto them, give them the Cooper's details and location, see if they took a call last night from Tina and if they did, who they sent out,' Ted told him. 'She'd also take a lift from someone she knew, of course. That's why I want witness statements from all of you of your movements from the moment you left the pub.

'You're grown-ups, sort it out between yourselves, get together, interview each other. These are routine witness statements only, at this stage, no one is a suspect. Treat it as you would for any other witness. And check alibis.

'We desperately need to find her personal effects, her mobile phone. Is he dumping stuff somewhere? If so, find it. Is he keeping their clothing and possessions as some sort of sick souvenir?

'Let's widen the search out from where ...' he hesitated for a moment, hating to use the word bodies when Tina was one of them, ' ... where these young women were found. Do a proper job. Do it for Tina.

'I've already talked to the Big Boss for the record. Someone needs to take my statement. Anything the slightest bit suspect anywhere, I want to know about it.

'If you don't like checking up on each other as a job, I'm just going to see Tina's parents to break the news, if anyone wants to swap with me?'

Chapter Thirty-seven

Ted arranged for a uniformed officer to go with him and asked for an unmarked pool car. He knew Tina's parents by sight, having met them with Tina at a police open day. They would know the moment he turned up on their doorstep on Christmas Day that it was the worst possible news. There was no point in signalling it to all the neighbours as well by arriving in a patrol car.

He knew the constable by sight but had to ask her name to remind himself. He was definitely not firing on all cylinders. She was clearly badly shaken up and had been crying.

'PC Heap, sir, Susan,' she told him. 'I'm … I was a friend of Tina's, we used to play badminton together sometimes.'

Ted decided to drive and opened the passenger door for the officer. As he sat in the driving seat, he said gently, 'There's no shame in crying, Susan. I cried myself when I first heard the news. Take a moment before we set off, get it out of your system. We're going to do possibly the hardest part of the job and we need to be totally professional when we do. '

As he hoped, his kind words meant she cried some more, but by the time they reached their destination, Handforth, she was fully composed and ready to do her job.

The house was a neat semi on an estate on the Wilmslow side of town. The front garden looked cherished. There were demurely twinkling silver Christmas lights festooned around the front window and porch and a festive holly wreath on the front door.

It was Mr Bailey who answered the door, for which Ted

was grateful. He greeted him formally, trying to keep his tone neutral. 'Hello, Mr Bailey, you may remember me, I'm DI Darling, this is PC Heap. May we come in, please?'

Ted could see at once from the man's eyes that he knew this was not going to be good news, or a social Christmas call. He said nothing, simply stood aside and motioned for them to enter. He indicated the first door on the right.

It was a pleasant sitting room, with an attractive bay window, in which stood a small but beautifully decorated Christmas tree, its lights flickering merrily. Presents were piled underneath it, and Mrs Bailey was sitting in a wing chair, facing the windows, fiddling to tie the ribbon of a small gift in her lap.

She looked up hopefully when the door opened but her face immediately fell and her hand flew up to her face when she saw the two officers. Her husband quietly crossed the room, sat on the arm of her chair and placed a protective hand on her shoulder.

'This is the inspector, love,' he told her, motioning the two officers to sit down.

Mrs Bailey's head started to shake vigorously from side to side and she began a monotone 'no, no, no,' as if she felt somehow that would ward off the bad news she knew was coming.

'I am very sorry to have to inform you both that Tina's body was found early this morning,' Ted began. 'She was close to the police station, her car was nearby. I'm afraid she was murdered. I am so sorry. I wish I did not have to ask but I am going to need one of you to come in to formally identify her body.

'I know it's of no consolation to you at this moment but I promise you now that I will get the person who has done this to your daughter.'

PC Heap now switched into professional mode. 'Shall I make a cup of tea for you both, Mr Bailey? Don't worry, I'll find where everything is.'

'Coffee,' the man said in an expressionless voice. 'Coffee for the wife, she doesn't drink tea in the mornings.'

He now had both his arms around his sobbing wife and was rocking her gently to and fro. He looked shell-shocked.

'When she didn't come last night, we thought she'd been held up at work,' he said blankly. 'We were surprised when she didn't phone us, she's always such a good, thoughtful girl, our Tina. We thought she'd be turning up any time now. The wife was just wrapping some silly little extra presents for her, for her stocking. We always do that, every year, even now she's all grown up.'

'Mr Bailey, is there someone who can come and be with your wife? I hate to press but we really will need you to come in and identify Tina,' Ted told him. 'I'll arrange for a car to pick you up when you feel ready, but it does need to be soon, please, so we can carry on with our investigations.'

'Good work, Susan,' Ted told the constable as he drove them back to the station. 'You held it together well.'

'Thank you, sir,' she said and blurted, 'Tina said you were the best boss on the force and I think she was right.'

'Sir, we've got an ID on victim number three, at last,' the DS told him as Ted trudged wearily upstairs into the office.

He sank into the nearest seat. 'Tell me,' he said.

'Nicola Parks. Started out as another runaway. Reported missing from her home on a farm at Sabden, in the Ribble valley,' DS Hallam read aloud from his notes. 'Disappeared just before her sixteenth birthday, never been back in touch with her family. Twenty-two when she died. Been in our area a year or so. Known as a drug user and small-time prostitute. No fixed abode, used to flit from squat to squat.

'Got form for minor offences like shoplifting and handbag snatching. Did a couple of short custodial sentences. She seemed to regard that as a good way to get a few hot meals and some showers.'

Ted sighed. 'So many runaways. Right, get onto the local nick – where the hell IS the local nick for up there? - and get them to send someone round to inform the family. But not today. She's been missing for six years, one more day is not going to make much difference in the greater scheme of things. Let them at least enjoy their turkey dinner and Queen's speech before they get the news.

'Where is everyone and where are we up to with Tina?'

'I've got Sal taking statements from everyone, sir, he has a good eye for detail,' Hallam told him. 'I said he should use your office, I hope that's all right? Virgil's been on to the AA, but there was no call from Tina last night. He's gone back onto the streets to see if anyone saw anything.'

'Good work,' Ted said shortly. 'Right, here's the plan. There is no overtime available, so it's a case of juggling everyone's hours to give us the cover we need. Get everyone together and split the time up between you. Half on, half off all the time until further notice.

'Let me see Sal's witness statements as soon as possible. I can do some alibi checking, free someone else up. I can do it on the basis of ringing round with festive greetings.

'I'll be in tomorrow early but not around – it's Tina's post-mortem. Professor Gillingham has cancelled his skiing trip so he can do it himself.'

It was the dark of early evening when Ted got back to the house. Inside the warm and festive sitting room, Trev and Willow looked cosy and contented, sitting close together on the sofa, buried under a heap of cats, watching television.

'Hi, Willow, Happy Christmas,' Ted bent over the back of the sofa to plant a kiss on each of their cheeks.

'So sorry, Ted,' she said. 'This must be really dreadful for you.'

Trev untangled his long frame from its covering of cats,

followed Ted into the kitchen and gave him a hug.

'Long day,' he said, 'and probably one of your most difficult ever, I imagine. Do you want to eat? There's plenty of food left over.'

Ted gently pushed him away to arm's length so he could see his face and said, 'Not over yet. I need to go back out and I need you to do something for me.'

Trev immediately looked suspicious and a little worried. 'What is it?'

'First, I need you not to ask any questions. Please?' Ted looked at him earnestly. Reluctantly, Trev nodded his agreement.

'I need to borrow the bike,' Ted said. 'I'll be back very late, but I will be back, so I need you not to worry. Enjoy your evening with Willow. Watch Downton, like we planned to do. I will be back.'

Trev adored Downtown Abbey. He hung on to every caustic word uttered by Maggie Smith as the Dowager Countess. It was probably the part of a traditional Christmas he enjoyed the most, watching it with Ted.

'Please stay safe,' Trev told him. 'Any problems at all, phone me.'

Ted nodded. He went to find his motorcycle leathers, his kitbag and the bike keys, then he was gone into the cold frost of Christmas night.

Chapter Thirty-eight

Ted kept the powerful bike to a sensible speed as he wound his way through the quiet streets, heading for the motorway.

His emotions were boiling to such a point that he doubted his ability to control them for much longer. He was in a state where he badly needed to hurt and be hurt.

There was only one dojo in the country where he knew he could find what he was looking for, and it wasn't close to. Even on Christmas Day, a couple of quick phone calls had been all it took to set things up for him.

He was going somewhere there would be no referees, no rules and no quarter given. He knew he was taking an enormous risk, not just with his career. But he needed to find an outlet so he could keep control in front of his team and find the clarity of mind to bring the investigation to a successful conclusion.

Once onto the motorway, almost deserted at that time on a Christmas evening, Ted opened the big bike up and let it have its head until it was nudging close to the ton and more it was easily capable of.

He knew it was only a matter of time before the blues and twos of a patrol car caught him up. He just hoped he could retain sufficient control of himself to get to his destination without being arrested or decking some poor officer who tried to stop him.

He obediently pulled onto the hard shoulder in response to the signals from the patrol car which came up behind him. But it was his warrant card he fished out from inside his leathers, rather than his driving licence.

Ted didn't think he could despise himself much more than he already did by playing that trick. He detested officers who pulled rank in any circumstances. He felt he could just about justify to himself doing it in this instance.

He could see in his mirrors that the driver was staying with the car, no doubt checking the bike's registration, while the passenger was approaching him slowly along the hard shoulder, easy to spot in his fluorescent stab vest.

'Good evening, sir,' the constable began. 'In a bit of a hurry tonight, are we?'

Ted had peeled off his helmet and his eyes were blazing angrily.

'May I see your driving licence and documents, please, sir?' the constable was still polite and correct.

'You can see my warrant card, Constable,' Ted snarled, thrusting the document into the younger man's face. 'And if you have any degree of common sense about you, you will not delay me.'

The PC snapped to attention and looked extremely awkward. Right now, Ted loathed himself even more.

The officer wasn't done with his attempt yet, and Ted admired his courage and his commitment to his job.

'Please, sir, will you at least slow down?' he said. 'Riding like that, you're going to kill someone, and probably not just yourself.'

'Thank you, officer,' Ted growled, replacing his helmet. He roared off before the PC had even had time to get back to the patrol car.

'What the fuck?' his colleague asked him, when he got back into the vehicle.

'A very bad tempered DI on some sort of mission,' his oppo said. 'I can think of lots of ways of committing career suicide that would be less painful than tangling with that little bastard in a mood like he was in.'

His mate laughed. 'Just let him go, then, and hope he only kills himself?'

'All three wise monkeys rolled into one, me. See no evil, hear no evil and speak not a fucking word about apeshit crazy DIs roaring round our patch like Easy Rider.'

Even keeping the Triumph to a ten per cent margin of error above the speed limit, it ate up the miles over the Pennines towards their destination. Ted was a competent biker though lacking any of the flamboyant flair of Trev. The dojo Ted was heading for was in an extremely rough part of a city's outskirts.

He was not remotely worried about leaving Trev's precious bike outside. Even without the goon on the door, whom Ted could see as he pulled up, no one, without a death wish, would dream of nicking or damaging anything from that location.

The door guard had folded arms across a thick barrel chest, bushy eye brows which merged as one, pulled down in a permanent scowl. He made Giant Haystacks look like he was into serious crash dieting. Ted knew he was there to ensure they were not disturbed, under any circumstances.

It had been a long time since Ted had been on the floor as often as he was in the next forty minutes or so, not since his school days as a runty kid, the target of all the bullies. Both his body and his morale were getting a good kicking.

But slowly, doggedly and against all the odds, he kept picking himself back up until he was, literally, the last man standing. And each time he got back up, he felt his drive and determination coming back.

His self-confidence had been badly dented this morning with the news of Tina's murder. He had been in a bad way, a low place. Now, finally, self-belief was starting to creep back and he felt able to get back on the proverbial horse and ride into battle.

By tacit agreement, there was not a single mark on his face, but most of his body was covered in red marks and he suspected that, by tomorrow, it would look like an abstract work of art. His right hand was so sore he could barely bend his fingers. He just hoped he would be able to control the Triumph on the journey home.

He was pleased he had had the presence of mind to put a zip-up fleece-lined hoody and sweat pants into his kit bag. There was no way he could get his customary polo neck on with all his muscles screaming at him for mercy. Somehow he managed to get into leathers and boots. His socks utterly defeated him, so he simply screwed them up and stuffed them into his kitbag.

He was also thankful he had thought to put a back support into his bag. From the way his kidneys felt, he suspected he might be peeing blood for a few days.

He didn't think anything was actually broken, at least not badly, just perhaps redesigned a little. Like himself, his opponents had all been extremely skilled martial arts fighters. Despite breaking all the normal rules, they were sufficiently in control to inflict pain yet stop short of serious injury. Ted had found what he'd come looking for.

The Triumph had never been ridden as slowly and carefully as it was on the way back, which seemed to take at least three times as long as the outward journey. Ted strongly suspected that if he happened to meet the same patrol car as before, they would pull him over again, convinced it had been stolen by someone's granny for a geriatric joyride.

He was freezing cold and starting to stiffen up all over by the time he arrived home. He only just managed to open and close the garage door, to make sure that Trev's baby was safely locked away for the night. It was late and there was no sign of life about the house. Just a few disgruntled cats, waiting up for him, opened reproachful eyes when Ted came in as quietly as he could, dumping his kitbag in the hall.

It seemed to take him forever to peel himself out of his

leathers and boots but he somehow managed it, although he had to leave them in a heap in the hallway. Bending down to put them away was just beyond him.

He limped painfully up the stairs, slipping out of hoody and sweat pants as he went. He had no intention of taking pain killers. His body needed to hurt a little, to give him back his focus.

Unusually, Trev stirred and went to sit up as Ted padded into the room. He'd clearly been worried about him.

'Don't put the light on,' Ted told him quietly. It even hurt him to speak. 'It's not pretty. But I'm all right.'

He sat carefully on the bed and eased himself painfully under the duvet. The bond between them was so strong that Trev knew instinctively what had been going on.

Gently and carefully he folded his arms around Ted, who surprised both of them by quickly falling into an exhausted sleep which was peaceful and untroubled.

Chapter Thirty-nine

Ted was awake well before his usual time, knowing he had an early start for the post-mortem, and that it was going to take him a long time to manage to get dressed. Trev had slept fitfully. He kept checking to make sure Ted was all right, and he woke the minute his partner started to move.

'Can I put the light on?' he asked quietly, not wanting to wake Willow in the next room.

Ted started to laugh, but revised his plan as pain shot through his battered body. 'It might put you off your breakfast,' he said. 'I'm fine, honestly. I'm sorry I worried you. Go back to sleep.'

He took a long shower, as hot as he could stand it, trying to ease stiffened muscles. His body was starting to turn some rather impressive colours. Dressing was hard but he managed it, just, opting for wide neck T-shirt and sweatshirt as the polo neck was out of the question.

He received a text from Hard G saying he was ready to start. He headed straight for the hospital and pulled on coveralls, after a struggle, before joining the Professor, with Tina's body laid out on the table in front of them.

He'd been to more post-mortems than he cared to count and, armed with his menthol sweets, had a great track record of not being ill. As the Professor made the first incision into Tina's skin, he only just made it to the nearest sluice before he lost his green tea, the only thing he'd had that morning, apart from the sweets which joined it.

The Professor gave him a surprisingly sympathetic look.

'It's hard, I know, old boy, when it's someone you know, and someone I suspect you were fond of. I'm afraid this is going to be very difficult for you. I made a brief examination before you arrived and it's not very nice.'

He began to speak for the tape, mentioning Tina's age, height and weight, then added, 'Light brown hair, blue eyes. Does that mean that all four of your victims now were blue-eyed? Did the young lady who had them removed have blue eyes and was that significant in some way?' he asked.

Ted nodded. 'She did and it's one possible link we've been looking into. But aren't blue eyes the most common? It may be merely a coincidence.'

'Nearly fifty per cent of people in Britain have blue eyes, dear boy, so good luck if you do try to make something of that route.'

He continued with his observations, noting aloud that the wound to the throat was once again a left-handed cut, made with a thin blade like a scalpel. Once again, he remarked, there were signs that the body had been thoroughly cleaned, making any chance of detecting the killer's DNA extremely slim.

'There's this same little scratch on her right buttock,' he pointed it out to Ted, 'just as we found on the last victim. I'm sorry to say I have not yet had the blood analysis results back on that victim so I'm not in a position to tell you what it was. It seems lab technicians have to have their festivities, resulting in a backlog, which is very inconvenient for us.

'I will send Tina's blood for analysis and will try to get the results hurried up a bit. My best guess still remains some sort of powerful intra-muscular sedative.

'Now for the bit you're not going to like Ted, and I will try to break it as gently as I can, without my usual vulgarities, which I know offend you at the best of times.

'There was, as before, evidence of some very rough sexual activity. There was vaginal penetration pre-mortem and there was this.'

He picked up a clear plastic evidence bag from one of the nearby surfaces.

'This is a butt plug, and a particularly formidable one. It was inserted anally pre-mortem and I can find no trace of any lubricant being used. All I can say is that if Tina was not sedated and was not used to such things, it would have been extremely painful.'

Ted didn't think he had anything left to throw up. After several minutes of dry heaving over the sluice, he was convinced he had lost part of his stomach lining.

'If you were in any doubt, Ted,' the Professor continued, 'I would say you are dealing with one extremely sick individual and that the sooner you get him – or her – off the street, the better.'

'Her?' Ted echoed, aghast. 'You're surely not remotely suggesting that a woman would be capable of doing this?'

'Physically? Yes, almost certainly, with the formidable array of sex toys on the market these days,' he replied. 'Psychologically? Emotionally? Don't make the mistake of thinking women cannot commit heinous crimes as well as men. There is precedent – look at Rosemary West. One of only three women in Britain sentenced to die behind bars.

'Or what about, now here's something you might not have considered, a couple at work. Him to do the sexual stuff, her to slit the throats? Again, there are precedents. Both West and Myra Hindley were operating in conjunction with a man.

'I can imagine a certain type of couple would find it the ultimate sexual thrill. Some murderers kill at the point of ejaculation as they find it intensely stimulating. I can just imagine the depravity of a certain type of couple if he was satisfying carnal lusts whilst she was busily slitting throats. But I hasten to add that that is merely a theory, and a pretty wild one, as well.'

Ted shook his head in bewilderment.

'Every time I think I've plumbed the depths of human

depravity, someone comes up with evidence that I have not, yet. Roger, can you manage without me now? I'm really having a lot of difficulty with this conversation at all, let alone in front of Tina.'

'But of course, dear boy,' the Professor replied. 'I still have a lot of work to do here. I'll email you my results when I've finished. I'll probably fly out to St Moritz tomorrow, if all goes well, but I will try and chase up any results for you, so that you have them as soon as possible.'

'Thank you. Oh, and Roger, can I just ask you, purely as routine, for your movements after you left The Grapes on Christmas Eve?' Ted asked. 'As we were all collectively amongst the last people to see Tina alive, I've been asking everyone, and checking alibis.'

'Yes, of course, I quite understand,' Hard G said. 'As I told you when I popped in, I had the blonde job outside in the Jag, so as soon as I left, we went back to the Edge, ate a light supper, drank rather a lot of champagne then, erm, well, predictably, enjoyed an awful lot of bedroom activity.

'The dreadful call from the coroner yesterday morning interrupted us, but as I was already too far over the limit either to drive or to carry out a post-mortem, we drank some more and I let the blonde job console me as only she knows how.'

'Thanks Roger, and thanks for sparing me too much detail,' Ted said. 'We will, of course, again as a matter of routine, have to check your alibi with the young lady in question. Can you give me her name, please?'

'Ah, Ted, how embarrassing!' the Professor exclaimed. 'Is it Linda or Belinda? Something like that. Or was that the one before? I have no idea about a second name, I never keep them long enough for it to become necessary to know. But I will be seeing her in a day or two, I hope seeing rather a lot of her, so I'll ask her and I can text you her details, and her mobile phone number so you can get in contact with her.'

'Do you not have her number on your phone?' Ted asked.

The Professor gave him a pitying look. 'Oh, please, dear boy. My women chase after me. I absolutely do not make the running. Why would I want to phone them?'

Ted smiled and shook his head. 'Have a good delayed Christmas, Roger, and thanks again for taking the time to do this. I really appreciate it.'

'I may be crass, my boy, but you can rely on me to afford Tina the consideration and dignity due to her. She was a remarkable young woman.'

Chapter Forty

DS Hallam was working at his desk when Ted got back to the station. No one else was in sight.

'Anyone using my office at the moment, Mike? he asked.

'No sir, everyone's out,' he replied. 'I'm just going over everyone's witness statements and noting alibis to be checked.'

'Great,' Ted said. 'Come on, I'll show you mine if you show me yours.'

Hallam gaped at him open-mouthed.

'Don't worry,' Ted told him, 'I'm just trying to be mildly amusing after a truly crap morning. Witness statements, about Christmas Eve. I'll take one from you, you take one from me.'

Knowing how fast the DI was capable of moving, the DS was surprised at his slow and stiff progress to his office. He saw him wince involuntarily as he sat down.

'You all right, boss?' he asked. 'You look as if you've been in the wars.'

'Absolutely fine, Mike,' Ted said with a small smile.

'You can't kid a kidder, boss,' Hallam said. 'I know the look of someone in pain.'

'Martial arts training that got a bit enthusiastic,' Ted said and would have shrugged, had it not been too painful. 'Now, tell me about your Christmas Eve, from the moment you left The Grapes.'

'Not much to tell really, sir,' the DS replied. 'I think we were the first to leave. I drove home, we helped the mother-in-law to bed as she was tired – she gets tired very quickly since the accident - then packed the kids off quite early. Then we just did our Christmas preparation, really. Wrapped presents, got things ready, had a fairly early night.'

'So your wife and mother-in-law can corroborate your movements?' Ted asked.

'Yes, sir,' Hallam said rather hesitantly. 'Will that be necessary? It's just that the wife … She's having a bit of a hard time of things at the moment. I try not to involve her in stuff.'

Ted raised an eyebrow. 'Stuff?' he queried. 'Stuff like the murder of a valued colleague?'

'Sorry, sir, of course, that came out all wrong,' the DS looked awkward.

Ted leaned back in his chair and looked at him. 'Is everything all right at home, Mike?' he asked. 'If there are problems likely to affect your work, I'd prefer to be kept in the loop. If you feel you can talk to me, I'm always available.'

DS Hallam flushed red and mumbled his thanks, but said nothing further.

'So to recap, your wife and mother-in-law can alibi you but, for instance, if either you or your wife or even both of you had gone out later on that evening, would the mother-in-law have known?'

'But we didn't, sir,' the DS said rather too quickly, then followed up, 'but no, I suppose she may not have heard if we had done.'

Ted nodded. 'All right. This is just purely routine for all of us at the moment. Right, my movements. I took the bus in on Christmas Eve morning as I left the car for Trev to bring in all the food. After everyone had left The Grapes, he and I stayed to have a drink and a chat with Dave, the landlord, then packed everything up and went home. We didn't see either Tina or her car on our drive home.

'By the time we'd unpacked things it was getting late. We watched a bit of something mindless on television, and I have no idea what it was, then we went to bed.'

Ted could see that the mental image was a difficult one for

the DS.

'So your, er, your …'

'My partner, Mike,' Ted smiled, 'Trev is my partner. And yes, he can confirm that. So unless you have come across any discrepancies in any witness statements you've taken or gone over so far, I would say we are right back on the starting blocks with a big fat zero.'

Ted stood up to put his kettle on. 'Green tea?' he offered the DS.

'No thank you, sir,' the DS sounded as if it had been an indecent proposal, but then continued, 'I really can't see where Tina's murder fits into this at all, boss. In fact, there's a bit of a discrepancy between the first victim and then the second and third. Maggie Fielding and Nicola Parks were runaways, Vicki Carr wasn't.'

Ted interrupted him. 'Have we actually checked that, for a fact?' he asked. 'Have we gone through her history to see if, perhaps as a young, rebellious teenager, she ran away from home or got into any other trouble? If not, why not?'

'We haven't, boss. We should have done. I'll get someone on it straight away. But then if that is the link between the victims, where does Tina's death fit into it? I'm assuming she was never a runaway? But again, I'll get someone to check.'

'Someone I know has a good saying, Mike. If you hear the sound of galloping hooves and you're not on the plains of Africa, it's more likely to be horses than zebra,' Ted told him. 'Most likely reason for a police officer involved in a case like this to finish up as a victim?'

'Getting too close to the perpetrator, boss,' Hallam said. 'So are you saying that someone who was in The Grapes that night is our killer? And that Tina knew that and talked to them, trying to flush them out? But then she talked to a lot of people, including me. And the DCI. Er, has he been excluded, sir?'

'At this stage, I'm satisfied that the Big Boss is not our man,' Ted said tersely. 'Mike, there was stuff that came out at

Tina's post-mortem that I'd rather the rest of the team didn't know about unless it becomes absolutely essential. But the Professor did say he couldn't entirely rule out the involvement of a woman in the killings. If not as the killer herself then possibly as an accomplice. Or that perhaps we're looking for a couple.'

The DS looked absolutely flabbergasted. ' A woman, sir?' he gaped. 'But how is that even possible?'

'Believe me,' Ted told him, ' there were things the Professor was telling me which were definitely in the category of Too Much Information. Tina was very clever, very quick to see things from an unexpected angle. What's that current phrase I dislike so much? Thinking outside the box. There is just the possibility that she had an idea which she was working on, or that something she said to someone that evening made them realise she was starting to close in. She needed to be removed.

'So now I hope you can see why it is so important that we look closely at the movements of everyone who was there that evening, even if it goes against the grain, feels uncomfortable or annoys our Significant Others.'

'Sir, I'll also send someone round to The Grapes to talk to the landlord and the bar staff. They will need to be eliminated too, they were all there that night.'

'Good, that's more like it, we need ideas like that,' Ted said. 'We're missing something here, something simple. Think horses, not zebra. Our killer is clever, very clever, but if we plod through routine work, we're going to find something basic he's overlooked and then we'll have him. Or them.

'We need to redouble our efforts to find a murder weapon and trace the clothes and personal possessions of all four victims.

'In a few days, we'll all be at Tina's funeral and that's going to be very hard for everyone who knew her. I want us to be able to stand there with heads held high knowing we have either got him or our noose is tightening very quickly around his neck.

'Speaking of the funeral, I want everyone there that day, and I do mean everyone. Not just out of respect for Tina, which I hope goes without **S**aying. But I want to know who everyone is who attends, what their connections were to Tina, and what they were doing on Christmas Eve.

'At the end of the day, it may be a grunt, but short of a miracle, that's going to be the thing that leads us to this killer – solid, routine police work.'

Chapter Forty-one

With the news of Tina's death, and particularly the fact that her body had been dumped so close to the station, it was now not just Pocket Billiards that Ted had to dodge whenever he arrived for work. There was also a determined press pack, more or less camping out on the police station steps, lying in wait for a lead.

The observant ones had picked up on the fact that Ted was always an early bird and they were often there when he arrived. He always tried to dodge them by using a back entrance, but they sometimes caught him on the car park and trotted across with him, microphones and cameras thrust into his face.

Ted disliked the press and media on principle and went to great lengths to avoid them. In the case of Tina's death, he couldn't trust himself to talk to them, even if he had been authorised and willing to do so. It was too raw a subject.

Inevitably, with four murder victims and no suspect in custody, the questions were getting more probing, even accusatory.

Crossing the car park felt more like running the gauntlet or walking the plank to Ted. He usually managed it by imagining speedy ways to dispatch each of them using martial arts.

'How is it that the Stockport Slasher is still at large, Inspector?' asked one particularly obnoxious reporter, walking half backwards so she could make eye contact as she threw her questions at him. 'With the resources at your disposal, how is it that he was able to go on and kill a member of your own team?'

Ted stopped so abruptly that she almost fell over. He

looked at her long enough for the silence to become uncomfortable, his eyes flashing warning signals. When he finally spoke, his voice was level and measured as he reminded them all, yet again, that all their questions needed to be addressed to the Press Office.

Although he was small, quietly spoken and extremely polite, the woman had read something in his gaze which had unsettled her. She made no attempt to follow him any further as he continued his way to the station.

Despite his bruising, aches and pains, Ted took the stairs three at a time, eager to get back to work. Perhaps this would finally be the day when they saw some sort of a breakthrough.

In fact his first phone call of the day was Tina's father, phoning to let him know that Tina's body was being released to them and the funeral would take place early in the New Year.

'Our daughter is dead. Delaying the funeral won't bring her back to life, so we've taken the first available date that we are allowed to,' he said in a dull voice, as if he were talking about booking the car in for a service. Ted was glad the man had reached the stage of numbness in his grief, to help him get through the difficult times to come.

It was to be a burial, he explained, and gave Ted the date and time. 'I hope you will be there, Inspector. I know my daughter thought very highly of you. She was always telling us you were the best boss on the force,' his voice choked slightly.

'Tina was a very valued member of my team, Mr Bailey. I and all her colleagues will be there for her. And I promise you again, we are going to catch her killer.'

'Oh, I know you will, Inspector,' Bailey said. 'Tina told us you always got your man. She said you were like a terrier after a bone. That made us laugh. She always had a funny way with words, did our Tina.'

Ted went into the main office to pass the information to the team. They were all in again, back to working standard hours now Christmas was behind them.

'Do we send flowers?' he asked them. 'What would Tina have wanted? I'd like to do something from the team, but it's a question of what.'

'I know she liked flowers, sir, but I'm not sure how she would think about expensive ones just to … ' Rob started but broke off, then regained control and continued, 'just to wilt away on her grave.'

'A charity donation, then?' Ted asked. 'Anyone know what charities interested her?'

'Dementia, boss,' Rob said, 'her granny's got Alzheimer's.'

Ted felt a fleeting moment of shame that he didn't know that.

'Sir,' young Steve piped up. 'What if we get some flowers for the church, for Tina, then make sure they go to an old people's home afterwards?'

'Brilliant idea, Steve,' Ted said. 'Can I put you in charge of sorting that out? Do you know what Tina liked, favourite colour, special flower, that sort of thing?'

'Oh, yes, sir,' Steve said, going red but looking pleased.

Ted could see from his expression how much he had idolised Tina and just hoped, if she had been aware, she had let him down gently. He felt sure she would have; she was that kind of person.

'Right, listen up,' he said to the team. 'The funeral is going to be a hard day for all of us. Tina was a colleague and a friend. But please remember, no matter how hard it is for us, it's a hundred times worse for her parents. So I want dignified professionalism from all of you. Do your grieving before or after, but not at the funeral.

'Remember, too, that you will also be there to work, not just to pay your respects. Eyes and ears working overtime, please. I want to know who everyone is at the funeral, all their connections to Tina. And watch everyone. Look for any body language that's not quite as you would expect at such

215

an occasion.

'Right, Steve, you're in charge of flowers. No idea how much these things cost these days so I'll start you off. Nobody feel you need to give more than you can afford. You know Tina would have hated that. And remember to ask the Big Boss, too. I'm sure he'd like to contribute and he doesn't bite – often. Tell me if you need more from me.'

Ted dropped a banknote on the young TDC's desk and the rest of the team started getting out their wallets to make their contribution.

The DS stood up and started to go through his pockets, looking acutely embarrassed. 'Sorry, guys, you're never going to believe this but I really have left my wallet at home,' he said. 'I got it out this morning to give the kids some spending money, must have forgotten to pick it up again. I'll give you mine tomorrow, if that's all right?'

Ted dropped another note on the desk and said, 'You can owe me, Mike, rather than owe young Steve. And as the funeral is at eleven, we'll have a quick round at The Grapes afterwards – my shout – to say our own goodbyes to Tina.

'Don't forget, the most useful thing we can do for Tina now is to catch her killer. It may feel like we're getting nowhere at the moment but it's this routine work that's going to get us to where we need to be.

'Keep at it. We'll get there.'

Chapter Forty-two

The church was crowded on the day of the funeral. There was a large uniformed presence, from Tina's days in the Uniform branch, with colleagues from that period of her career to act as coffin bearers. The Divisional Commander was also there. She made time to have a few formal words with Ted, expressing her condolences and asking for a progress report. Ted didn't have much to offer, other than yet more assurances.

Steve had done the team, and Tina, proud, with a magnificent bouquet of pink roses and white lilies, and a card with all their names on.

There was still no sign of the DS, but the rest of the team had arrived. Trev had taken the morning off work to attend, to pay his respects to Tina, and to support Ted in what he knew was going to be an extremely difficult day.

Ted dispersed his team around the church where they could discreetly watch those present. He put young Steve nearest the door to check names. There was a book there so that those present were able to sign themselves in. It was a long shot, trying to spot a murderer in a crowded church, but right now long shots were all that they had left.

Mr Bailey had asked Ted to say a few words, as Tina's boss, which Trev had helped him prepare the evening before.

As funerals go, it was a good one. He knew his team members were all feeling the same acute sense of loss as he was when, after the service, they saw the coffin carrying their friend and colleague lowered into the ground. Ted stepped near enough to place a hand on young Steve's arm when he saw he was struggling for control.

The mood in The Grapes afterwards was subdued. DS Hallam had still not appeared and despite checking his phone frequently, Ted had no word from him to explain his absence. He was seething by the time they returned to the station.

DS Hallam was sitting at his desk when they came in. One look at him showed he was in a terrible state, beaten and bloody, both eyes blackened, a nose which looked broken.

Ted strode past him, muttering, 'My office. Now,' through gritted teeth.

Hallam rose painfully and followed him, keeping his head down. He made sure he shut the door himself. He didn't think he was up to witnessing another kick-trick.

Ted nodded to the spare chair and said, 'Sit down, before you fall down,' then put his kettle on. 'Now, tell me what the hell happened and how you managed to miss Tina's funeral?'

'I was mugged, sir, they took my phone,' the DS said without looking up.

Ted slammed his hand down on his desk in front of Hallam, so the man jumped involuntarily as he raised his voice.

'For god's sake, Mike, stop the bullshit. I don't interfere in anyone's private life but yours just spilled over into the workplace.

'So, let me tell you how it looks from where I am standing, and then perhaps you will give me your own account of what is really going on.

'You don't have any money to chip in for Tina's flowers,' Hallam started to interrupt but Ted held up a hand to stop him. 'You've had a couple, if not more, serious goings-over, and remember I know a lot about such things.

'On the morning after Tina's murder, with a scalpel, you turn up to work with a fresh gash on your hand and yet another implausible story of a domestic accident. You can see how this is starting to wear a bit thin, can't you, Mike?

'Let me put a possible scenario to you, and then you can

tell me why it's not the right one. A family man, under a lot of stress at home, wife perhaps not as loving as she once was. Plenty of street girls available, and in fact, the perfect cover to go looking for them, handed to him on a plate by his boss.

'But street girls cost money, of course, and when you can't pay up, if they have a pimp who's doing the job as he should, you're in serious danger of getting a beating at best. The less money you have, the more of a pasting you get.

'Now, just suppose for a minute, that our man gets his jollies by doing away with the girls either during or after the sex act. Then one night he picks up the wrong girl, one with a pimp who's watching her closely, worried about losing one of his girls. So when he wants to get up to his usual tricks, the pimp is there in a shot and beats seven bells of hell out of him.'

DS Hallam was still looking at the floor, shaking his head slowly from side to side, although it was clearly painful to do so.

'You're so wrong, sir, it's almost funny,' he said quietly.

'So tell me, damn it,' Ted snapped. 'You were cagey, to say the least, about your alibi for the night of Tina's death. I cannot continue to ignore whatever it is that's going on when it's having such an effect on your work.

'Your absence from Tina's funeral, without a very valid excuse, risks seriously damaging your working relationship with the rest of the team. I need to know what is going on.'

'I'm too ashamed to tell you, sir,' Hallam said, so quietly that Ted had to lean forward to hear him.

Ted stood up and went into the outer office, where the team were all at their desks working. 'I need you all out on the streets, now, doing police work, doing your jobs. Move it. Maurice, you're senior in here at the moment, get the team mobile. Get them working on that idea we talked about.'

Ted looked hard at Maurice Brown, hoping the usually insensitive DC would pick up on what he was really saying. For a moment, the man simply looked blankly at him until the penny dropped.

'On it now, sir,' he said, standing up. 'Right, everyone, you're all needed to work this latest idea the boss told me about, I'll fill you in on the way. I think it should take us about half an hour, boss?' he looked to the boss for confirmation that he had got the right end of the stick.

Ted threw him a grateful glance and said, 'Thanks, Maurice, I'm sure half an hour will be long enough to come up with some answers.'

The team trooped out of the office. Ted returned to his, made two cups of green tea, liberally laced with organic honey and put one in front of DS Hallam before sitting down with his own.

'Right, Mike, we have an uninterrupted half-hour. You need to tell me what's going on, and you can tell me what's going on,' he said quietly. 'If it has nothing at all to do with work, you have my word that it will go no further than this office. But I need to know.'

'It's the wife, sir. She hits me,' Ted could hear the self-loathing in his voice as DS Hallam spoke. 'Knee-high to a bloody grasshopper and she beats the shit out of me.'

He had pulled out a large handkerchief and even though he still refused to raise his head, Ted could tell his DS was in tears.

Of all the answers Ted had prepared himself for, this was not at the top of his list. He bought himself some time by saying, 'Drink your green tea, Mike. It tastes disgusting until you get used to it, but it has the advantage of being sweet and wet.'

The DS took a gulp. 'Bloody hell, sir, how do you drink this stuff?' he said, but at least he now looked up from studying the floor.

'How long has this been going on? Ted asked gently.

'We were having a few problems before the mother-in-law's accident,' he said, and was managing now to hold eye contact for a few moments at a time. 'Joan always had a bit of a short fuse. It just used to be the odd slap, though.

'When she had to give up her job, things changed completely. She loved her work, everything about it. She didn't want to give it up, didn't want to move back to Stockport, didn't want to be stuck at home all the time as a home carer. She started using the lad's baseball bat on me.'

'Have you spoken to anyone about it?' Ted asked.

'Are you kidding, sir?' the DS looked horrified. 'Look at me, I'm a six-foot tall copper, Joan is a five foot nothing midwife. I'd never live it down.'

'There's specialist help available to you, and to your wife, and you certainly do need it. This cannot go on,' Ted told him. 'Does she hit the children?'

'Oh good god no, she's as soft as butter with them. She's not even particularly strict with them, although she used to be a right little dragon of a theatre sister,' Hallam said.

'What about the mobile phone thing? Is it related that it's always been her who's answered whenever I've called you at home?' Ted asked.

The DS nodded. 'She's insanely jealous, convinced I'm having affairs right, left and centre,' he snorted. 'I couldn't, anyway, she has me so scared I'm not up to much. She lets me bring the phone to work, of course, but takes it off me when I get home and goes through every incoming and outgoing message and text. I delete things, obviously, but if ever I forget …'

'And the money?'

'That too. I'm not allowed any cash, in case I spend it on my so-called other women. She lets me carry a credit card because she can check up on anything I spend.'

'And the wound to your hand on Christmas Eve? What was the real cause of that?' Ted asked.

'Because I talked to Tina in The Grapes. It was just a brief conversation, work stuff, but the wife saw us talking and I paid for it later on. The boiling water, too, that was her.'

He made direct and steady eye contact with the DI for the first time since they had started to talk. 'I didn't kill anyone, sir, and certainly not Tina.'

'I believe you, Mike,' Ted said reassuringly. 'Thank you for telling me. Now, this is what is going to happen next. You're going to take some sick leave ... ' he waved away the protest the DS started to make. 'That was not a suggestion.

'I'm going to make a few phone calls, get you the right sort of help. Professional people, Mike. No one will judge you. I certainly don't. Most importantly, we're going to see that your wife gets the help she clearly needs.

'Once that's all sorted, you're going to come back to work, bright-eyed and bushy-tailed, and none of the team will know a thing. Trust me.'

Chapter Forty-three

If Ted didn't have a single new lead to go on in the days after Tina's funeral, at least he didn't have another body. The case was a long way from being over, he and the team were still working flat out, but there were no more bodies – yet.

Trev suggested they take advantage of the relative calm while they could and have a postponed Christmas dinner. He once again suggested they invite Willow, as he said she had something she wanted to tell them.

It still felt wrong to Ted to be celebrating anything with Tina barely cold in her grave but he knew he owed it to Trev for all his unending support to agree. He once again told him to invite Willow to stay over.

The chosen evening was a deceptively mild one, for January, and they were able to enjoy drinks on the small patio of the garden behind the house. Ted and Trev had erected high mesh netting all around the garden in an attempt to deter any cats from wandering onto nearby roads. There was a construction like a fruit cage, where Ted grew his lilies, keeping them out of feline harm's way because of their toxicity to cats.

Willow had been trying to learn the cats' names. She knew they all had a Queen connection, hence Freddie and Mercury, and she thought it hilarious that it meant having a cat called John.

A robin was chattering cheekily at them from an ornamental cherry tree in the garden and one of the cats, with luxuriant, long blonde fur, tipping to rich chocolate at the ends and points, was advancing stealthily towards it, belly low to the ground, tail tip twitching menacingly.

'Which one's that?' Willow asked.

'Roger, the wanton killer,' Trev said, hurrying after him, scooping up a furious, growling cat, whose blue eyes flashed with anger at being interrupted.

Willow threw back her head and laughed. 'Oh, how very apt,' she said. 'I can't think of a more appropriate name for a psychopathic killer than Roger.'

'Why do you say that? Ted asked, intrigued. 'Does our Professor have real skeletons in his cupboard?'

'If he has, he never let me see them,' came the quick reply. 'But seriously, nothing about him would surprise me. There is an incredibly cold and cruel streak about him. A lot of people said about Jimmy Savile that nothing that ever came out about him would surprise them. I'm like that with Roger.'

'Interesting,' Ted said. 'How long did you live with him?'

'Oh, the blonde jobs are never allowed to live with him,' Willow told him. 'We're allowed to stay over for shagging purposes but never, ever, to dream of moving in so much as a change of undies, except in your own bag. I actually lasted a couple of months, which is close to a record.'

'I've always thought it a fascinating house,' Ted said musingly. 'Have you seen all round it?'

'Ted, stop being such a policeman!' Trev told him. 'Right, I'm ready to dish up, so come in, sit at the table, and no more shop talk, Ted. Willow, I'm dying to hear this news you have for us.'

'Well, I've met someone new,' Willow told them as they sat at the table. 'I think it might be pretty serious. Tall, dark, very dark, black, actually, and totally ripped. A model, like me, which is how we met.' She smiled happily at them and added, 'I feel so safe when he's around.'

Trev leapt up to give her a hug and a kiss. 'That's fantastic news, I'm so pleased for you. You deserve someone lovely after Hard G. What's his name?'

Ted also leaned over to give her a kiss on each cheek.

'Ebony,' Willow said and winked. 'But he's no more an Ebony than I am a Willow. His real name is Rupert, it just doesn't go with the image.'

'I still can't see why you were ever with Hard G in the first place,' Ted said. 'Sorry if I'm out of line asking that, I'm just curious.'

'I don't mind talking about it,' Willow assured him. 'Revolting as Hard G is as a person, it did get my photo into Cheshire Life and Tatler, being seen out with him. And he is an accomplished lover, if you don't mind things a little rough. Accomplished and insatiable, largely due to an inexhaustible supply of little blue pills from the family pharmacy.'

'I'm still intrigued about the house,' Ted said. 'I imagine he has an extensive wine cellar, knowing his expensive taste?'

'So he told me,' Willow replied, 'although I never saw it for myself. The house is huge, but I was more or less restricted to the bedroom, bathroom and the main reception rooms. But yes, there's a wine cellar, a game larder, even a cheese room, I believe. I understand some of the cellar rooms are climate controlled for storing his most precious things.

'There's also a fully functioning laundry down there. As you probably know he is obsessed with clean bed linen daily, and at least three clean shirts a day. And some sort of big incinerator thing, a bio-mass boiler, I think he said. He's also obsessive over personal documents, always prefers to burn stuff rather than putting in out in dustbins.'

'Does he just have the two people looking after him?' Ted asked. 'It seems a colossal workload for one couple.'

'Oh no, the Collinses are more like directors of operations,' Willow explained. 'There's a professional cleaning firm that comes in daily, with industrial machines to clean right through. All the food is courtesy of outside caterers, the bed linen goes out for professional laundering most of the time. Mrs Collins sees to his shirts herself in the cellar laundry.'

'Have you been to any of his overseas properties?' Ted asked. 'Fabulous meal, as ever, Trev,' he said as an aside.

'I was really looking forward to going to one of the winter resort ones this year, but he got tired of me and dumped me first. I adore skiing.'

'Do you know where all the overseas ones are? Could you give me a list of them?' Ted asked her.

'Ted!' Trev said, 'you are being decidedly policeman-like at table. What are you up to?'

'Sorry, I'll stop,' Ted smiled at him. 'But if I'm very good and eat up all my greens, will you let me ask Willow just a few more questions over coffee? And I'm going to need your help, too. I'll need to borrow your linguistic abilities.'

Trev sighed theatrically. 'Which languages?' he asked.

'Not entirely sure yet but I'd say certainly French, … what do they speak in Switzerland?'

'French, German, Italian and Romansh,' Trev replied. 'I may struggle in Romansh.'

'I'm not sure where you're coming from Ted, but I'm guessing you might want to add Spanish and possibly Portuguese,' Willow said.

'Does Roger just have the Jag or does he have any other cars?'

'Ted, we're not at the coffee yet!' Trev chided him.

'I know, I'm sorry, I'll make it up to you, promise,' Ted said, clearly without a shred of true remorse. 'Just this one more question, then I will be good, honestly.'

'I've only ever seen the Jag, but I haven't been in the garage and it is huge,' Willow told him. 'The Collins have a big old Mercedes estate, a real old bus, but immaculately kept. Roger is as anal about the cleanliness of his motors as he is about his bedding.'

'Trev, just one more thing … ' Ted ducked as Trev hurled half a bread roll at him. 'I may need you to take some time off tomorrow morning, to make these phone calls for me. They may be urgent.'

Ted managed to keep quiet through the rest of the meal. As Trev was serving coffee, he asked Ted, 'You're surely not thinking of Hard G in terms of being a suspect, are you?'

Ted looked pointedly at Willow. Much as he liked her, he was not about to start discussing a case in detail in front of her, especially as they'd not known her long. He barely discussed his work with Trev.

'It's just a couple of things Willow said which made me think of a completely different angle that I'd like to explore. It's going to mean phoning round a few countries though, which is why I need your help. You know I can just about order a coffee in French and that's my limit. Is Switzerland on the same time as us?'

'An hour ahead,' Trev told him. 'I'll phone work first thing and say I'll be in later. It's just as well my boss thinks I am the greatest thing since sliced bread, he won't mind. But you are so going to have to make this up to me somehow.'

'It might not be the best of times for me to ask Hard G for the loan of that ski chalet he offered me,' Ted warned him with a wink.

Chapter Forty-four

Ted phoned Maurice Brown's mobile first thing. With his DS temporarily out of action, he needed someone to head up the team when he was not there. Maurice was the longest serving of them all, though not the brightest, but Ted hoped that asking him to step up might just produce a bit of inspiration from him.

'Maurice, it's the boss,' he said. 'The DS is on sick leave for a bit, though it's nothing too serious. I'll be in later. You know what needs working on. Can you make sure the team are on it, then fill me in when I get back. Any problems at all, phone me. Don't try flying solo if there's too much turbulence.'

As soon as Willow had left for work, Trev asked him, 'You can't seriously think Hard G is your killer, can you?'

Ted sighed. 'I really am right out of ideas and clutching at straws on this one,' he admitted. 'But there were a few things Willow said which got me thinking. I'm not a bad copper and I've got nowhere at all on this one. No traces, no DNA, nothing.

'But what if I really was up against the best forensic pathologist in the country? I wouldn't find anything, would I? Especially if he was also the person who did the PMs on three of the bodies. I've been going nowhere fast, even to the point of asking Jim for his alibi.'

'What help do you need from me, then?' Trev asked.

'I'm going to have to go to the Big Boss with a good theory and plenty to back it up. I need a search warrant for Hard G's place and we certainly aren't going to get that on a whim. So

I'm going to need something substantial to offer for reasonable grounds.

'We know Hard G has property all over the place, in Europe and beyond. We've now got the list Willow gave us of where the properties are, the ones she knows about. I want to make contact with the local police in each area and find out, just on the off-chance, if they have any disappearances or unsolved murders on their books which match our killer's MO. That would be pretty strong grounds to look more closely at our slippery and odious friend.

'And you heard what Willow said, it sounds as if his cellar would be the ideal place to get up to the tricks the killer got up to. With his obsession for having everywhere cleaned, it would be very difficult to find any traces of anything, but we might just get lucky.'

Trev whistled admiringly. 'I have to say, when you decide to go out on a limb, you do it big style! This is your wildest idea yet. I know you don't like Hard G – I can't stand the man – but really? Murder? And killing Tina? After he called in especially to bring us that lovely hamper?'

'Thanks for reminding me,' Ted took out his phone and dialled Hard G's number. He got his answering service. 'Roger? Ted here. Hate to hurry you but I'm still waiting on your call about the latest blonde job's name, when you have a minute. Give me a call, when you're back in the country. We could do coffee. Thanks.'

Trev made fingers down the throat gagging gestures at him. 'Do coffee?' he asked, 'Since when did you ever do coffee?'

Ted smiled. 'Just trying to avoid arousing his suspicions or he may not come back. The thing is, he told us the current blonde job was waiting for him outside in the Jag but we never saw that, and he's not provided a name for us to verify the alibi.

'He could have slashed Tina's tyres, waited outside for her, then offered her a lift. Handforth isn't far out of his way, driving back to the Edge, and she would probably have accepted a lift from him as she knew who he was,' Ted said. 'I don't think she liked him much but she would know how slim her chances were of getting a taxi on Christmas Eve. With two tyres slashed, she couldn't just change for the spare and again, where was she going to get a new tyre at that time the night before Christmas?'

'I'm stunned, I really am,' Trev said. 'Right, tell me who I'm phoning and what I need to say and let's get started.'

Ted watched in silent admiration as his partner switched effortlessly between French, Italian, German and Spanish to make the calls. Ted made careful notes of the results. He'd asked Trev to ask exclusively about the last twelve months to begin with. The theory was still so incredible he wasn't sure if it would go anywhere. It quickly became apparent that it would.

There was a definite pattern emerging from countries in which Hard G owned a holiday home or his family had one, which he used from time to time. Young women found dead, either strangled or with their throat cut and signs of violent sexual activity either prior to or at the point of death. They were almost always women who would not be immediately missed, sometimes runaways, sometimes working as chalet maids who moved around a lot, making them hard to trace.

After about the sixth phone call had paid dividends, Trev asked, 'Do you want me to carry on or is that enough to be going on with? It's looking as if you might be right.'

'I'm not sure if I'm pleased or not,' Ted said. 'It still seems so far-fetched. I can't get anywhere further unless I can get a search warrant and I can't see that being easy. I need to sell the idea to Jim first, which may not go well. "Boss, you know that a while ago I thought you were the murderer? Well now I've decided it's actually the country's leading forensic pathologist". He's really going to love that.'

'There is the added factor that there hasn't been another

death here in the time Hard G has been out of the country,' Trev pointed out.

'Circumstantial,' Ted said dismissively, playing devil's advocate with his own theory. 'On the one hand, it sounds totally incredible. On the other, it answers a lot of questions. Notably why we've got nothing out of any of the post-mortems.'

'So what's next?' Trev said, putting the kettle on.

'I can't do anything more now, not unless and until the Big Boss backs me in trying to get a warrant for Hard G Towers,' Ted said. 'We need to get a look in those cellars, see exactly what sort of a set-up he has down there. It sounds like the ideal place to keep bodies cool before dumping them.'

'Good luck with that,' Trev said fervently. 'Tea, before you go?'

Ted shook his head. 'Not sure that all the tea in China will make it any easier to sell this idea to the Big Boss. I'll see you later.'

Maurice Brown seemed to have things under control when Ted went into work, a little to his surprise. Ted caught up quickly with who was where, then went in search of the DCI, after a detour to arm himself with green tea. He decided after all that he needed a clear head for this.

The DCI looked bone-crushingly weary. He looked up hopefully when Ted walked in. 'Ted, tell me you have some good news in the shape of a strong new lead,' he said. 'The top brass are all over me like a rash and I need a lifeline.'

'I have a strong new lead,' Ted told him, sitting down uninvited.

'Really?' the DCI visibly perked up. 'What is it?'

'I have a possible new suspect and I want to apply for a search warrant to confirm my suspicions,' Ted said.

'I'm liking this. Who is it?'

Ted took a deep breath, then plunged in at the deep end.

'Professor Roger Gillingham,' he said.

For a moment, the DCI just looked at him in bewilderment as if he hadn't heard him properly. Then he erupted.

'What the hell are you talking about, man?' he bellowed. 'Ted, what has got into you? Have you started drinking? Are you taking drugs? Not so long ago you thought I was the killer. Now you're pointing the finger at a highly respected pathologist. You bloody well better have some good sound reasoning behind your theory.'

Ted produced the notebook he'd used for jotting down the findings Trev had made during the morning's phone calls.

'First off, the Professor has no verifiable alibi for the night Tina was killed. He came to The Grapes, as you know. He said the latest blonde job was waiting in the Jag outside and that they went back to the Edge together, but he conveniently can't remember her name so anyone can verify that.'

The DCI scoffed. 'Don't be ridiculous, you know he never knows their names half the time. There are so many of them and they change so quickly.'

'We know the Professor has holiday homes all over Europe and beyond, either in his own name or owned by the family company,' Ted continued, unperturbed. 'I've done some ringing round and found an interesting pattern emerging.'

He referred to his notes. 'Close to his winter sports home in St Moritz, in the last few months, a chalet maid vanished and was later found dead with her throat cut, having been involved in some pretty heavy-duty sex shortly before death.

'Near to his home in Como, Italy, in the last six months, one girl has been reported missing by friends and another has been found dead, also with her throat cut. A similar thing emerged on the French Riviera, near to where he has the use of an apartment.

'There are others, I can list them if you like. I haven't yet tried his South American homes because of the time difference.'

'You managed to speak to all these forces in other countries and make yourself understood?' the DCI asked suspiciously.

'Trev helped me,' Ted admitted.

'What?' This time the DCI's roar must have been clearly audible to the whole of Ted's team, out in the main office. 'You start on a line of enquiry like this without discussing it with me first, and you bring in a totally unauthorised civilian to work with you? Ted, I should put you on a disciplinary for this.'

Ted shrugged. 'I didn't mention it because I was afraid this would be how you would react, Jim. It's incredible. It's abso-bloody-lutely incredible. But when you've calmed down a bit, have a serious think about it and tell me if it doesn't finally answer a few of our questions. And then can we talk again about getting a search warrant?'

Chapter Forty-five

Ted decided to give the Big Boss a few hours to subside to a low simmer before trying to talk to him again before he left for the day.

He tapped lightly on the door and put his head round first. 'I come in peace,' he said, with a smile.

The DCI waved him in. 'Come in, Ted, we need to talk,' he said.

'Sounds ominous,' Ted said, as he sat down.

'If, and it's a bloody big if, you want me to take this latest insane idea of yours seriously, you've got a long way to go to convince me you're on the right lines,' he said. 'So start out by giving me a motive that makes any kind of sense.'

'Sexual gratification,' Ted said promptly. 'There is a strong indication that all of these victims, including those who have come to light in other countries, were subjected to rough sex either just before or at the point of death, which suggests a deviant sexual motive. And I have it on good authority that the Professor likes it rough, the rougher the better.'

'My God, the very thought makes my skin crawl,' the DCI said, shaking his head. 'All right, I know it happens. I'm still struggling with the Professor as a suspect but I'm working on it. So why make it personal to you? Why the messages?'

'That has me stumped at the moment,' Ted confessed. 'Mocking me because I haven't caught him yet? Some grudge he has against me that I'm not aware of? Trev and I have thrashed him at badminton every time we've played him – maybe he's a bad loser?'

'Not funny, Ted,' the DCI growled. 'And why Tina? Of all people, why her?'

'That would be the ultimate taunt to me, Jim, taking one of my team right out from under my nose. That's why I absolutely have to check his alibi for Christmas Eve. And at some point, I'm going to want to talk to his staff.'

'This is a political minefield,' the DCI warned. 'If we get this wrong, I can kiss goodbye to any chance of ever making Super and you are likely to be directing traffic for the rest of what's left of your career. It's not just the Professor's position in his field, it's the family connections, too.

'PharmaGill is one of the richest companies in the country. They will pay for top lawyers to fight us every step of the way, so we need to be one hundred per cent sure of ourselves and not go off half-cocked. I know you're very good at playing it by the book, Ted, and that's going to be essential on this one.

'The first thing you need to do is check that alibi. Carefully and discreetly. Your whole theory hangs on that at the moment. If the alibi is tight, the rest of it is bobbins, and the deaths in other countries are nothing but coincidence.

'Wait until you hear from him, check out the alibi then report back to me and we'll decide what action to take next. Don't, I repeat, Ted, don't, whatever you do suddenly decide to become a cowboy for the first time since I've known you and go riding off in lone pursuit on a white charger.'

Ted smiled. 'The only time I've ever ridden a horse was on Blackpool beach when I was a kid and I fell off when it sneezed,' he said ruefully. 'No danger there, Jim.'

Ted was just getting into his car when his mobile phone rang and the display told him that it was Hard G.

'Ted, dear boy,' the Professor's voice said, as soon as he accepted the call, 'so sorry not to have got back to you before. I've been rather more busy with the après than the ski, if you follow my meaning, so now here I am, breathlessly contrite, phoning you back as requested.'

Ted kept his tone neutral and professional. 'Thank you, Roger. It was just a prompt to remind you I still need the name of the incumbent blonde job on Christmas Eve, as we're checking everyone's alibi for that night, purely as a matter of routine.'

'Ah, perfidy, thy name is woman! And in this case, forever nameless woman. You won't believe it. As I told you, I sent the blonde job, Linda, Belinda, Bindy, whatever she was called, on ahead to St Moritz in the Gulfstream on Boxing Day whilst I was working on poor Tina with you.

'When I finally got away and flew out to join her, I discovered she'd had a quite spectacular party in my chalet, left it in the most appalling mess and gone off with a young ski instructor. The last I heard, they'd gone on to deliver a yacht from the Riviera to the Antilles.

'She did leave me a scribbled note, but her handwriting is so bad I'm still none the wiser as to her name, I'm afraid. Luckily there was no shortage of candidates to take her place. I'm so sorry I can't help you further, old chap.'

'No problem at all, Roger,' Ted replied, his mind working overtime. 'When are you back?'

'Flying back in on Friday morning, giving myself the weekend to catch up on what's been happening, ready to start back in harness on Monday morning.'

'That works in rather well for me,' Ted told him. 'I have to pop over to Handforth on Friday, to talk to Tina's parents. I was wondering, if it's not too much trouble, if I could call in on you afterwards? There are a number of baffling factors about this case I'd really appreciate the chance to discuss with you in more detail. Your workplace is too depressing, mine is too busy. I'm not far from your doorstep that day, so I wondered if I could be cheeky and call round?'

The Professor laughed. 'Ted, you naughty boy, I know exactly what you are really up to!'

'You do?' Ted said in surprise.

'Yes, indeed. You know Mrs Collins will welcome me back with freshly baked cakes for afternoon tea and you want to gatecrash. You are always welcome to do so, dear boy, please do come. Just let me know what time and I will make sure she has the kettle on.'

Ted recounted his day to Trev when he got back. 'You really fell off a pony when it snorted?' Trev laughed. 'You never told me before. Wish I could have seen that. But seriously, you be careful, going to beard the dragon in his den. If it is Hard G, you could be putting yourself in danger, if he thinks you're on to him.'

'I doubt he does,' Ted said. 'If I'm right about it being him, then surely he's mocking me all along because he thinks I'm too stupid to solve the case, not a worthy opponent for him. I've not said anything to make him think that's changed. I've just asked him about a routine piece of police work.'

'I don't like the sound of the missing Lindy-Bindy,' Trev said. 'It could all be perfectly genuine but there again, maybe she's his latest victim out there. Do you want me to phone the Swiss police again and get more details of the one who was found dead there?'

'Thanks, but better not. I got a bollocking from Jim for involving you at all and I've promised to play it by the book for now.'

'Well, at least take someone with you on Friday, someone nice and solid,' Trev said. 'What about Maurice?'

It was Ted's turn to laugh. 'If I turn up at Hard G Towers for a tea party with Maurice in tow, I might just as well arrive on blues and twos, dangling handcuffs and shouting "You're nicked, mate". Maurice doesn't exactly do subtle. I'd rather go on my own, it would look more natural.'

'And be twice as dangerous. Please, Ted, take back-up or I'll worry.'

'I'll think about it, I promise,' he said. 'I just don't want to do anything at all to arouse his suspicions. If I make the wrong move now, all he has to do is jump on the Gulfstream and he's out of my reach for ever more.'

Chapter Forty-six

Ted was really surprised when a light knock on his door a couple of days later was followed by DS Hallam stepping into the room. His face was still badly bruised, though the damage was subsiding, but he looked a completely different man. There was a spring to his stride and a whole new air of confidence about him that Ted had not seen before.

'Don't worry, sir, I have a note from me mam saying I can come back to work,' the DS joked. 'Seriously, I have a note from the medic to say I'm fit and, thanks to you, things on the home front are absolutely bloody marvellous. I should have spoken to you a lot sooner.'

'Come in, Mike, sit down,' Ted told him, genuinely pleased to see the improvement. 'Green tea?'

The DS laughed. 'That might just give me a relapse, boss. So, do you want to bring me up to speed, so I can hit the ground running?'

'Are you sure you don't need more time, Mike? There's just a possibility things are about to get a little bumpy around here.'

'I don't need more time, boss. The people you put me in touch with were incredible. Everything has been sorted out very quickly and the relief is enormous. The wife is clearly seriously ill and they helped her to recognise that. She's gone quite meekly into Cheadle Royal.

'Her sister has moved in to look after the mother-in-law and help me with the kids. Peace is restored and look, boss,' he pulled out his wallet and handed Ted the money for Tina's flowers he owed him. 'I'm even in charge of my own finances again.

'It sounds to me as if you're in need of a good steady bagman to watch your back. And I hope you know, boss, that if you had any doubts about me before, after what you've done for me, I know that I owe you big time and I won't ever forget that.'

Ted waved away his protestations. 'Just looking after a valued team member, Mike, like any good boss should do.'

He quickly filled the DS in on where he was up to with his current thinking and watched his jaw drop as he heard the latest theory.

'Bloody hell, boss,' was all he could manage, to begin with.

'The DCI thinks I should be certified,' Ted admitted. 'I'm still trying to check out the Professor's alibi for Christmas Eve, so far without any success. The Big Boss won't let me go any further until I get somewhere with that.'

'Do you know where PharmaGill keep the Gulfstream, boss? I could see if I can find out if it did fly on Boxing Day, with a passenger on board, and if anyone has any idea of the passenger's identity. They may have to log such information with flight plans, perhaps.'

Ted stared at him in open admiration. 'Blimey, Mike, it's good to have you back,' he said. 'When you come out with stuff like that, I think the killer is right and I am too thick to be a match for him. Get onto it as soon as you can and keep me posted. Keep it under wraps for now though, eh?

'Oh, and Mike, I'm going to see the Professor on Friday afternoon, for a little chat over tea and cake, which is always very good. Trev doesn't want me to go alone. Do you fancy coming with me? Like you said, I need a good bagman. It's not strictly on the level, and the Big Boss doesn't know about it...'

'I did say it and I meant it, sir. I'm your bagman, from now on.'

On the drive over to Alderley Edge, Ted told the DS, 'I don't often do it, but I did tell the Professor a little white lie on this occasion. I said we were calling on Tina's parents in Handforth first. I thought it sounded less suspicious than coming over specially to see him. So if he asks, that's what we've been doing.

'You're sure the Gulfstream didn't take off to anywhere on Boxing Day?'

'As sure as I can be, boss,' the DS said. 'I couldn't find any evidence that it had, but it definitely flew to St Moritz on the twenty-seventh of December. I really want to speak to the regular pilots about the twenty-sixth, to be positive, but I thought that would alert the Professor that we were on to him, so I've left it for now.'

'Good thinking, Mike. Now, when we get there, let me do the talking. Just sit back and enjoy the cake. I've given the Professor our ETA so he is expecting us.'

When they pulled up outside the Professor's impressive home, the Jag was parked at the bottom of the broad steps leading up to the striking stone portico. The DS was clearly a little shocked at the sight of the opulent house and the expensive car. Ted and he were just getting out of the humble Renault as the Professor appeared at the front door.

'Ah, two for tea, how delightful,' he beamed and ducked back inside the half-open door.

Something about his movements kicked in Ted's sixth sense for danger and flooded his body with adrenalin. He was already diving sideways to knock the DS to the floor as Hard G reappeared, with the side by side barrels of a Purdey raised and pointing to where their bodies had been a split second before the dive. He calmly squeezed the trigger.

The DS, being taller, was higher up and slower to hit the ground. Some of the shot hit him and Ted felt blood splatter onto him. He had Hallam down and he kept him there whilst the Professor nonchalantly dropped the Purdey into the passenger seat of the Jag, jumped in after it and roared away in a spray of gravel, without a backward glance at the two men on the floor.

The DS was struggling to sit up. 'I'm fine, boss, it's just flesh wounds. Get after him, for god's sake.'

Ted sat up carefully, looking down at the man. He could that see he was right. Most of the blood was coming from a nick to his right ear, but there was no sign of any serious injury and the DS was most insistent.

'Go,' he said, brandishing his mobile, 'I can call for medical assistance myself, and back-up.'

As Ted got to his feet, there was another roar and Trev's Triumph came hurtling up the drive, skidding to a halt right next to him. Trev half tossed Ted's helmet to him, shouting, 'Get on, quick.'

Ted had one last glance at his DS, who waved him away impatiently, then hurdled onto the bike, jamming on his helmet and bellowing through the intercom, 'What the hell are you doing here? Do you know how dangerous this situation is?'

'You seriously think you could follow him in the Renault? The Jag can do a ton and a half. Even the Triumph can't match that head to head but at least we can keep him in sight while you call for back-up,' Trev said, as he set off in pursuit, handling the big bike with ease. 'Speaking of which, you better do it, and quick.'

Ted was already through to the control room using his helmet's in-built Bluetooth. 'This is DI Darling. Shots fired. I have an officer down, repeat, officer down,' he gave the location of the Professor's house. 'I am in pursuit of the perpetrator who is still armed and should be considered extremely dangerous.

'The vehicle is a Jaguar XK-E, British racing green, cream top, registration number Hotel 4 Romeo Delta Golf, I say again Hotel 4 Romeo Delta Golf.

'I believe he may be heading for the PharmaGill company

airstrip, where they keep a Gulfstream jet aircraft. Request an armed response unit. I suggest you try to clear a route for him, he's not going to stop.'

The DCI's voice came online. He must have been notified the minute Ted's call came through. 'DI Darling, cease pursuit immediately. I repeat, cease pursuit.'

'Signal is poor, incoming calls breaking up,' Ted lied shamelessly. 'Request you listen without interrupting. We now have the suspect on visual. I repeat, suspect in sight.'

'Ted, back off, dammit!' the DCI bellowed.

'Suspect is turning left, left, left, onto the A535. Speeds are excessive. Whatever you do don't try to intercept him at that speed,' Ted continued, totally ignoring the DCI. 'Try to clear some road ahead for him as best you can. He's ignoring all traffic lights and stop signs.

At a roundabout ahead of them, a police patrol car came out of the side turning and took up pursuit, behind the Jag and in front of the bike.

'I now have visual of a patrol car in pursuit. Suspect is speeding up in response. For god's sake, clear him some road ahead. Don't try to stop him anywhere there is traffic about, it will be carnage.

'We need a reception committee as near to the airfield as possible, where it's relatively quiet. Stingers and armed response.'

The DCI tried a gentler approach. 'Good work, Ted, back off now and leave it to the patrol cars.'

'Signal breaking up,' Ted said again. 'Still have him on visual, he is still heading for PharmaGill. The speeds he's driving at, he's going to be there very shortly. Where are we at with armed response?'

'Mobilised, Ted,' the DCI said, 'but it will take a while.'

'Alert PharmaGill and the nearest Air Traffic Control to what's happening. That Gulfstream does not leave the ground!' Ted shouted. 'We're approaching another roundabout ahead. I can see another patrol car manoeuvring to try to cut him off. Tell the bloody fool to stay where he is, then to follow when we're past! Let him through. Let's shepherd him to the airfield where we can at least contain him, away from too many people.

'ETA at the airfield is now less than ten minutes. Do you have stingers in place?'

'Affirmative stingers, negative on armed response as yet, but they're mobile,' the DCI said. 'Ted, I'm warning you, do not try to approach this suspect if he is halted by the stingers.'

Ted ignored his boss and didn't reply or acknowledge his order.

Trev's skills with the bike were impressive, even at the speeds they were going, round bends and roundabouts. The tarmac was flashing past in a black blur. They now had a patrol car in front and one behind them, with the Jag still effortlessly holding its lead.

Cars trying to join the road where skidding to a halt on smoking tyres and swerving out of the way of the Jaguar. Mercifully, so far, there had not been a collision with another vehicle, but Ted could see it was only a matter of time before there was.

'I have visual on the airfield now and can see further patrol cars ahead, so I'm hoping they do have stingers out. Remind all units that the suspect is armed and has already fired once.'

'Remind yourself too, Ted,' the DCI muttered.

'Any word on DS Hallam?' Ted asked.

'Ambulance is on site and confirms the injuries are not life-threatening,' the DCI replied.

'Shit! Ted said loudly as the Jag ran over a stinger laid across the road near an entrance into the airfield and started to swerve alarmingly all over the road. A second stinger further up the road on the other side of the gateway made sure there was no air left in any of the white-walled tyres. The Jag went into a spin and took a nose dive into the shallow ditch at the side of the road.

Ted was off the bike before it had fully come to a halt and running at top speed, crouched low, up behind the Jag. He leapt onto the back of the crashed vehicle just as a badly shaken Hard G was trying to gather his wits and reach for the Purdey.

He didn't even see Ted coming until he found himself suddenly immobilised in a neck-lock with one arm behind his back.

'You're nicked, mate,' Ted couldn't resist saying, then, more formally, 'Roger Gillingham, I am arresting you for the attempted murder of DS Mike Hallam and on suspicion of the murders of Vicki Carr, Maggie Fielding, Nicola Parks and DC Christina Bailey. You do not have to say anything. But it may harm your defence if you do not mention when questioned something which you later rely on in court. Anything you do say may be given in evidence.'

The uniformed officers were closing in, looking a little warily at Ted, despite having been reassured over the radio that he was a plain clothes officer. One of them sensibly lifted the Purdey out of harm's way, aware as he did so that it was probably the most expensive firearm he had ever handled.

'Get an ambulance and get the Professor checked over thoroughly before he's brought to my nick for questioning,' Ted told them, slackening his grip enough to flash his warrant card for them all to see. 'Someone cuff him carefully, but don't move him in case of injury. Don't hurt him at all, whatever you do. I've not hurt him, just immobilised an armed suspect with minimum force. And he is not to be left unattended at all for any reason.

'Tell the hospital I want a full psych assessment on him before I interview him, and tell them that that is not a request. I don't want to give his legal team any excuse to get him off. When Armed Response arrive, I want them babysitting him at all times.'

The Professor remained tight-lipped and silent, only a

supercilious sneer and slightly raised respiration betraying any emotion.

Trev had propped the bike on its stand and was sauntering over, smiling at the excitement of it all. Despite the seriousness of the situation, he hadn't had so much fun on the bike since he'd got it. He'd certainly had it up to speeds he wouldn't dare even to attempt normally, knowing how angry Ted would be if he got himself a speeding fine, or even a ban for excessive speeds.

Ted jumped down off the Jag and walked towards him with a face like thunder.

'You are in so much trouble,' Ted told him menacingly as he approached.

'God, you're sexy when you're angry,' Trev told him, and laughed.

Chapter Forty-seven

Trev dropped Ted off back at the Professor's house to collect his car. He knew he was still angry with him for taking such risks so he didn't push his luck, just gave him a brief peck on the cheek and rode away.

The place was already starting to look like a crime scene. Scene of crime investigators had arrived and were setting up. There was a uniformed presence at the gateway checking anyone arriving, and Rob and Virgil were already on site.

'How's the sarge, sir?' they asked Ted, as soon as he arrived.

'As far as I know, it's not serious,' Ted told them. 'He took a bit of shotgun blast but we managed to duck most of it. Luckily the Professor only fired off one barrel.

'How are we doing with search warrants? I want every inch of this place going over with a fine- tooth comb. I also want the two members of staff, Collins, their name is, taken in to the station separately and kept separate at all times, to be interviewed at length.'

'The Big Boss is sorting warrants out now, sir,' Rob told him. 'He told us to tell you he wants to see you the minute you get back, no excuses. Not sure he's going to present you with a big bunch of flowers, boss.'

Just for a moment, Ted grinned conspiratorially at his team members, then his serious face went back on.

'I want statements from the pilots of the PharmaGill Gulfstream, confirming its whereabouts, especially over Christmas, backed up by flight plans they filed, and details of any and all passengers. And they can forget about any confidentiality crap. I want full details.

'Find out which firm has been doing the cleaning here and I want statements from them. Anything at all unusual they noticed at any time, no matter how seemingly insignificant. I'm guessing they will have been paid well above the odds, as will the Collinses, to turn a blind eye and develop a poor memory, so we need to impress on them the seriousness of this enquiry. And mention the words accessory to murder enough times to rattle them.

'I've had the Professor taken off to hospital for a physical check-up after the crash and a psych evaluation before I question him. He will have the best legal teams in the country at his disposal. I bet London silks are already fighting over him, so I don't want any errors anywhere.

'This means you do not go over that threshold into the house until you have search warrants in your hands. I may be being over cautious on that, but I'm not taking any risks at all. This is a crime scene, outside the house, stick to going over that while you wait. And sort the Collinses out early on; I don't want to give them time to be cooking up a story between them.

'Right,' Ted said resignedly. 'I better get back to the nick and go and see the Big Boss. But at least we have a strong suspect under armed guard, which is a big step forward. Remember, a thorough job.'

The DCI's first words to Ted when he walked through the door were a growled, 'I hope you're covered in Teflon, Ted, because you're going to need it to stop this lot sticking. What the hell were you playing at?'

'Catching a killer, boss,' Ted said innocently.

'Don't get clever, Inspector,' the DCI said warningly. 'With an officer injured in circumstances I knew nothing about, there will need to be an enquiry and you know it. What were you doing at the Professor's in the first place, without first discussing it with me as I had instructed you to?'

'We were invited to tea,' Ted told him, looking totally unperturbed.

'This is not the time to play the smart arse for the first time in your career, Ted,' the DCI told him 'I'm a whisker away from suspending you. Don't force me into it. Tell me what happened, and first of all, tell me what the hell Trev was doing involved in all this, playing cops and robbers on that bike of his?'

Seeing Ted's surprise, he said, 'Oh yes, I've already spoken over the radio to the officers on the scene about exactly what happened. Luckily for you, they have all confirmed that you apprehended the suspect using minimum force. One even went on to say you had taken great care to immobilise the Professor's neck in case of spinal injury.'

Despite the seriousness of the situation, Ted couldn't suppress a grin and made a mental note to find out who the officers at the scene were and thank them.

'Jim, you're right and I apologise,' Ted said, realising the need to show some contrition. 'We got an early indication that the alibi for Christmas Eve was not reliable. I wanted to try talking to Roger in an informal setting, to see if he might just say something of some use to us.

'I had absolutely no cause to suspect that he was on to us or that he would use a firearm. I imagine it was the sight of two of us arriving when he thought it was just going to be me for a cosy chat that tipped him over the edge. When he first opened the door there was no sign of the shotgun. It was just when he ducked back inside we thought something fishy was going on and both managed to dive out of the way.'

'I've spoken to DS Hallam, too. He says it was you who dived onto him, knocking him out of the line of fire and probably saving his life,' the DCI said. 'It's that act which is making me hesitate over kicking your arse all round the office and out on your ear.'

There was a long pause, then the DCI softened and said, 'That, and the knowledge that I couldn't do it anyway, even though I badly want to.'

'Sorry, Jim,' Ted said, sounding much more sincere this time. 'I should have consulted you. You just seemed so against the idea, so I wanted to work it up a bit first. I put one of my team at risk in doing so. I consider myself duly chastised.

'Now, as for Hard G, I really have done everything by the book. I know the kind of defence team he will be able to afford and I'm not giving them any chance anywhere on procedural points. I've had him shipped off to hospital under armed escort and have asked for a thorough physical and a psych evaluation before I begin to question him … '

'Stop right there,' the DCI said, shaking his head firmly. 'You will not be interviewing the Professor. You are already too close to this case, too personally and emotionally involved. You have also shown me that I can't trust you on it. I will be conducting the interviews with Professor Gillingham. At the very most, you may get to sit in with me.'

'It's my case, Jim,' Ted said aghast. 'You can't take it away from me now!'

'You said yourself, he will be using the best defence team money can buy,' the DCI said. 'If you do or say the slightest thing that's out of order, you will effectively blow the whole case out of the water before we have even begun. Where's the sense in that? If we want him put away for life, and we do, we have to be squeaky clean.'

'What if I promise faithfully not to lay a finger on him, sir?' Ted asked.

'Well, now you really have me worried,' the DCI replied. 'When you start calling me sir in private, for probably the first time ever in our acquaintance, it makes me seriously concerned that I can't trust you.'

He gave Ted a long, hard look then finally said, 'All right, this is how we're going to play it. You are going to interview him, with DS Hallam present, if he's pronounced fit to work. I am going to talk to the DS first to tell him exactly what I expect from him. There's going to be a uniformed officer just inside the door at all times.

'I am going to be watching and listening to you on the two-way the whole time. The slightest, and I do mean the slightest, hint of anything that is not by the book, and you are off this case completely. That is your first and final warning. Is that absolutely clear, Inspector?'

Chapter Forty-eight

For the first time in weeks, Ted was home at a reasonable time. Trev was in the kitchen, starting to prepare a meal. He looked a little apprehensive as Ted walked in.

Ted went over to him, put his arms round him and hugged him fiercely.

'Sorry,' he said. 'You were looking out for me and I behaved like a grumpy old git. Thank you. But please, promise me you won't ever put yourself in danger like that again.'

Trev hugged him back in relief. 'I was just worried about you,' he said. 'I never for a moment thought Hard G would do anything like that. I was more worried about what you might do to him if you got an inkling that it really was him who killed Tina.

'I followed you from the station. I saw the whole thing from the gateway, in case you need another witness. How's Mike?'

'Nothing serious, thankfully. They had to dig a couple of pellets out of his shoulder but he was lucky.'

'Not lucky,' Trev said, 'you saved his life. I saw it.'

Ted shrugged it off. 'I just needed to make a soft landing for when I hit the ground. Are you cooking, or shall we go out somewhere, get a meal?'

'I've not really started anything yet. That would be good; where did you have in mind?'

'Let's do something a little crazy. Go somewhere we can sit high up and watch the world going about its business. Go hill walking, maybe.'

BABY'S GOT BLUE EYES

'On a dark winter's evening? That is crazy,' Trev laughed.

'Do you fancy chips?' Ted asked. 'I have an idea.'

'A bag of chips, you cheapskate? Go on then. I'll grab my warmest coat, sounds as if I am going to need it.'

They stopped for fish, chips and mushy peas, Ted's swimming in vinegar, then drove up to the Ridge beyond Marple and parked the Renault at the end of a rough track. They walked along it in the darkness until they found a drystone wall to sit on.

Spread out in the distance was the Cheshire Plain, with the twinkling lights of towns and conurbations, and in the dark night sky above them, the constant passage of planes with landing lights on, making their final approach to Manchester Airport.

In the middle distance was a dark line of wooded hills, visible even in the darkness because of the light pollution. Alderley Edge.

Ted stared silently towards it as he munched his fish supper, deep in his own dark thoughts. Acutely aware that it was almost certainly where Tina spent her last hours alive. Hoping against hope that she had been drugged and didn't know too much about it.

Neither of them spoke until the last chip, pea and morsel of fish in crunchy batter had been eaten, papers carefully scrunched up and stuffed back into the bag they came in, to be taken home with them for disposal.

Trev wiped chip fat from his hand onto the grass then draped an arm round Ted's shoulders. 'It wasn't your fault, you know. Tina. Nor any of the others. You're a good man, a good copper. You were just up against a complete crazy. You said yourself Jim didn't believe your theory. No one could have seen Tina's death coming.'

Ted was still looking across to the Edge, but his mind was playing the post-mortem scene over and over, the last time he had seen Tina.

'She thought the world of you, Ted, you know she did,' Trev told him. 'She wouldn't want you beating yourself up like this.'

Ted gave a long sigh and turned his gaze away towards the distant lights. 'I wonder if Rosalie is out there somewhere? It would be good if we could find her and bring her back alive. You know it's going to kill Jim if she's found dead, don't you?'

Trev shook him gently. 'Hey, you, what kind of a date is this? A bag of chips and a lot of gloomy talk? You've had it very tough, but the worst is over now.' Then he managed to raise a small smile from Ted by misquoting a line from his favourite film, Blazing Saddles. 'Hey, you got the bad guy.'

'I couldn't have got through it without you. I don't know what I'd do without you,' Ted said, with feeling.

'Silly old fool,' Trev laughed. 'Like I'm going anywhere. Come on, brisk walk in the moonlight then an early night for you. Next you've got to make sure you nail the bad guy.'

Chapter Forty-nine

The Professor was brought to the station for questioning the next morning, certified as physically fit by the hospital where he had spent the night, passed as fit to be questioned by the duty psychiatrist.

The Collinses were both resolutely refusing to say anything, other than giving the basics about their duties working for the Professor. Their loyalty and silence had clearly been bought at a high price.

They had been kept at the station overnight in separate cells. Virgil and Rob would continue questioning them right up to the twenty-four hour deadline then, if necessary, they would apply for an extension. Ted was adamant that they must know something and that only loyalty to the Professor, or heavy bribes, was keeping them silent.

DS Hallam was back in work, his right arm in a sling, the right side of his head heavily bandaged, but in extremely high spirits.

'I hope you're okay about us having body piercings and jewellery, boss,' he joked. 'I've got such a big hole in my earlobe I'm thinking of getting one of those big black saucer things to stick in it, like a Goth.'

Ted and the DS had been summoned to see the Big Boss first thing, for a final briefing on the interview.

'By the book, Inspector,' the DCI emphasised. 'I'm taking a risk trusting you on this so don't let me down. If we lose a conviction because of any rough stuff or anything at all dodgy, you know you will never work again.

'DS Hallam, I know you're not up to full strength, but I'm counting on you to keep a lid on things in there. This must not get out of hand. Am I making myself clear?'

Both men nodded and the DCI continued. 'They've already got the big guns out. His brief has arrived from London, from a firm with a fearsome reputation. Right, you know what you have to do, so go and nail the bastard.'

On their way down to the interview room, the DS said, 'I meant what I said to the Big Boss, sir. I may only have one arm today but I will use it if I have to. Because your career is worth too much to let you waste it on this bastard.'

The Professor was looking remarkably composed, even slightly amused, by his circumstances. Ted assessed his lawyer with a glance. The obvious price tag of the man's suit told him all he needed to know about the level of law firm he was from.

Ted kept it totally brisk and formal, acutely aware of the DCI watching him through the glass, and the tapes rolling to record his every word and movement.

'Professor Gillingham,' Ted began formally and politely, 'I would first like to ask you about your movements on the twenty-fourth of December and the morning of December the twenty-fifth. This is in connection with the death of Detective Constable Christina Bailey.'

Hard G's lip curled in a superior smile. 'As I already told you, old boy, I was with my lady friend of the moment, whose name I have been unable to supply since I generously flew her out to St Moritz on Boxing Day, where she promptly disappeared with some young ski instructor.'

'Professor, we have checked carefully with Air Traffic Controllers both here and in Switzerland and we can find no record of PharmaGill's Gulfstream having flown anywhere on the twenty-sixth of December, certainly not to Switzerland as you claim. Can you explain that, please?'

'You don't have to say anything at all at this stage if you choose not to, Roger,' the brief was quick to remind him.

A flash of something like annoyance passed fleetingly across Hard G's face. Ted was guessing he was so unfamiliar with the mundane details of everyday life that the possibility of things like logging flight plans had not occurred to him.

'Can you please tell me, Professor, if you saw DC Bailey at any time on the twenty-fourth of December, after you left The Grapes public house?'

'I saw rather a lot of an entirely different young woman, as I have already told you.'

'Professor, we have been making enquiries with other countries and have discovered that there have been a number of other killings very similar to the ones here, at places where you have holiday property. St Moritz, Como, Faro ... would you like me to go on?'

The annoyance was clearly anger now. The Professor's jaw was clenched and his knuckles where whitening.

'If you had no involvement in any of these killings, would you like to tell me what prompted you to open fire with a shotgun when DS Hallam and I visited your house, at your invitation, for tea and cake yesterday?' Ted asked calmly.

The explosion, when it came, was sudden and unexpected to most of the watchers. The Professor leapt to his feet, overturning his chair, and lunged across the desk at Ted. Ted's training had enabled him to anticipate the action. His reaction was so swift that both DS Hallam and the constable by the door struggled to describe what happened, when asked to make statements about it afterwards.

The videotape later confirmed the speed with which Ted rose and used the other man's superior height and weight against him to take him on over the desk to finish up with his face against the wall, his legs spread to the point where he had no purchase to lunge again. One of his hands was maintained with light pressure, doubled back against the joint so that the least movement would be rendered extremely painful.

'Inspector Darling!' the DCI's voice barked over the

intercom at the same time as both DS Hallam and the constable sprang forward to assist, although neither of them was truly sure whether they should be tackling the suspect or the DI.

Ted's voice was completely calm and totally under control. 'There is no problem at all, Chief Inspector. The Professor is completely unharmed, merely restrained with minimum force. He simply lost self-control for a moment. I am more than happy to release him once I have his assurance that such behaviour will not be repeated.'

The lawyer was looking extremely uncomfortable. He was also utterly bewildered by the speed of events, but even he would have to concede later on in a statement that his client had made the first move and that Ted had merely reacted in self defence without inflicting any injury.

'Do I have that assurance, Professor?' Ted asked his prisoner.

'Take your hands off me, you filthy little pervert!' Hard G spat in a low voice, all pretence of bonhomie now abandoned.

Still speaking calmly, Ted said, 'For the purposes of the tape, in case it was unclear, the Professor said "Take your hands off me, you filthy little pervert".'

'Sit down, Roger,' the brief said nervously. 'You're really not helping yourself by this behaviour.'

With great effort, Hard G relaxed and said, 'Please let go of me. I will sit down, and I will answer your questions.'

Ted released him immediately. A somewhat subdued Hard G quietly resumed his seat next to his brief, who was still looking extremely ill at ease.

'I suppose this is the moment when I am meant to say "It's a fair cop, guv, you've got me bang to rights",' Hard G said mockingly.

'Roger, I really do advise you not to say anything further at this stage,' his lawyer told him. 'Inspector, I request a break from interview so I can take instruction from my client in private before we continue.'

Hard G waved him down. 'It is over. Finally. There is no point in fighting the inevitable.' He looked hard at Ted and continued, 'I never thought you would have the intelligence for this. You were so wide of the mark, so much of the time. Even when I left you glaring clues you were too stupid to see them for what they were.

'It began abroad, as a little holiday treat to myself. I discovered once, quite by accident, the supreme thrill of climax at the point of a partner's death. It was not intentional that time, a little choking to make it more exciting, pressure sustained a moment too long. But it became addictive, even more so when I started to use a scalpel blade.

'I kept it out of this country to begin with – what is that vulgar phrase about not shitting on one's own doorstep? But then there was you, Ted,' he said and now there was real loathing in his tone of voice.

'I find your disgusting proclivity quite revolting. It makes me sick to think of what you get up to. And you were so successful, you seemed to manage to solve every case which came your way. I thought it was about time someone set you a true challenge.

'It was almost too easy. I picked the first girl at random. She knew me by sight, I'd eaten at that bistro on many occasions. It was easier to pick her up than you might think. The charms of the Jag, no doubt. She was even happy to go for a drink with me, where flunitrazepam took care of the rest of the evening for me.

'To save you looking that up, it's the generic name for Rohypnol. I, of course, used the PharmaGill brand,' he said condescendingly.

'After that, I saw how it could become a game we could play, you and I. I began to throw in some more elements, just for fun, which I knew were of special interest to you. Runaways, of course. I know how you profess to be so concerned about your boss's missing daughter, yet you've totally failed to find her.

'Blue eyes, as well, since you drool so offensively over the eyes of the young thing you live with. And then the biggest clue of all. The butt plug, with Tina. I thought even someone as stupid as you would finally make the connection, but no.

'I'd moved on from flunitrazepam for the later victims. I'd found the most delightful ketamine-based cocktail from our veterinary range. So simple to administer. A gallant gentleman helping his lady passenger on with her seat belt. A small, discreetly concealed syringe. A tiny scratch they barely noticed.

'It had the delicious advantage of rendering my victims almost zombie-like – completely immobile and unable to react but still conscious and fully aware. That added an enormous frisson to the whole thing.'

There was a sudden silence in the room, apart from the sound of the DS and the officer by the door both swallowing hard. Hard G's brief was white in the face and looked in grave danger of being sick. Only Ted remained in total cold control.

Quietly, the DCI came into the room behind him and cautiously put a gently restraining hand on his shoulder. 'Book him,' he said quietly.

Ted turned to the DS and the Uniform officer. 'Take him to the custody sergeant, get him charged with all four murders plus the attempted murder of DS Hallam. And throw in attempting to murder me with a firearm, and assaulting me in here as well. If we're going for a whole-life term, we may as well not spare any ammunition.'

Chapter Fifty

As soon as the Professor started to talk, there was no stopping him, as if he relished boasting of his exploits. Every time Ted interviewed him he divulged more and more, totally ignoring all the advice of his lawyer. He seemed to take pride in his cleverness.

Early on, he had a visit from his elder brother, the CEO and purse-string holder of the family company. He was appalled, seemingly not by the fact that his younger brother was admitting to the murder of so many young women, but that the firm's own products had been involved. He took immediate steps to remove the Professor from all involvement with PharmaGill, as a director and shareholder, effectively drying up his funds at a stroke.

Even the Professor's respectable salary as a forensic pathologist, of itself now frozen, was not sufficient to attract the interest of the big law firms who had previously been fighting over him, and their interest quickly cooled. There was no kudos in defending a seemingly lost cause. He was quickly whisked away and remanded in custody, awaiting a date for a preliminary trial. The London lawyer of the expensive suit was not seen again.

The press pack had gone wild with the news of who was in custody. Ted and the DCI were under siege at the station until they agreed to a brief appearance in front of the cameras, on the station steps. Ted refused to dress up this time, preferring to flaunt his Mossad agent look, simply glaring from camera to microphone to reporter.

To celebrate the end of a long and difficult case, Ted and Trev had invited Willow to dinner with her new man, Rupert, the male model. Over coffee Trev and Rupert discovered a mutual passion for motorbikes when Rupert mentioned he often had to pose, leather-clad or partially so, on some of the most expensive and glamorous bikes on the market.

When he mentioned having sat on a Ducati Desmosedici wearing nothing but a leather thong, Trev was drooling so much that Ted and Willow rolled their eyes at each other and went out to the kitchen together to start the washing up.

Willow planted a warm kiss on Ted's cheek and said, 'Thank you so much for lending me Trev to get over Roger. He is so utterly gorgeous I would take him off you if I could, but it's impossible. Nobody could. He absolutely adores you.'

'I can't imagine what he sees in a grumpy old fool like me,' Ted said self-effacingly.

'He loves you. Don't ever try to understand, just accept and enjoy,' Willow said. 'And don't you dare put yourself down, Ted Darling. You are an adorable man and very well named.

'I know you hate dressing up but I do hope you will at least hire, if not buy yourself a suit for the summer.' She smiled shyly at him. 'I know we've only known each other five minutes but Rupert and I are planning on getting married. But it's a secret, we haven't told anyone yet.'

Ted gave her a hug and a kiss, covering her in soap suds from the washing up. 'For you, I'd consider wearing a dress,' he smiled. Both he and Trev had quickly grown very fond of Willow.

Things were quietly calm at work, with the huge pressure of such a difficult case lifted from the shoulders of everyone involved. Ted could not get over the incredible change in the DCI since the arrest of the Professor.

He seemed years younger, suddenly. In particular, he had been so impressed to see how the DS had turned his domestic life around that he suddenly found the strength to set his own house in order. With Mike Hallam's permission, Ted had filled in the Big Boss about what had been going on. It seemed to galvanise him into action.

One day, when his wife returned home for a rare visit, after apparently spending the weekend with a lusty young traffic cop from another division, she found her belongings packed and waiting on the doorstep and the locks changed.

She fled home to her mother's, hoping things would quieten down. But the first post she received there was a solicitor's letter, informing her that the DCI was filing for divorce on the grounds of her adultery.

Ted and the DCI were enjoying a relaxed chat in the Big Boss's office at the end of the day. The DCI had just told Ted the top brass were so impressed with his work that not only were they no longer talking about disciplinary action because of his unorthodox behaviour, they were once again dangling the carrot of a commendation in front of him.

As before, Ted's answer had been to ask him to tell them where to stick their offer, in the most diplomatic way he knew.

Ted was pleased that he was back on the same easy and companionable terms with the Big Boss, whom he liked and respected so much. Their friendship had been sorely put to the test by the case, but it had survived.

The DCI's apologies had been profuse that he had been slow to accept Ted's theory, which had proved to be correct, but Ted quickly waved them away. The whole thing had been so crazy he had not entirely believed it himself, until the Professor started to talk.

The search of the house on the Edge had been most revealing. As Ted had suspected, not only did the Professor have the facilities to store bodies at low temperatures in his cellar rooms, there was also a room equipped much like his post-mortem suite at the hospital, where he could carry out whatever acts he chose without risk of disturbance.

His previously loyal staff, the Collinses, on hearing the word 'accessory', had each, individually, started to sing like a canary. Although the Jaguar was antiseptically immaculate, inside and out, the forensic team did find one single hair from Tina in the old estate car the staff used. Clearly, with the intervention of Christmas, and his boss away skiing, Mr Collins had not been quite as careful as usual with his valeting of the vehicle.

It seemed the Jag had been the pick-up vehicle of choice, but the estate car had clearly been more practical and less noticeable for disposing of the bodies.

'A good outcome in the end, Ted,' the DCI said, pouring himself a small Glenfiddich from a bottle in his desk, 'purely for medicinal purposes,' he told Ted with a sly wink. 'Such a tragic shame about young Tina, but I don't see how anyone could have seen that coming and prevented it.

'I still can't quite understand it all. If Hard G hated your lifestyle so much, why that business of dancing with Trev and, er, you know …' Jim was never comfortable talking about anything which alluded to Ted's sexuality.

'Fondling his bum and getting a stiffy?' Ted smiled. 'We'll know more in the lead-up to the trial, if we get a clue as to whether he is going to plead guilty meekly or launch some sort of defence.

'It's not my field of expertise at all but, with his background – prep school, public school – I suspect Hard G may well have encountered his fair share of shirt-lifters, as Mike Hallam once so eloquently put it. Either the experience disgusted him to a point beyond reason or, and this is just a guess, he found he enjoyed it more than he had been brought up to believe he should.

'That would explain his behaviour with Trev, and also his obsession with dominating the blonde jobs, playing the rough caveman all the time. The constant conflict may be what finally led him to crack up, or at least that would be my best guess.'

The DCI was by now squirming with discomfort with mental images he could clearly well do without.

His phone rang, interrupting them, and he picked it up, saying, 'DCI Baker.'

Immediately, big fat tears sprang to his eyes and started to roll down his cheeks. Ted felt as if he had just been kicked in the stomach.

With a shaking hand, the DCI reached out to put the call onto speaker-phone so Ted could hear. A familiar voice, breathless, full of emotion, racing through the words without a pause between them, was saying, 'Daddy? Is it true? I heard Mummy's gone? Can I come and see you? I want you to meet your grandson. And my husband.'

The End

22208295R00158

Printed in Great Britain
by Amazon